Hidden Ball Trick

S.E. Martin

Apostrophe H

eBook Edition ISBN-13: 979-8-9988419-2-7

Paperback ISBN-13: 979-8-9988419-3-4

Cover design by: All Write Well

For all the Chelsea girls who've lost their shine. There's a Wes out there waiting for you.

Prologue
Ká:lahsé / Lacrosse

Wes

It's a beautiful day to play lacrosse.

The crisp November air bites at the exposed skin on my forearms, goosebumps forming on the constellations tattooed there. There's a slight breeze, making me grateful I packed a sweatshirt. There's not a cloud in the sky. Just sun, wind, and the game the Creator gifted to my ancestors—who passed it down to me.

My Buffalo Outlaws teammate, Zeke Jacobs, invited me to practice on the Seneca Nation's Cattaraugus Territory, and I jumped at the opportunity. After I was drafted to the National Lacrosse League, I moved to Western New York and I've struggled. I'm lonely, missing family and friends back home in Green Bay.

"I hope you're not feeling too discouraged about being assigned to the practice roster," Zeke says as he parks his truck.

"It's a long season, and you showed a lot of promise in training camp. I know you'll be a starter soon."

I smile at his praise. "Thanks, Z. It's all good. I'll get a shot."

I'm used to working my tail off. My five-foot-eight frame has been underestimated throughout my entire career. I may be vertically challenged, but I'm used to working for every opportunity. I quickly read offenses, breaking up plays before stealing the ball and scoring on the other end.

Field lacrosse, played outdoors with ten players on each team, has been my passion since I was young. In the past year I've also sought opportunities to learn the smaller, indoor version of the game, referred to as box lacrosse. It's the national sport of Canada, but much harder to find played in the United States. Professional leagues exist for both forms of the game, and I want to be one of the few Americans to make a difference in both.

I grab my equipment bag from the back seat. "Thanks for inviting me out. It's rough, being away from my Oneida Nation community in Wisconsin."

"Yeah, man. Come on out anytime. You're welcome here with other Haudenosaunee people."

Zeke is fast becoming a friend. He's mentored me as I adjust to playing professional box lacrosse.

"How's your new apartment? Are you all moved in?" he asks as we walk towards the Cattaraugus Community Center.

I cringe. "It's—it's OK." I picture the yellowing carpet and crumbling drywall back at the only place I could afford near the city.

"So, it's a shithole?"

"It's a shithole. But it's fine, really." I adjust the bulky bag on my shoulder. "With any luck, I won't be home that often between training and working."

"Are you getting a nine-to-five? Makes sense, especially given the peanuts you make on the practice squad."

"There's a gym where some of the Outlaws are personal trainers. I've got an interview next week."

Zeke nods. "That's smart. You can make your own schedule, and the owners will understand the weird hours we keep because of the team."

We head to the playing field behind the building. Two women are already there, passing a lacrosse ball back and forth. Their movements are relaxed and loose, their laughter floating over in the breeze.

They turn as we approach, and their reactions could not be more different. One of them freezes, while the other breaks into a wide and easy smile.

"Zeke Jacobs. Long time no see," the second woman says.

"Hey Chels." Zeke embraces her warmly.

Her rich chestnut hair is pulled up into a high ponytail. She's clearly an athlete, with the body to show for it. Her legs are toned and shapely in royal purple running shorts, with the rest of her hidden beneath an oversized University of Albany sweatshirt. My gaze locks onto her, unable to be torn away from her broad smile and warm brown eyes.

"I've been back in Cattaraugus for a few weeks now. We're getting ready to start our season soon." My attention finally catches on Zeke's voice mid-conversation. "This is my teammate, Wes. He's Oneida."

I swallow nervously, cover it up with a smile, and hold my hand out to her. "Nice to meet you."

She raises her eyebrows and returns my handshake. A spark shoots through my fingers and into my arm. "Chelsea John. I'm Oneida, too. Who's your family?"

"My mom's Kay Patterson, but she moved out to the Wisconsin community in the 90s. I'm not sure who's left in New York from our family." I shift from foot to foot, my gaze on the ground. "We've never visited."

Chelsea's jaw drops. "Of course I know who Kay is! Your grandmother is a Bear Clan Mother. Your cousin Jessica is one of my best friends."

"I've got a cousin my age?" I ask with a grin.

"You have *so* many cousins," Chelsea emphasizes. "You should come visit!"

"Maybe I will."

"Would you ladies be opposed to playing pickup ball with us?" Zeke interjects.

"Not as long as you don't mind getting your asses handed to you," Chelsea teases. She elbows her friend, who still hasn't said a word.

I give her a lopsided smile. "Bring it on."

"And this is—" Zeke begins.

"I'll set up the goal," the other woman interjects, spinning to head towards the net.

I frown. There's clearly something I'm missing here.

"Give her time," Chelsea says quietly to Zeke, scooping up a loose ball.

I reach around Zeke to grab the equipment bag. "I'm going to help with the net. See you in a minute."

The other woman walks back from the Community Center carrying a large sheet of plywood. I drop my bag on the ground and jog to catch up with her.

"Want me to grab that?" I offer.

She shakes her head. "I've got it, thanks."

She did indeed have it. She sets the board down next to the net without a hair out of place or looking out of breath.

"I'm Wes, by the way," I say. "I apologize for Zeke's lack of manners in not introducing us."

Her lips twitch. "I'm Genny. Zeke and Chelsea are friends of mine from high school."

"Nice to meet you, Genny."

I hold the wood in place while she begins tying it to the crossbar of the net.

"So, you're from the Oneida rez in Wisconsin?" Genny asks. "I've never met anyone from out there."

I nod and adjust my grip so she can reach a new section. "My mom was born and raised on the New York reservation, but she moved out to Green Bay before I was born."

"Did she have friends or family there?"

"I don't know, actually. She doesn't talk about it much."

My mom's life in New York has always been a mystery to me and my sister. We've tried to get her to talk about it over the years, but she's kept the details to a minimum. I don't know who in my family is left there, and the gaping hole in my family tree haunts me.

She steps back to admire her handiwork. "This should hold, as long as no one rips a shot too hard." She glances over at me. "I'm looking at you two professional slingers."

"Hey, I'm just a defender." I rattle the net to see if I can knock anything loose. "Talk to that brooding hulk you call a friend."

She laughs, but a shadow passes across her eyes as Zeke and Chelsea arrive.

"Do you want to play with pads?" Zeke asks.

"Don't have any," Chelsea responds. "Why, are you afraid we'll hurt you?"

I chuckle under my breath. *I like this one.*

"If you want us to go easy on you, just say so," he replies with a teasing grin, dumping lacrosse balls out of the duffel bag.

"Simmer down, hotshot," Chelsea grabs a ball and places it in the middle of the field. "Let's do this."

"You cover Chelsea," Zeke tells me. "She's squirrelly."

"I can imagine." I look over at where she and Genny are strategizing.

"I've got Genny. I know how she plays."

"I don't know that this approach is going to help your case with her, man. I've seen you with women."

He fixes me with a pointed look, and I grin.

Chelsea and I set up for the opening faceoff. I set my knee down near the ball and try to remember strategies for coming up with the win.

"You probably don't take many faceoffs." She looks down at me with a smile.

I laugh. "Gee, I don't know how I'll manage."

"Do you need me to teach you a few things?" Her eyes sparkle as she gets to her knee and places her stick in the improvised faceoff circle. I notice she's using a stick like mine, and not the flatter head designed for the women's game.

"What makes you think I'd be the student?" I mirror her positioning. *Have I taken faceoffs before? Of course. Am I any good at it? Hell no.*

"Just a guess."

"I like being underestimated. Keep it up."

"Down. Set. Go!" Genny calls, and we both dive for the ball.

Chelsea clamps her stick over the ball, and I'm already losing this matchup. I use my weight advantage to muscle her over until the ball pops free.

"Oh, so you don't play fair. Got it," she says, reaching for the ball, but I've already scooped it and passed it over to Zeke.

I shrug. "I've got a low center of gravity, what can I say?"

"You're fun-sized. Makes it easier to get around you."

My grin grows. "Look who's talking, pipsqueak. You're shorter than I am."

A surprised laugh escapes her lips. "I don't think I've ever been called small in my life."

Several yards away, Genny puts a move on Zeke and scores. *We're in trouble.*

After hyping up a dejected Zeke, I retrieve the ball and place it back in our circle. It's his and Genny's turn to face off, and hopefully they don't kill each other.

"What's with these two?" I ask Chelsea as we wait for them to get set.

She glances over, the corner of her mouth lifted in amusement. "What do you mean?"

"It's obvious they have some kind of unresolved issue."

She clears her throat. "You'd have to talk to Zeke about it. I'm forbidden from commenting due to Girl Code."

"Ah, a sacred form of governance. I wouldn't ask you to break that."

They seem relatively in place, so Chelsea calls out for the faceoff to begin. Zeke and Genny wrestle for control, neither of them giving up an inch. The seconds tick by without a clean win.

"Hey! Hurry it up, you two!" I call out.

"If I had to guess, I'd bet those two like each other more than they realize," Chelsea says. "Maybe the Medicine Game will do them good today."

Genny finally comes up with the ball, swinging her stick and pushing it to a waiting Chelsea as Zeke pulls her to the ground.

Chelsea scoops the ball and takes off towards the net, but I have her blocked. Genny is out of commission as someone to pass to, so Chelsea has to get creative. She dodges and bobs in an attempt to buy time and keep the ball away from me. Each time she makes a move towards the net, I slash at her stick and force her to protect the ball.

"What's wrong, Rookie? Don't want to play rough with a girl?" she heckles.

I grin. "You want to play rough?"

"With you? Hell yeah." She winks and shuffles to her right.

I follow her movement and realize too late that it's a trap. I try to recover from committing too soon, but she spins out in the opposite direction.

I fall on my ass as she runs around me, scoring easily.

Genny whoops from the ground where she's tangled up with Zeke, her arms raised in victory as Chelsea jogs over to high five her.

I sit on the grass, laughing to myself as Zeke makes his way over.

"She's a master trash talker, man." He shakes his head.

"I see that," I chuckle, watching Chelsea help Genny up from the ground.

I'm a sucker for a woman who challenges me, and Chelsea John does that in spades. I don't typically take kindly to getting embarrassed on the field, but she could walk across my chest in cleats and I wouldn't mind.

We wind up playing for over an hour. I enjoy watching the banter and affection between the three friends. It reminds me of my friend group in Wisconsin, and I'm hit with a new wave of homesickness.

We work together to clean up once we've exhausted ourselves. I set to work on the net, fiddling with the knots holding the plywood in place. I glance up to find Chelsea smiling at me. My heart skips a beat as I return her smile.

"You prefer playing with a men's stick?" I attempt small talk and immediately realize that was the wrong thing to ask.

Her eyebrows go skyward. "Excuse me?"

I swear internally. "I just mean—not that you can't use whichever style of stick you want—"

She watches me squirm, the corner of her lip turning up.

I blow out a shaky breath. "Tell me about your stick choice. I'd love to learn."

Her eyes dance. "I only use a woman's stick if I'm playing outdoors on a team, which I haven't done since college. For everything else, I prefer the men's stick." She leans against the net while I continue untying the plywood. "Although I'd argue against the terminology when women use the same stick style as men in box lacrosse."

I look up. "You play box?"

"Yeah, but watch out for your–"

My distracted fingers loosen the second-to-last knot enough and the sheet of wood comes crashing down on top of my toes.

"F—!" I hiss and attempt to cover the litany of curses trying to fly out of my mouth.

"Jesus, man." Chelsea laughs as she quickly grabs the board and pulls it out of the net. "Are you OK? Might need to amputate."

I bite my cheek as the pain radiates out from my foot. "I'm good. Just embarrassed."

She leans against the goal post. "You should be. Not sure how you're going to come back from this."

"Serves me right."

She cocks an eyebrow.

"You're—" I blow out a pained exhale. "You're really pretty. I lost my focus."

I look up and see surprise and softness cross her face. "Oh. I'm...sorry?"

Launch one, Wes.

"Sorry enough to give me your number? You could show some pity for an amputee."

Her sharp laugh echoes across the field. "Points for audacity, I'll give you that. Especially after the stick comment."

"So, that's a...?"

She looks away, and my stomach sinks.

"You're probably already seeing someone," I blurt out.

"I'm not."

"Did I ruin my chances by dropping plywood on my foot like a dumbass?"

Chelsea giggles, and it's the best damn sound I've ever heard. It's genuine, joyful, and a little wicked.

"I just got out of a relationship, and I plan to be single for a while," she responds hesitantly.

Disappointment floods my veins. "I get it; I've been there. No worries."

"And definitely no lacrosse players. I've seen enough."

It's my turn to raise my eyebrows. "Is that a challenge?"

She chuckles. "No. Just a statement."

"If you say so."

She takes the plywood from me and brings it back inside the community building. My eyes follow her movements, appreciating her strength and beauty.

"You seem happy." Zeke smiles as we get into his truck.

I lean my head against the back of the passenger seat. "I am. That was fun."

"It really was."

Chapter 1

Six Months Later

Chelsea

I'm unapologetically a rez girl. I swear too much, laugh too loud, and know there's nothing more terrifying than a pissed off Native woman. I fight hard, love harder, and throw boys around on the lacrosse field for fun.

Which is why it pains me to admit that after decades of calling the Oneida Nation home, I'm feeling the itch to leave. I've long felt a tension between celebrating that I live on the ancestral homelands of my people while also craving big dreams. I want to explore the world and share my beautiful culture with everyone I meet. I want to play lacrosse at an elite level, including representing my nation at the Olympics in a few years. I want to take chances and push myself out of my comfort zone.

Every time I've tried, I've inevitably been pulled back to rez life. I missed my chance at a fresh start when I moved home after college graduation. The rez and I fit together like a well-worn pair of slippers, and it was easy to fall back into its grooves.

Today I'm working at the Shako:wi Cultural Center on my reservation. It's a soaring white pine building showcasing thousands of years of Oneida history near Utica, NY. It's a testament to the resiliency of our people after we very nearly lost our homelands following the American Revolution. My part-time gig here has turned into an unexpected blessing, as I can flex my cultural knowledge to visitors *and* pull a much-needed paycheck.

My friend and roommate, Jessica Parker, wanders out from her post in the attached gift shop. "What time are you off?"

My tongue pokes between my teeth as I push a needle through a string of beads, anchoring them to the felt I'm working on. "Five, so I'll close up if you need to head out early."

"I have the night off from the casino, so I'm good to stay." Jess leans on the counter. "What are you making?"

I angle my beadwork towards her. "Some floral hair clips. They'll be perfect for pow wow season and all the summer festivals."

She gasps softly. "I love those. Do you want to sell those in the gift shop, or wait for the Strawberry Festival?"

"Probably the festival, although I've got some earrings to work on at home that could get listed here." I slide more beads onto my needle.

"You're so talented," she murmurs, watching me work.

"I could teach you sometime," I offer.

She shakes her head. "I've never been good at making things with my hands."

"That's not true!" I weave between beads and pull the string tight as I finish a row. "I have faith you could pull off beading."

The door chimes as it opens. We have visitors.

A middle-aged couple enters, their eyes wide as they take in the abundance of beautiful items around the building: the sacred medicines of sage, cedar, sweetgrass, and tobacco; multiple styles of wooden lacrosse sticks; rows of shiny purple wampum; and brightly colored displays of traditional regalia such as ribbon skirts and feathered *kastowíhe* headdresses.

"Welcome to Shako:wi Cultural Center," I greet them, coming around from behind the large reception desk as Jess scatters to her post in the gift shop. "I'm Chelsea. What brings you here today?"

Their gazes dart around the surroundings.

"Hi, Chelsea. I'm Mary, and this is my husband, Richard," the woman says warmly. "Aren't you friendly?"

"We spent the day at Turning Stone and saw this on a map. We didn't know what it was, so we figured we'd stop by and find out," Richard says.

I smile. The Nation's casino brings in revenue for the community, and we benefit from their visitor traffic as well. "Did you have a good time there?"

"Oh, yes. It's great fun. I played the slots, and Richard tried his hand at Blackjack." Mary's lips quiver upward. "Can't say we had much luck, but we did have a nice day."

"So, what is this place?" Richard asks bluntly. "Is this a gift shop?"

I'm used to whatever people throw at me here, so I launch into my prepared remarks.

"I'm so glad you asked! This is the cultural center of the Oneida Nation. We're the original inhabitants of this land. This is a place for people, inside or outside of our community, to encounter the history and future of the Haudenosaunee."

He furrows his brow. "Haudeno-what now? I thought this was where Indians live?"

"*Richard,*" Mary hisses through her teeth, elbowing him in the side. "Don't use that word! It's not polite."

I smile kindly. "It's OK. Native people will sometimes call themselves Indians, but we prefer if others refer to us as Indigenous Peoples or by the name of our tribal nations." I gesture for them to follow me. "It can be a bit confusing if you're not used to it. Let me show you something that should help."

I lead them over to a display featuring a map of New York State with several areas highlighted.

"The Haudenosaunee are a confederacy of six tribes whose ancestral homelands are here in New York. You may have heard us referred to as the Iroquois in the past, but we choose to use our traditional name now."

"I know about the Iroquois!" Mary beams. "We live in Rochester, and there are lots of Iroquois names there."

"See? You've got it. The tribal nation that's closest to you is the Seneca." I point to different places on the map. "In the rest of the state you'll also find the Mohawk, Tuscarora, Cayuga, and Onondaga Nations. We're very similar people, but our languages and clans evolved over centuries to be a little different from each other."

Mary nods with wide eyes. "Can you all understand each other?"

"There are a lot of similarities between our languages. There are variations in words and phrases, and definitely in spellings. Oneida looks a lot different from Seneca, for example, which is where my dad is from." I show them some Oneida words written on a nearby sign. "See these letters that look like upside-down V's? You don't see those in other Haudenosaunee languages."

I guide them through the rest of the Center, answering their questions about traditional dress, the origins of lacrosse, and basket weaving. They don't know much about Haudenosaunee culture, but they're curious and open-minded about learning. By the time they finish exploring the exhibits and visiting the gift shop, it's time to close for the day.

"Thank you so much, Chelsea," Mary says with a warm smile. "You're so knowledgeable, and we really appreciate you taking so much time to teach us about your culture."

Richard holds out his hand to me. "Yes, thank you for answering all our questions. I know I'm not always good at knowing the right thing to say." He side-eyes his wife, and I smother a smile.

"You two are great. Please come back and visit anytime!" I shake his hand.

"How do you say 'thank you' in your languages?" Mary asks.

"It's *ya:wʌ́* in Oneida, or *nya:wëh* in Seneca." I sound out the words slowly for them.

"*Ya:wʌ́*, Chelsea," Mary says.

"*Nya:wëh,*" Richard chimes in.

17

My heart grows two sizes. Few things are more fulfilling to me than making connections with people seeking to understand and appreciate my culture.

"*Nyóh*, Mary and Richard," I say with a wave as they exit. "Have a safe trip home!"

I collapse into a nearby chair once they depart. "Whew. That was a marathon visit."

"And you were amazing, as usual," Jess says, plopping into the armchair next to me. "You've got this Academic Chelsea persona you slip into when you're explaining history and traditions to non-Natives."

I chuckle. "It's honed by my years in college and working here. I love it."

She gets to her feet. "Let me close out the register and finish up."

I close my eyes. "You're the best, Jess. *Ya:wʌ́.*"

She putters around the building, and I pull out my phone to disassociate with some scrolling. I open social media to find notifications waiting for me. A slow smile creeps across my face as I click through.

I shot Wes down six months ago when he'd asked for my number, but the boy was nothing if not persistent. A couple of months later, he requested to follow me on Instagram with the accompanying message:

Wes: Does this count if it's not your number?

My stomach had flipped then, as it did now seeing that he'd liked my most recent post about playing for the indoor Women's Major Series Lacrosse league in Fort Erie, Ontario this coming summer. I'd taken a few years off from organized lacrosse after college, not exactly on purpose, and this was an important step in getting my game back on track.

He also left a comment:

> *Watch out, WMSL! This one will knock you on your ass and score in the same breath. Congrats on your new opportunity, Chelsea!*

"What are you smiling about?" Jessica asks from the cash register, and I jump in surprise.

"You scared me!" I clutch at my chest.

"Sorry." She grins. "You were so smiley over there."

I swallow. "I just got a nice comment from your cousin on IG. He congratulated me on making the Fort Erie team."

She lights up. "I hope he comes for a visit. I'm so excited to meet him finally."

My skin warms at the thought of seeing Wes again. He was cute, funny, *and* Native, which has been hard to come by in my dating life. He's also a professional lacrosse player, which is number one on the Avoid This list I've been curating since I ended a relationship last November. I'd dated plenty of players, but the last one in particular did a real number on me. I have no interest in repeating the experience.

But Wes also celebrated my accomplishments, respected my boundaries, and dropped a sheet of plywood on his foot because he was busy looking at me. I'm not conventionally attractive, with some extra thickness around my waist and thighs due to a love of athletics and fry bread, so I'm not used to a guy embarrassing himself on my account.

He's been following me online for months and hasn't once tried to ask me out or sent creepy messages. He seems like a genuinely nice guy, which I hope isn't a ruse. After all, it had been with my most recent ex.

"All right, we're all closed up." Jess slides the cash register shut with a *ding*. "Ready to head home?"

"So ready." I pocket my phone and push down all thoughts of the guy who was tempting me to throw my No Relationships For Now resolution in the trash.

Chapter 2

Latiy^thos

Planting / May

Wes

I toss several balled-up pairs of socks into my suitcase from across the room. They narrowly miss the orange bucket collecting water dripping from the ceiling. My landlord has been "stopping by soon" to fix the problem since April.

The Outlaws leave for Calgary in the morning to play for the NLL championship. It's a three-game series, so we'll be back in Buffalo a few days later. I don't need to pack much, but my mind is racing and making it difficult to put together an appropriate amount of clothing for the trip.

My rookie year has been full of ups and downs. I started the season on the practice roster, which wasn't unexpected given my comparatively short history with box lacrosse. I worked my ass off for months getting stronger in the gym, studying game film, and adjusting to the speed and flow of the indoor game. Coach Travis called me up to start a few times before it stuck, and I'm acutely aware of how lucky I am to be playing as a starter as we head into the championship series.

I don't take this opportunity for granted, not for an instant. My mind wanders as I think back eight months ago to the night I was drafted, and I smile at the memory.

It was the most important night of my life, and I was huddled over a steaming pot of corn soup.

"You can add the kidney beans now, Wes," my mom called from the living room where she was pulling out patterned blankets and helping guests find places to sit in the cramped space.

I dumped two cans of beans into the simmering concoction and gently stirred. "Katie," I hissed at my little sister, who'd been trying to creep past the kitchen without being noticed. "Can you take over so I can watch the draft?"

Katie groaned. "I'm trying to avoid all these people. Do I have to?"

"I'd like to know when I get selected." I paused. "*If* I get selected."

"Wesley, come," my mom insisted, to my relief. "Katie, find your father and have him finish the soup."

My sister glared at me and I stuck my tongue out at her.

I graduated in May after spending four years playing Division I lacrosse at Marquette University, and this was the next step in my quest to play professionally. Unlike the top prospects, who were superstars at elite schools, I had no assurances of being selected. What I did have was talent, a hardworking mentality, and a passion for the game that transcended typical athletics.

"Come squeeze in here, Wes," our family friend Helen said with a smile, patting the slice of couch cushion available between her and my mother.

"We're so excited for you," her husband Edgar said from a nearby armchair. "We've watched you grow up and become such a good representative of the Creator's Game."

My mom put her arm around my shoulders and squeezed me. "This has been a long time coming. I'm so proud of you."

I ducked my head. "We don't know that I'll be drafted."

"You will." My dad entered from the kitchen, drying his hands on a towel. "These teams will see your highlight film and your background as a Haudenosaunee player. You're special, kid."

"There are other Indigenous players in this year's class," I reminded him. "I'm not any different from them."

"Remember when you jumped and stripped the ball from above during that game against Syracuse?" Edgar said. "No other defenders make plays like that, and you make them regularly." He tapped my leg with his cane. "You're going to be a star, I know it."

The first-round picks rolled in, then the second. I didn't give it much thought, but I heard my mom make a disgruntled noise each time a pick was announced. The third-round went by, and my stomach started to clench. By the end of the fourth-round I was pacing between the kitchen and living room.

I mentally flipped through what my next steps would be if I wasn't drafted: I'd call every team to see if I could attend training camp and compete for a spot; I'd coach at my high school for a year and give back to the community; I'd work on a new strength training plan; I'd—

My mother screamed from the next room, followed by bursts of yelling and whooping from the others. She ran into the kitchen and grabbed me, roughly pulling me to her for a hug.

"Buffalo!" she gasped.

My heart stuttered with disbelief. "What?"

My dad wrapped us both in his arms. "You're a Buffalo Outlaw, kid. First pick of the fifth round."

"Are you sure?"

He laughed. "Yes, I'm sure. My eyes still work, although I may have lost an eardrum to your mother back there."

"I'm so happy for you." My mom wiped away the tears streaming down her cheeks. "You've worked so hard for this. And you'll be close to other Native communities out there. There are Seneca and Tuscarora reservations nearby."

I kissed the top of her head. "And it's not far from the Oneida rez in New York, right? Maybe I could visit where you grew up."

She stilled in my embrace. "Oh, I don't know if that's a good—I mean, it's quite a drive. And I'm sure you'll be so busy with the team."

I caught my dad's concerned glance her way. I opened my mouth to respond when my phone buzzed in my pocket.

"Who is it?" My mom asked.

I furrowed my brow. "Not sure. It's a 716 area code."

She brightened. "That's Buffalo! Answer it!"

I quickly slid my finger across the screen. "Hello?"

"Wes? This is Coach Travis calling from the Buffalo Outlaws. How are you doing tonight?"

I swallowed nervously. "I'm good, Coach. How are you?"

"I'm great now that I have a hell of a defender coming to my team this year."

I bit my lip to hold back a grin. "Thanks, Coach. I'm really excited to be a part of the Outlaws organization."

"I'm glad to hear that. I've got our captain, Jamie Montour, on the line with me. Jammer, you there?"

Jamie Montour was a bona fide superstar, the player that every Indigenous youth looked up to. *And I'm going to play with him.*

"Hey, Wes. Welcome to the Outlaws." Jamie's smooth voice came across the line.

"Thank you so much. It's an honor." My voice cracks with nerves on the last word.

"You're the best young defender I've seen in years. I've been in Coach's ear in the lead-up to draft day. I can't tell you how excited I am to have another Haudenosaunee player on the team, especially one as talented as you. I'm Mohawk from Six Nations Reserve in Canada, and we also just traded for Zeke Jacobs, who's Seneca from Cattaraugus Territory south of Buffalo."

Creator was really working overtime, because I couldn't think of a better place for me to wind up.

A chunk of plaster falls from the ceiling and into the five-gallon bucket by my bed, startling me back to the present. I make a mental note to text my landlord *again* and fight off a wave of homesickness.

I flop onto my bed and pull out my phone. *I've earned a little break, right?* I check my various social media apps and notice I have a message waiting for me on Instagram. My heart leaps. *Could it be?*

Disappointment prickles my chest when I see someone else's name in my inbox, and not Chelsea's. Each time I have a new message I hope it's her, but so far that dream has yet to become reality.

> **Hailey:** Hey Wes! It was great seeing you at the gym again today. I know you're going to have a great game in Calgary this weekend! Want to grab a drink once you're back in town?

Hailey and I keep similar hours at the gym, and we've spent time chatting amicably with each other between sets. She's a Buffalo girl, super nice, pleasant to talk to...but I'm not interested. I haven't been interested in anyone since I met Chelsea.

It feels crazy to be so taken with a woman I've met only once. It's embarrassing to admit she captivated me and has me comparing all other girls to her. I should be agreeing to drinks with the pretty blonde who regularly checks me out during squats, but instead I'm wondering how to let her down gently. I type a quick reply to Hailey.

My phone rings in my hand, and my sister's name and face pop up. I answer with a grin.

"Hey Katie."

"Hey, loser. Are you ready for your big championship adventure?"

I exhale loudly and roll over onto my pillows. "I hope so. I'm almost packed and trying not to feel too nervous. My flight's in the morning."

She scoffs. "You should see how anxious Mom is for you. She's going to gnaw a hole in her medicine pouch at this rate."

Laughter bubbles from my chest. "You're home from school for the summer, I take it?"

"Freshly home in Green Bay, big brother. It's an exciting life I lead."

I prop my arm behind my head to settle in comfortably. "How are Mom and Dad otherwise?"

"They're good. Dad's been walleye fishing at every opportunity, and Mom's been hanging out with her friends from work. Not that you asked, but I've been doing a lot of sleeping and eating."

"Such a college kid," I tease. "Hey, speaking of Mom, I've been meaning to tell you about this girl I met from the Oneida reservation in New York."

"Ooh, a girl!"

I roll my eyes. "Not like that. She knows our family."

"For real?"

"Yeah. She recognized Mom's name and knew our grandmother. Why hasn't Mom ever mentioned her mother to us?"

Katie blows out a breath. "Your guess is as good as mine. I've never understood why she's so tight-lipped about her life before she met Dad. Maybe she has a secret family out there that she likes better than us."

I chuckle. "Well, it piqued my interest. I have a week off next month, so I'm thinking of driving over there to check it out. I won't know anyone, but it would be meaningful to see where Mom's from and maybe stop by a museum or something."

"Let me know what you find, Detective."

"Will do." A drop of water plops next to my head. "Dammit. I need to call my landlord. I'll talk to you soon, OK?"

"Good luck, Wes. *Kunolúkhwa.*"

"Love you too, Katie."

Chapter 3

Chelsea

The Buffalo Outlaws have a chance to win the championship tonight, and I don't know what to do with my nervous excitement.

The Outlaws have been my favorite team since I was a little girl, even when all they did was lose. I lived with my dad near Buffalo while I was in high school, and we bonded over watching games together.

"Are you going to watch the game with me, Jess?" I call into the kitchen as I pull up the stream on TV.

"If I have to," she says. "I can think of twenty other things I'd rather do than watch yet another lacrosse game. I maxed out watching my brothers play nonstop."

"You don't want to see your cousin?" I ask, accepting a Genesee beer from my friend.

"Oh, that's right!" She plops next to me. "I forgot he plays for the Outlaws."

We clink bottles as the teams emerge for warmups.

"There he is." I gesture as Wes jogs by the camera. "Number thirty-three."

"Oh, gosh." Jess brightens. "He looks like my mom!"

"I thought so, too. It's his eyes; they're kind." He bumps shoulders with Jamie Montour and knocks him off the ball with a laugh. "They're light, though. Kind of green."

"White dad," she says knowingly, and I chuckle. "It's not his fault."

My phone buzzes as the players are lining up for the opening faceoff.

> **Lake'niha:** Are you watching the Outlaws game?

> **Me:** Yep. Jess and I just turned it on.

> **Lake'niha:** We'll see what they're made of tonight. It's a big opportunity for them to put the series away early and not have to play Game 3.

> **Me:** That would be amazing! I'll believe it when I see it :)

"Is that your dad?" Jessica asks.

"How'd you know?" I glance up in surprise.

"You always smile when he texts."

My smile grows wider. My dad has always been the one man I could count on.

I reach for my beading tray so I can work on some earrings while the game is on.

My nerves get the best of me, and my beadwork lies unattended late in the fourth quarter. The Outlaws just scored to go ahead by one goal, but their opponent, the Calgary Stampede, are pushing hard with less than a minute remaining in the game.

I message my group chat with Genny and her sister Mackenzie. They decided to attend the game at the last minute, and I can't imagine how tense the environment must be at the Outlaws' arena, nicknamed The Hideout.

> **Me:** This game is so stressful! How are you two holding up?

> **Mackenzie:** Genny looks like she needs a barf bag, but we're hanging in there

> **Mackenzie:** She's not touching her phone, so we can talk about her all we want

Me: Thinking of you, Gen! Does Zeke know she's there?

Mackenzie: Nope. Not sure if she'll want to talk to him after the game or not. We'll see how things play out.

"Well, shit."

I look up to see the Stampede score the game-tying goal with seconds to spare.

"We're going to need another drink to survive overtime."

"Agreed." Jessica hops up and heads towards the fridge. "I'll grab them. I'm too nervous to sit."

"I thought you were sick of watching lacrosse games?" I tease.

"That's before I had a cuz in the pros! I'm invested now."

We pace around the television. It's Sudden Victory format, so the first team to score wins the game. If that team is the Outlaws, they'll win the championship.

"Tell me about Wes," Jessica asks, her eyes glued to the TV.

My stomach somersaults as I think back to our first meeting, where we'd clicked immediately. He made me laugh, took whatever shit I threw at him, and played a damn good game of lacrosse. It was a dangerous combination for me and put him firmly on my Avoid This list.

"He's really nice," I reply. "Not full of himself like some of the professional players."

"Like Brock."

I shudder. "He's definitely not like Brock."

"Thank Creator, because I hated that guy."

Of all the boneheaded crushes I've had, Brock was, by far, the worst. He was handsome, charismatic, and an absolute snake. He loved to shower me with attention in public before belittling me behind closed doors.

"Why are you bothering with this?" Brock had asked over my shoulder as I reviewed the Women's Major Series Lacrosse registration form last year.

"Because I miss playing, and this gives me something to work towards," I replied.

He scoffed. "That league is a joke. It's not worth the effort to get yourself back in shape."

My chest was heavy with shame. I'd gained some weight since I stopped playing lacrosse, and knew it would be a hard journey back in the gym. "I know it's not comparable to the NLL, but it would feel so good to be back on a team again."

"Whatever." He started scrolling on his phone. "It's your decision, but I think it's a waste of time."

It killed me to admit I'd let his discouragement prevent me from working towards my dreams. I'd left my application unfinished that year. It wasn't the first time I had gotten distracted by a man and let my goals fall through the cracks, but it was the most painful. I didn't tell my friends a fraction of what he routinely said to me, because I was too humiliated.

Jess' gasp brings me back to the game. Zeke poke-checks the ball from the stick of a Stampede player before scooping it up and charging down the floor. He fakes out the goaltender and hits a perfect shot, sending the ball into the back of the net.

The Hideout goes absolutely berserk. The goal horn blares, and the camera shakes from fans pounding on the glass. Jessica and I scream and throw our arms around each other. The Outlaws do the same, piling on top of Zeke to celebrate his championship-winning goal.

"You're my good luck charm!" I exclaim. "You watch one game and they win the whole damn thing. This hasn't happened since I was a kid!"

The camera soon pans across a gaggle of players and I see Wes, his championship ball cap turned backwards and a wide smile splitting his face.

"He's cute," Jessica says. "We need to find him an Oneida girl out here."

My last sip of beer goes down the wrong pipe, and I cough aggressively.

"Do you know anyone who would be good for him?" she continues. "We just need to avoid Bear Clan relatives."

I pound my chest as my cough dies down. "I'll have to get back to you on that one."

Much to my shock and delight, Zeke is announced as the Most Valuable Player in the playoffs, and he thanks Genny in his speech. Those two have a long and painful history, along with a recent breakup. *Maybe that's about to change?*

> **Me:** OH MY GOD

> **Mackenzie:** DID YOU HEAR THAT?!

> **Me:** Tell me she's running into his arms right now

> **Mackenzie:** She just left! I hope she's able to make it onto the floor.

> **Me:** I need play-by-play reporting, Kenz.

> **Mackenzie:** I'll do my best. It's a madhouse here, so I can't see much.

I smile, but my heart hurts. Genny's about to reunite with Zeke, and Kenzie recently paired off with his brother Jordan. That just leaves me and my incredibly single ass. *Sigh.*

A wave of sadness hits me unexpectedly. Jess is my only friend I see with any regularity. I have Mackenzie and Genny, but we live several hours apart, and visits are few and far between. I'd rather be a nun than still be with Brock, but I can't deny that I miss having a romantic partner to share my days with.

Who am I kidding? That was never Brock, either. Brock has the emotional intelligence of a fruit fly, if I'm being generous. He did more harm than good in my life. But this is the first time I've been single for a long stretch, and it feels uncomfortable. I'm a serial monogamist, used to distracting myself with relationships, and I'm determined to break that bad habit this time around.

The Outlaws are passing the NLL Cup around. My breath catches as Wes is handed the trophy. He raises it above his head hesitantly, and the home arena roars its approval. His face lights up with a smile, and my insides twist painfully.

I had a fantastic time playing lacrosse with him. Some men are resistant to playing with women, acting like we might break if they touch us. Wes gave me too much room on our first series, and I burned him for a goal. He came right back and gave me everything he had after that. I loved that he matched my physicality. It challenged me to get creative with the ball. And I sure didn't mind how nice he was to flirt with, either.

The TV feed ends as the players are still celebrating, and I feel a sense of loss. *Maybe I should send him a quick message of congratulations. That would be the nice thing to do, right?*

I pull up his Instagram profile and lazily scroll through his posts. They're full of college lacrosse memories, his home in Wisconsin, and a few from his debut year with the Outlaws. He shared photos of Lake Michigan, sunrises over his backyard, and the night sky.

He seems like someone I'd enjoy talking to and spending time with.

I can keep lying to myself, but he made an impression on me all those months ago. I know it's the right thing to avoid hopping into a rebound relationship, but sometimes I regret turning him down.

He probably doesn't think about me at all.

My own profile shows the inaccuracy of that thought. He's liked just about everything I've posted since January, when he started following me. He leaves thoughtful and encouraging comments on my posts. And he's never once shown up in my DMs asking for anything more.

I kind of wish he would.

I tap to send him a message before I can change my mind. My fingers fly across the screen, typing out a message I hope comes across as polite and unbothered. *Nothing to see here.* I re-read it a dozen times and tweak my phrasing. My heart is pounding, which annoys the shit out of me.

"I'm heading to bed," Jess calls from the kitchen as she refills her water bottle. "I'll see you in the morning."

"I'm right behind you. Night, Jess."

I close my eyes and hit Send.

Chapter 4

Wes

The Outlaws afterparty is wilder than my usual scene, but it's a lot of fun.

I sip my whiskey and chuckle as our resident goal-scorer and party animal, Sawyer Lane, climbs onto the bar to drink from the NLL Cup. *If I lie low, maybe he won't notice me.*

Zeke, Genny, and I are chatting at a nearby table. Well, we're chatting in between the reunited lovebirds making out across from me. I truly don't mind. I'm just happy they were able to patch things up.

Genny giggles as Zeke whispers in her ear, so I take the opportunity to check my phone. I've had messages rolling in from friends and family, and I don't want to miss anyone.

I tap out a response to my parents, who texted that they were back at their hotel and would see me the next day. I'm thrilled they were able to make it out to Buffalo for the game and celebrate with me on the floor. I open Instagram and groan at the wall of direct messages waiting for me. *This may take a while.*

I'm about to navigate away when an unexpected name catches my eye and causes my heart to leap into my throat.

Chelsea John.

I nearly drop my phone on the table in my haste to click on her message.

> **Chelsea:** You looked good out there tonight, Rookie. Congrats on the championship.

My smile knows no upper limit. I'm pretty sure it must be visible from space.

"What's up?" Genny asks, her head tilted with curiosity.

My body buzzes with excitement. *She thought about me.* "Nothing, I just—" I memorize the contents of Chelsea's message before setting my phone down to be polite. "I just heard from someone I didn't expect to."

The party picks up after that, with Sawyer bulldozing through with tequila shots at one point. I excuse myself to use the restroom while he launches a campaign for more drinks.

I tuck myself into a corner and eagerly pull my phone back out. I've been crawling out of my skin waiting to write back to her.

> **Me:** Thanks! Hearing from you is almost as good as lifting that Cup. How've you been?

It's close to midnight, and I can't imagine she's still up. *Maybe she's just being polite.* My thoughts pinball around my brain for thirty seconds before I raise my thumb to darken the phone screen.

That's when I see a bubble pop up, indicating she's typing.

I bite my knuckles to stifle my excitement.

I assume she tolerates my presence as her social media follower. I try to be her hype man, but resist going beyond that. She told me she wasn't interested in anything more, and I respect that, even though it kills me. She's my lacrosse playing, badass, Oneida dream girl. I hope one day she'll give me a chance to prove myself to her.

> **Chelsea:** Pretty good. Trying to figure out what I want to be when I grow up. Easy stuff like that. How about you?

> **Me:** Been busy hypnotizing the team into keeping me on the starting roster. Living out my childhood dreams. Liking your Instagram posts. The usual.

> **Chelsea:** Don't let them know you can't defend a girl. That's reputation-ruining.

> **Me:** A PRETTY girl. Coach would understand.

I crane my neck to see if my friends have noticed I've been gone for a while. They look sloppy, so that should buy me some time.

> **Chelsea:** How many drinks have you had out of that Cup?

> **Me:** You think I would drunk text you?

> **Chelsea:** I kinda thought you would've by now, to be honest

"Wes!" Sawyer stands on a bench to flag me down.
I groan. "Gimme a minute. I'll be right there!"
Is she flirting with me?

> **Me:** Disappointed?

> **Chelsea:** Maybe a little

Definitely flirting.
A million possible responses clatter through my head, but I don't want to risk ruining this tenuous connection.
Sawyer jumps out of nowhere and tackles me against the wall.
"Dude. Come on, let's close this party out in style." He pulls me back towards our table as I frantically try to type out a message. Just as I'm about to hit Send, another comes through.

> **Chelsea:** Have fun and be safe tonight. Congratulations again.

Dammit, Sawyer.

People begin peeling off not too long after that.

"I'm probably going to head out," I announce. *I need some time to reconsider my life in light of the perfect woman sliding into my DMs.*

"You OK to drive?" Zeke asks.

"Yeah, I'm good. I've only had a couple of drinks, and I've been pounding water all night."

"All right, man. Take a few days off, and then we're right back at it with training camp." He grins and raps me on the back. Zeke and I play on the same professional field lacrosse team in the summer, and this will be my first year in that league.

"No rest for the weary, huh?"

"You mean, no rest *for the winners!*" Sawyer throws his arm around my shoulder and forcefully rubs my head.

I elbow him in the side. "Go to bed, Lanes. Your pillow is calling."

"With her sweet siren song, yes." Sawyer ducks away from me.

I toss off one last message to Chelsea as I walk to my car back at the arena.

> **Me:** Sorry to miss my chance at drunkenly serenading you tonight. Rain check?

The drive back home is short with so few cars out this late. I roll over the next morning feeling dazed. I'd fallen asleep in my contacts and my suit, with my phone still in my pocket. A kick of adrenaline floods my system when I remember last night's conversation with Chelsea. I open Instagram and pump my fist when I see a new message from her.

> **Chelsea:** Good morning, champ. Hope you had a great time partying it up last night

I smile from ear to ear. *I've got a chance, and I'm not going to squander it.*

Chapter 5

Aw^híhte'
Strawberries / June

Chelsea

I t's late Friday afternoon, and Shako:wi is dead.

I haven't seen a visitor for over an hour. I've re-organized the bookshelves by color and counted the items in the gift shop. Twice.

I light the contents of the smudge bowl near the entrance. The familiar scents of sage, cedar, and sweetgrass waft up, the sacred smoke surrounding me with its healing tendrils.

I scroll through my Instagram messages. I'd been hoping to hear from Wes, but so far he hadn't reached out today. *That's a good thing for my resolution...right?*

I read through our last few weeks of correspondence since I first messaged him. I smile re-reading his words, savoring the curiosity and thoughtfulness he brought to his questions about my life.

Wes: What are you up to this weekend?

Me: Working and beading, mostly. I'm trying to save up so I can move closer to Canada for lacrosse opportunities

Wes: I'd love to see some of your beadwork

Wes: It stinks that there are so few leagues for women players

Me: *picture of long fringe earrings with a moon phases pattern*

Wes: You made those?!

Me: Yep. I sell pieces online and at craft fairs when I can

Wes: Those are incredible. You're really talented! Could I commission you to make earrings for my mom and sister sometime?

My cheeks warm at his praise. *He's probably just being nice so he can get in my pants.*

The idea isn't unappealing, but I can't let myself fall back into this trap. I'm twenty-seven and ready to get a hold of my life, which includes a distinct lack of immature men.

I set my phone down with a sigh, pushing it from view and pulling out my latest book instead. I started it last night, and I'm already hooked.

The door chimes jingle as someone enters. I quickly scan to the end of my paragraph, trying to finish before needing to put the book down.

"*Shekólih*, welcome to—"

My breath fails as I look up to see Wes walking in the door. He stops in his tracks when he sees me, but then a wide smile lights up his face.

"It's you." His eyes sparkle.

"What are you doing here?" My heart races at the sight of him. We haven't seen each other since we met, and watching his games on TV hasn't adequately prepared me for how attractive I find him.

He props his elbows on the counter in front of me. His arms are tan from the summer sun, and I'm hopelessly distracted. "I'm visiting the ancestral homelands. What are *you* doing here?"

"I work here."

"Clearly. You told me you waitressed at a restaurant in Utica."

"I lied."

"I see that." His green eyes sparkle as he looks down at where I'm sitting. "Did you think I would stalk you?"

I clear my throat and stick a bookmark in my novel. "Would you like me to show you around?"

"I'd love that, but I'm also interested in what you've got there." He gestures to the novel I'm attempting to discreetly tuck away. "I didn't know you liked to read."

Shit. I'm caught completely unprepared for this conversation.

"It's, uh—a romance." I feel my cheeks flush.

"Very cool. Do you mind if I check it out?" Wes asks. He looks so darn innocent, and I feel a giggle start to bubble up in my throat. *He has no idea what he's walking into.*

I cringe and hand him the book. "I doubt you'd be interested."

"I'm interested in anything you find interesting." He flips it over and skims the back cover. The edges of his lips lift in a smile. "Hockey players?"

"I know it's not exactly classic literature, but it's a fun read." I shuffle some papers at the desk in an attempt to look unbothered. Brock had been so dismissive of my reading preferences, and I've learned to keep those under wraps.

He thumbs through the pages. "Can't say I've read this genre before, but I'll try anything. I'll see if my library has it." He hands the book back across the counter.

My eyes widen. "You want to read a romance novel?"

"Sure, why not?"

"It's...spicy."

He raises an eyebrow. "Tell me more."

My blush deepens, and I duck my head to hide it. "Well, I mean—"

"Is there *kissing*?"

I smother a smile. "There's more than kissing. Think you can handle that?"

"Oh my. I'll dig my pearls out of storage so I can clutch them." He leans forward. "We could talk about it together, like a book club."

The laugh I've been holding back finally escapes. "You're in for a wild ride."

He bites his lower lip. "I think I'm going to need a preview of this book now."

"All right. You asked for it." I flip through until I find a steamy scene. I hand the book to him with my finger holding it open to the correct page.

"Should I be nervous?"

"Yes, because I'll be judging you based on your reaction."

"The stakes are high. Got it." He settles into one of the cozy chairs in the area featuring Indigenous-authored books.

I pretend to scroll on my phone, but in reality I'm watching his every move. *Is he going to be cool or weird about it?* Reading is a big part of my life, and while I don't expect a guy to enjoy the same books, I at least expect him not to be a judgmental jerk about my home library.

Wes looks unphased for several pages before I notice his eyebrows tick slightly upwards.

Here we go.

I lean forward to observe him more closely.

He flips to the next page and crosses his ankle over his knee.

"How're you doing there, tough guy?"

He smiles but doesn't take his eyes off the page. "Just fine."

"Do you need some water, or..."

He glances up at me. "Are you having fun?"

"A tremendous amount."

He chuckles and goes back to reading. A page later he shifts in his seat, and it occurs to me I should have considered he'd *enjoy* the scene.

My stomach clenches at the thought, and my breathing picks up slightly.

Another page turns. He brings a hand to his jaw and starts rubbing his beard.

I'm no longer pretending to do anything other than stare at him.

His eyes dart to the opposite page, and he imperceptibly bites his knuckle.

I stabilize my hands on the counter as my legs feel gelatinous.

He adjusts his position and coughs into his hand. His eyes flick up and catch mine. "Damn, Chels."

Is it too late to crawl under the desk and pretend I'm not here?

"Not your cup of tea?"

"No, I—" Wes clears his throat. "This is really fun. I'm definitely going to read the rest of the book." He blinks slowly. "I like how much you surprise me," he says quietly.

Dammit. He passed the test.

I set down my phone with a clatter. "Ready for that tour?"

We walk around the Center together, making easy conversation as he takes in the various cultural artifacts. We climb the sweeping staircase to the second floor, and his eyes light up as the colorful stained glass window in the building's eaves comes into view.

"That's gorgeous," he says. His eyes skate over the wolf, bear, and turtle surrounding the white and purple Great Law of Peace from our national flag. "I love the depictions of the three clan animals, and the wampum belt."

"Isn't it stunning? That's my favorite part of Shako:wi."

Wes wanders over to the basket making exhibit, reading through the informational placards. "I'm embarrassed to admit I don't know anything about this tradition. I never saw anyone make these in Wisconsin."

I stand next to him. "That's probably because the practice didn't start here until after we lost most of our land. It was a survival tactic for people to make and sell wooden baskets to settlers. By then, your group had already left in search of better living opportunities in the Midwest."

He glances at me. "I didn't know that," he says quietly. "I never considered how devastating it must have been for the Oneida here to lose so much of their community after already losing their land. People would have lost family and friends, and they never saw them again."

I nod. "It was a painful time. I wish our two communities could be closer."

We slowly walk past the remainder of the basket displays.

"Do you want to grab dinner with me tonight?" He doesn't take his eyes off the exhibit.

I suck in a breath. It would be so easy to say yes. It would be a natural extension of our time together today.

"I have plans already. I'm sorry."

"No worries." I notice him swallow. "Anything fun?"

"Dinner with a friend. Actually, it's—" I cut myself off.

He glances over when I go silent. "What's that?"

"Nothing." I wander towards the next display case.

The entrance door dings as it opens. *Shit*.

Jess smiles when she notices me on the ledge overlooking the lobby. "Hey, girl. Ready to close up and get some dinner?"

I smile tightly. "Yeah, just give me a minute."

"I should get out of your way so you can head out," Wes offers.

Shit. I won't be able to live with myself if I don't tell him.

I scratch the back of my head. "Actually, I have someone for you to meet."

He tilts his head.

"Do you remember when I said I was friends with your cousin?" A smile tugs at the corner of my lips. "She's here."

His eyes widen.

"Come on. I'll introduce you." I gesture for him to follow me, but he remains rooted to the spot. "What's wrong?"

He shifts awkwardly on his feet. "Are you sure she wants to meet me?"

"Jess is kin. She's going to be over the moon!"

"I'm not from here." He looks at the ground. "I'm not sure why my mom left, or why we've never visited. I'm only half Oneida."

I'm so used to seeing him confident that it takes me aback to see his insecurity.

"Don't fall for that colonizer shit." Without thinking, I take two steps forward and pull him into a hug. "You're *Onyota'a:ká*. We're your people, and you belong here."

He relaxes into me, and I tighten my hold on him. He smells like fresh pine, and it overwhelms my senses.

"This is your home. We've been waiting for you," I assure him, resting my cheek against his shoulder. "You're just as Oneida as everyone else here."

His shaky breath skates across my cheek. "*Yaw□ko*," he thanks me.

"*Nyóh*." I look up at him, and our lips are so close it sends a shot of desire straight to my core.

He looks into my eyes for a few seconds before pulling back. "All right. Let's get this family reunion started."

I grin and call downstairs. "Jess! I've got a surprise for you!"

"Ooh, I love surprises!" she responds.

"Come on." I tug on Wes' hand. "You're going to love her."

He squeezes back with a soft smile.

I hang onto him as we descend the stairs. Jess waits at the bottom, her head tilted in question.

"You wanted to meet your cousin, right?" I ask, unable to hide my smile.

Her eyes pop as she looks behind me. "Oh my God."

He waves hesitantly.

Jess bounds up the stairs, beaming with joy, and launches into his arms. "Welcome home, cuz."

He steps back into the railing, trying to gain his balance with a laugh. "Thank you. It's good to be here." His eyes are shiny with tears as he blinks, and it melts my insides.

"Gramma is gonna *freak out* when I tell her," she says excitedly. "Can I tell her?"

"Give the kid a chance to breathe, Jess," I laugh. "You'll scare him away."

"Sorry, sorry." She gives him one last squeeze. "Are you here for a while?"

His eyes are hesitant but happy. "I'm just here for a quick visit. I wasn't planning on seeing anyone." He shoots me a pointed look. "I didn't know Chelsea worked here."

"*Ow*!" I rub my arm where Jess smacks me.

"Please forgive my terrible friend. I'm dying to get to know you," she says. "Can you stay for dinner with us?"

I groan internally, but Wes flashes me a pitiful look, and I can't deny him.

"Yes, please come out with us," I say genuinely. "We'd love to hang out with you longer."

His eyes are hard to read, but they trigger a slow burn in my veins. "It would be an honor to join you."

I swallow. "You two catch up. It's closing time, so I'll get things finished and we can leave."

I smile to myself at the sound of Wes and Jess' laughter echoing through the Cultural Center as I verify the register and run through the closing shift tasks. His warm voice rumbles through my chest, and I take a deep breath. *It's getting harder and harder not to like him.*

"All right, friends. Are we ready to head out?" I turn off the main lights.

"Let's go!" Jess chirps, and we head to the parking lot.

Chapter 6

Wes

"I'm working at the casino after this, so I hope you don't mind we're eating here," Jess says as we enter a local sports bar. "It's just across the street."

"This is great," I say. "I haven't had wings in a while."

"They're not as good out here," Chelsea whispers to me. "They're better in Buffalo."

"I heard that!" Jess laughs.

"I speak the truth." Chelsea holds up her hands.

We order drinks and settle into our seats.

"What's it like out on the Wisconsin rez?" Chelsea asks. "I've never been."

I smile. "It's vibrant. The community is large but tight-knit. It's just west of Green Bay, on Lake Michigan."

"I bet that's beautiful," Jess says.

"It is. And the people are wonderful," I continue. "Everyone feels like family." I pause. "I've always wondered about my mom's family here, but we've been so loved there."

Jess stirs her Pepsi with a straw. "I wish things were different. We've missed out on your entire life."

"Do you know why my mom left?" I ask hesitantly. "The story she told us has always been vague, and I've wondered what she's leaving out."

"What has she told you?" Chelsea asks.

"That she wanted a fresh start after ending an engagement. She doesn't elaborate much beyond that."

Jess and Chelsea exchange looks.

"I take it there's more to the story?" I ask.

"I don't want to step on your mom's toes," Jess says, shredding her straw wrapper.

I shake my head. "No, I want to know. It feels important, especially now that I'm here and meeting you for the first time."

"I'm sure her version is different because of what she experienced." Jess takes a deep breath. "Your mom was engaged to a man here, Jeremy. He was the son of the tribal government leader. Their family was, and still is, very influential in the community."

I lean forward on my forearms.

"Your mom told her family that he was getting rough with her, but they thought she was exaggerating. They figured she was getting cold feet about settling down."

My glass of water is icy cold as I clench my hand around it.

"Kay always seemed hesitant about the engagement, from what I've heard. She'd graduated top of her class from nursing school, and she wanted to have more stability and independence than women from the older generations," she continues.

"Jeremy was traditional and wanted her to focus on raising kids as soon as they got married."

"Typical," Chelsea mutters.

"Years later, he got arrested for domestic violence. Multiple times. And every time the women dropped the charges or the police conveniently couldn't find any evidence."

My jaw ticks.

"Your mom was telling the truth, and our family failed her," Jess says sadly. "She tried to break off the engagement, but Jeremy's family pressured our grandparents to keep her in check. One morning they woke up and Kay was gone."

"Gone?" I blink.

"She left a note to say she was leaving, and couldn't tell them where she was going. She went into hiding for years out of fear that Jeremy would find her if anyone knew where she was."

She must've been terrified. I run my hand over my beard. "When did the family find out she had gone to Wisconsin?"

She shakes her head. "I'm not sure exactly, because I would've been young. I get the sense it wasn't until you and your sister were already born."

"Do you know if she knew anyone out there?" Chelsea asks me. "We've always wondered why she went there, and whether she had someone to stay with."

I blow out a breath. "I don't know exactly. She has some friends she's extra close with, and they're the closest thing we have to family there. It's possible she knew them beforehand, but I just don't know."

Jess squeezes my hand. "I know this is a lot to hear."

I squeeze back. "It is, but it's also making a lot of sense."

"Your dad's not Native, right?"

I shake my head. "He's not. He's from a Midwestern family."

"I've been told Gramma met him once, but she never talks about it."

I raise an eyebrow. "Really? As far as I know, my dad has never met her."

"I would guess there are some secrets left to uncover," Chelsea says gently.

"It seems that way."

"Tell me about your sister," Jess asks with a grin. "I hope I get to meet her sometime."

The three of us chat easily over dinner, sharing stories about our childhoods in the same cultural traditions nearly a thousand miles apart. Chelsea is at ease in a way I haven't yet seen, and it's a struggle to look at anything that isn't her bright smile. I wish we could do this more often.

"I hate for this to end, but I need to head into work," Jess announces once we've paid the bill.

"I'm so glad I got to meet you." I get to my feet and hold my arms out to her. "Thank you for welcoming me here."

"Are you kidding? It's a dream come true to meet you finally." She squeezes me. "Do you mind if I tell the rest of the family?"

Unease coils in my stomach. "Could you hold off for now? I'm sure it's fine, but given what you've shared, I'd like to talk with my mom about it first and make sure she's comfortable."

I'm rattled by what I've learned about my mom's past. I have a lot of questions for her at some point, but for now I need time to let the new information settle. I'm glad to have met Jess, but this has given me pause about opening up to the rest of the New York family.

"Of course. I want her to feel safe." She pulls out her phone. "Gimme your number and we'll stay in touch."

"I'll see you at home," Chelsea says to her friend as she heads out.

"You two live together?" I ask. "You're just full of surprises today."

She ducks her head. "I'm subletting a room from her for a few months while I figure out what I'm doing next. I love living here and working at Shako:wi, but I'm feeling drawn to challenge myself more."

"Would that mean leaving the rez?"

Chelsea nods. "It's nerve-wracking to consider, but yes. I've been working to get back into full-time lacrosse, and it's hard to stay in game shape out here without practice buddies. Syracuse or Buffalo would put me in a better location for summer league and casual play."

I bite my tongue before begging her to move and join my practices. The thought of her being in the same city lights up my insides.

"When does your season start?" I ask.

"It started at the end of May." She looks away from me. "It's a heck of a drive to Canada for WMSL weekends."

I cross my arms. "OK, what gives? You give me a fake workplace, neglect to mention you're roommates with my cousin, and you've been driving through my city for the past month and not saying a word?"

She cringes. "I'm a spy?"

"Have I come on too strong?"

She looks at her feet. "No, you haven't."

"Do you secretly hate me?"

A smile creeps across her lips. "Definitely not." She tucks some hair behind her ear and looks up. "Here's some honesty for you: I'm trying out for the Haudenosaunee women's national team this September. They're playing at the World Box Championships in Utica."

"No way! I feel like a dumb guy because I didn't realize women competed there, too."

"It'll be the first time! Only the men have played before this. Really exciting stuff." Her face lights up, and I'd do anything to keep that smile on her face.

"Rosters should be coming out for that in a couple of months, I think." I nudge her foot. "I'll look for your name."

She fidgets with her earring. "We'll see. Competition is tough for spots, since the championship only comes every four years."

"I have no doubt I'll see you there."

She smiles shyly, and I shift from foot to foot.

"Thanks for all the hospitality you showed me today." I shove my hands awkwardly into my pockets. "I figured I'd come out here and just drive around a bit. But this was much better."

"I'm glad you came by Shako:wi." We walk towards our cars. "It was really nice to see you again."

"It was." I scan her expression, trying to get a feel for whether she'd be receptive to anything more than a goodbye. "Now I have Spicy Book Club to look forward to."

She rolls her eyes. "I fear you're about to be very disappointed."

I chuckle. "It's going to be great. I love reading new things, and this book definitely got my attention."

She shakes her head and leans against her car. "I keep trying to get rid of you, and you keep worming your way into my life."

"You're not trying very hard. I believe you were the one who slid into my DMs a couple of weeks ago, Ms. John."

Chelsea hides a smile behind her hand.

"Speaking of which, are we going to conduct this book club by Instagram, or can I finally get your number?" I prop my hip against her passenger door.

She thinks it over, her eyes conflicted.

"I promise I'll be good," I continue. "I won't blow up your phone with messages. I won't drunk dial you. And I absolutely won't send unsolicited pictures."

She laughs. "Those sound more like threats than promises."

"Only if you ask nicely. I'm a real fun drunk texter."

"I bet you are." She bites her pillowy bottom lip before exhaling with gusto. "Gimme your phone."

Mentally, I unroll a *Mission Accomplished* banner with noisemakers and confetti. Externally, I calmly enter my passcode and hand her the device.

She taps out her name and number. "Don't make me regret this."

I consider a flirty comeback before deciding otherwise. She's like a wild animal I'm desperately trying not to spook, and I don't want to take any chances.

"I'll be on my best behavior." I accept the phone back from her and type a quick message. "You should have my number now, too."

Chelsea pulls her phone out and swipes to save my contact information. She glances at my arm as she's typing and does a double take.

Her hands are on me before I realize what's happening. She turns my forearm back and forth, inspecting the inky stars there.

My heart races at her touch. "Can I help you?"

She traces her finger down one of my tattoos. "*Ohkwaliko*? I didn't see him hiding in there before."

The June air is warm, but goosebumps prickle my skin. "The Great Bear, yeah."

"I love it." She smiles and drops her hands. I miss her warmth immediately. "That's so clever, using the constellation instead of the animal."

My stomach flips at her praise. "Thanks. It's for my clan."

"I know."

"Oh, you do? Were you trying to find out if we're related?" I smirk.

"You wish."

I scratch my head. "So, uh…which clan are you?"

She throws her head back in laughter. "I shouldn't tell you. That way I can watch you squirm for longer."

"I'm a worm on a hook for you, Chels."

She rests her head against the car and stares at me. "You're something."

"I'd be so good to you."

She smiles. "I almost believe you. And I like the *Shoresy* reference."

I clutch at my chest. "And you watch *Shoresy*, too? My heart can't take this. You're the perfect woman."

Her giggles light up my spirit. "Stop it."

"I can't. You're encouraging me." I grin and place my forearm next to her head.

Her breath catches, and she visibly swallows.

I lightly brush my fingers across her cheek, and her eyelids flutter closed.

"Wes, please."

"What's that?" I'm close enough to smell the lingering aroma of sweetgrass in her hair.

Her eyes open and lock onto mine. "Please don't kiss me."

Oof. That's a kick in the gut.

I hold myself still and try not to drown in the chocolate depths of her gaze. "I won't."

We stare at each other for a few moments. She licks her lips nervously, and it is pure torture to pull back from her.

"I should probably let you get home. I've got a long drive back to Buffalo." I put my hands back in my pockets so they're not tempted to wander again.

"Yeah." She roughly runs her hand through her hair. "I hope you have an easy trip back."

"Thanks."

She pulls a car key from her pocket and fiddles with it. "Come back sometime soon. There are tons more people for you to meet."

"I definitely will."

"Hug for the road?" She holds her arms out, and I gratefully envelop her. "I'm really glad to have you as a friend."

Double oof. "Me too. Thank you for welcoming me home."

"It's where you belong." She steps back and unlocks her car. "Oh, and Wes."

"Yeah."

She looks up at me with a mischievous grin. "I'm Turtle clan. So, we're safe."

Her car beeps, and she zips into the driver's seat before I can react.

"Oh, you—"

She waves at me as she pulls away, her eyes dancing with mirth.

I stand in the empty parking spot and exhale deeply. I have a lot to unpack on the drive back to Buffalo.

Chapter 7

Chelsea

M y phone rings while I'm elbow-deep in soapy water. I
glance over and swear.

I lost track of time and forgot that Spicy Book Club was
starting. I've been anticipating it with a mixture of excitement
and terror, and had planned to fix myself up beforehand.
Instead, I'm sweating in the late June heat while scrubbing
caked-on pasta sauce off a pan from last night.

I shake water from one hand and gingerly lift my phone. I
balance it on the windowsill above the kitchen sink and slide a
finger across to answer.

"Well, hey." Wes' warm voice fills the room.

"Hey. Sorry, I'm just finishing the dishes." I blow damp hair
from my mouth as I reach for a sponge. "Jess will be home soon,
and I promised I'd have these done before that."

"No problem." He sits back in his chair, a breeze ruffling his
dark hair and linen shirt. "You look great."

I laugh. "I do not. I'm a sweaty mess."

"I like your mess."

Warmth creeps up my cheeks. "Where are you? You look like an old, rich guy out on his yacht."

Wes chuckles, raising a glass of amber-colored liquid to his lips. "Definitely not. My apartment has very little going for it, but it does have a tiny balcony."

"Well, aren't you fancy?" I dry the pan and set it on the counter with a clatter. "I'm about to take an ice bath at this point."

He swallows and takes a deep breath. "It's a hot one, for sure."

"What are you drinking?" I ask.

"Whiskey. It's my drink of choice when I have a chance to put my feet up."

I stick out my tongue. "Blech. Whiskey tastes like lighter fluid to me."

He chuckles. "It's an acquired taste. I can help you work up to it if you're ever interested in giving it another try."

A key rattles in the lock, and Jess pushes in the front door, sweaty hair clinging to her forehead. "It's too damn hot today!"

"Is that Jess?" Wes asks.

"That's our girl," I respond. "I was *just* finishing the dishes." I grin sheepishly at her.

"Mmm hmm, sure," she teases. "Hi, Wes!"

"Do you two want to catch up? I could use a quick shower," I ask.

"Sure, that'd be fun." She reaches for my phone. "Are you guys just chatting?"

"We're having a book club," Wes says.

"A book club?" Her eyebrows shoot up. "What kind of white people shit is this?"

"Blame Wes. It was his idea." I toss a rag onto the counter and make a beeline for the bathroom.

Ten minutes later, I'm feeling fresh and ready to get gross again in the next five minutes. I quickly braid my hair on my way back to the kitchen.

"Ready for your book club?" Jess asks.

I don't like the look in her eyes as she hands my phone back.

"Thanks for waiting," I say to Wes. "I felt icky."

"No problem. It was nice talking to Jess again." His eyes flick across the screen. "You still look great."

With wet hair and no makeup, I know I don't look my best. I tuck a lock behind my ear. "So, what did you think of the book?"

"I loved it."

"Really?"

"Yeah." Wes grins. "It was fun as hell. The main characters had great chemistry. The hockey scenes were cool. I like how we got to see the teammates interact and have their own personalities."

Jess hands me an ice-cold beer and clinks her bottle against mine as she walks by. "Thank you," I mouth to her. "So you actually did read the book?"

"Of course I did." He tilts his head quizzically. "Why wouldn't I?"

I take a sip. "Most guys think these types of books are silly."

"No way. It was a fun read. I *really* liked the female main character being on the team as well. That's a cool angle." He clears his throat. "So, uh, is this an accurate representation of what women want?"

A slow smirk grows across my face. "What do you mean?"

He scratches the back of his neck, and my eyes catch on the flash of triceps I'm given. "You know, the tall, dark, and handsome millionaire who's amazing in bed?"

I laugh loudly.

"What?" He smiles.

"You're missing the point."

"How so?"

"Why does she love him? Is it because he spends money on her?"

"Well, no."

"Is it because he's hot?"

"She definitely thinks he's hot."

I smile. "Yes, but the *reason* she thinks he's hot is that he makes her laugh, and he supports her. He thinks *he's* lucky to have *her*, and he shows her that with his actions."

Wes mumbles something under his breath.

"What's that?" I ask.

"Nothing. So, tell me more." He takes another sip of his beverage. "What else do you like?"

I tuck my legs underneath me on the couch. "Their chemistry's great. I love their banter."

"Me too. It really made me root for them."

"Same. And that makes their eventual, uh, spicy time that much better."

"Agreed." He pages through the book. "So, how's a guy supposed to feel like he can make a woman happy in the bedroom if this is what we're measuring up against?" He gives me a lopsided grin.

"Oh, please. The bar is on the floor."

He raises an eyebrow.

"It's not about any of the stuff that you're probably thinking of." My braid is starting to tug at my scalp as it dries, and I slowly pull it loose as I talk. "Women just want a man who makes sure she feels good, too. That it's not just all about him."

His eyes follow my movements as my hair comes undone. "Isn't that standard?"

"You would think so, but it's very hard to find."

His eyes slide back to mine in concern. "Seriously?"

"Seriously."

"What the hell is wrong with men?"

"That's a question I ask myself often."

"Wait a minute." He sits upright. "Are you telling me most men don't make sure a woman gets hers before he does?"

"Before? Sweet summer child, it rarely happens *after*."

He looks utterly gobsmacked. "Can I apologize on behalf of my gender?"

I giggle, fluffing my damp hair out into waves. "Maybe you could do a speaking tour to help educate your species."

"I might need to." He shakes his head. "Men are idiots."

"I'll drink to that."

His empty glass rattles on the table next to him. "So, what's the next book?"

My eyebrows go up. "You want to read another one?"

"Yeah. Hit me with your best shot."

I chuckle. "All right. I'll come up with something and send you a title soon."

"Can't wait."

I end the video call and drain the last of my beer. Jess wanders through as I'm rinsing the bottle.

"So. You and my cousin?"

I nearly drop the slippery glass. "What? No."

She taps her foot. "You're reading smut together?"

I laugh nervously. "It's not *smut*."

"Chelsea."

I avoid her gaze. "He saw me reading a book at Shako:wi and expressed interest in checking it out. That's all."

"I see how he looks at you."

I sigh. "I know he likes me. And I like him, too, if I'm being honest. But we're just friends, seriously. You know I jump into relationships, and I don't want to do that anymore."

She crosses her arms.

I drop the clean bottle into the bin of returnables. "I'm trying to start new patterns here, trust me."

She eyes me warily. "OK."

A few minutes later, I plop onto the couch with a tall glass of ice water and my phone, determined to find a new book for me and Wes to read together.

Chapter 8

Wes

I brought a list of questions to the next installment of Spicy Book Club.

Chelsea's commentary on what attracts women to these books got me thinking. I like to think of myself as a good partner, but it's eye-opening to see the themes broken down. How did I measure up against these book boyfriends?

Funny? *Check*. Supportive? *Check*. Make sure she enjoys herself during sex? *Double check*. What on earth is wrong with my fellow men?

Our last discussion was a window into Chelsea's world: her beliefs about herself, her views on men, and what she likes in relationships. She comes off as a confident woman who knows what she wants, but I've caught some insecurities that lie underneath: her surprise when I called her pretty the first time we met; her subtle blush whenever I've complimented her; and her hesitancy to share important parts of her life. I want to know more without being a creep. I'm treasuring our fledgling friendship the more I get to know her, and I want to protect that at all costs.

I came up with thoughtfully worded questions to guide tonight's discussion and promised myself I wouldn't flirt with her. Spicy Book Club isn't fun if the other person is trying to get you into bed, right?

That well-intentioned oath flies out the window the second she answers my call.

"Hey, Rookie." She's bathed in sunlight, wearing sunglasses, a wide-brimmed hat, and—*Oh, shit.*

I clear my throat. "Hey. It's hot again today, huh?"

"Yeah." She fans herself with her book. "I couldn't stand it in the apartment any longer. It's cooler outside than it is in there."

I bite my cheek to keep my focus on her face and not the straps of her vibrant green bikini top. *Creator help.*

"So, uh, different kind of book this time." I flip some pages in my notebook until I come to my list.

She grins. "I figured I'd throw you straight into the pool with a dark roman—Did you bring a notebook?" She pulls her sunglasses down to look at me.

"I did." I click my pen open.

"You're taking notes?" Her lips curl upwards.

"Think of me as an academic researcher. I'm studying women."

"I like your enthusiasm." She adjusts her position, and the phone briefly dips dangerously low.

I bite the inside of my cheek and wrench my eyes away from her curves. "You're going to have to give me details on what women like about a guy who stalks the main character, because I would think that would be a major red flag. To put it mildly."

Her laughter floats across the screen. "Well, yeah, in real life that would be a restraining order. But as an escape from reality, it's hot to think about a man being utterly obsessed with you."

"That's not creepy and overbearing?"

"It's about role reversal. We're used to seeing men hold the power in relationships. But here *she* has *him* wrapped around her finger because he is so consumed by her. He doesn't want to hurt her or scare her. He wants any possible crumb of attention he can get from her."

Never thought I'd identify with a stalker, but here we are.

"Do all of these books boil down to women wanting to be adored and cared for by their partners?"

"Pretty much."

I chuckle and lick my thumb to flip a page in my notebook.

"You are such an old man," Chelsea says. "No one turns pages like that anymore."

"It's effective. Otherwise, the paper sticks."

"No, it doesn't."

I smile and fold the notebook over. "So, women would be into this stuff?"

"What stuff?"

"The, uh—" I scratch the side of my head.

"We're adults. You can use your big boy words," she teases.

I blow out a deep breath. "OK. You asked for it."

"Oh, I'm asking for it."

This woman is impossible. How am I supposed to behave myself under these conditions?

I clear my throat and start counting on my fingers as I speak. "Dirty talk? Getting pinned against walls? Possessiveness?"

"I mean, every woman is different, so I can only speak for myself. But yes, yes, and yes."

I'm starting to sweat, and it's not just from the sun. I scribble randomly on my page, needing to do something with my hands but not coherent enough to write words. "Noted. Which did you prefer: the car scene or the woods scene?"

Chelsea whistles. "The *car scene.* That was really hot. I loved that he was so desperate to have her, and that he wanted to use his mouth on her."

I bite my knuckle to suppress a groan. It's probably frowned upon to get hard during Spicy Book Club.

"In these books, the men always love doing that. It doesn't feel like that's the case in real life, unfortunately." Her skin looks flushed.

"I'm going to guess that's because they don't know how to slow down and enjoy a woman." My voice comes out raspy. "There's nothing better if you commit to taking your time."

She's *definitely* blushing now.

"I take it you're someone who enjoys that?" She fidgets with the brim of her hat.

"Very much so." My hands tremble slightly as I raise my glass, gulping down some whiskey.

She hums quietly in appreciation, and I am absolutely getting hard during Spicy Book Club.

"Well, you should be happy to hear you're Book Boyfriend material, then."

I shake my head and set my drink down. "Not possible. I'm not tall enough."

Her laughter warms my insides. "The men are all over six feet, aren't they?"

"Seems that way. Us short kings can't compete."

She smiles slyly. "I'm not so sure about that. I like shorter guys, personally. Why would I need a giant when I'm five-five?"

"So, you're telling me there's a chance?"

She giggles. "Depends. Can you pick me up?"

"I'm certain I can, but get over here and let's be sure."

And there goes my No Flirting resolution.

Chelsea bites her lip. "I weigh too much. I'm an athlete."

"Baby, I bench press more than you weigh. I'm not worried."

She's visibly squirming, and I can feel every one of the miles between us.

"You good over there?" I ask quietly, unabashedly pressing my luck.

She blows a piece of hair out of her eyes. "I'm good. Just incredibly single."

"Me too."

Her gaze meets mine. "You're not seeing anyone?"

I shake my head. "Not for a while."

She looks down, fiddling with her book. "I suppose a little flirting wouldn't hurt, then? Between friends?"

My stomach flips with excitement. "Not at all. I like flirting with you."

"I don't want to give you the wrong idea." Her eyes flick back up to mine. "I like you, quite a bit, but I want to be careful with my heart."

I run my hand through my hair. "I would never push you. You call the shots."

Chelsea smiles. "Game on."

I'm not quite sure how it happened, but Spicy Book Club has gotten quite spicy indeed.

Chapter 9

Ohyótsheli'

Green Beans / July

Chelsea

The sun is shining on one of my favorite places in the world.

With the NLL in the offseason, most players fill in the gaps in their calendars, and paychecks, with other leagues. Zeke and Wes play pro field lacrosse for the New York Havoc, and this weekend they're in front of a home crowd in Albany, NY. Genny invited me to watch with her, since I'm between games for my own summer league.

"Does it feel good to be back?" Genny asks as we climb the bleachers. "I used to love coming out here to watch you play."

I smile and look around at the outdoor stadium where I played four years of lacrosse with the University of Albany. Genny had often made the long drive from Cattaraugus to see my games. "It does. I was so happy here. Lots of great memories."

I thrived in college. I was less than two hours from home in Oneida, but living away from the reservation for the first time. I was thrust outside of my culture, and it was a bumpy transition, but I enjoyed sharing my traditions with non-Natives. I missed my family and friends, yet I could be myself in a way I couldn't back home. I didn't have to live up to, or down to, anyone's expectations. It was freeing.

"I'm so glad you're back playing box this summer." Genny leans over to dip a tortilla chip into the package of nacho cheese on my lap. "I really think it's going to help you get your groove back."

"I think so, too. I lost a lot of confidence and direction when I fell away from lacrosse after college."

"You need the medicine of the Creator's Game," she says softly.

I nod. "You're right. As usual."

She smiles. "Speaking of getting your shine back, how's the single life?"

I groan. "It's fine. Better than rebounding with some loser."

She smiles sympathetically. "It's hard to be alone, though. It gets lonely, even with plenty to keep you busy."

I crunch on a chip. "Yeah, especially now that you and Zeke are back together and on your own little love island."

"Sorry not sorry."

"Yeah, yeah."

Genny and Zeke have been in love with each other since high school, but never could seem to get their timing right. I can't be happier that they're finally together, even if it reminds me of how much I miss having a partner of my own.

She cringes. "Kenzie too, I suppose. She and Jordan have been in the 'On' phase of their situationship for a while."

"I've been trying to tell you, I'm too single for our girls' group chat. You're all dating Jacobs brothers."

She laughs. "Do you want me to see if Miles is available?"

I stick my tongue out at her. "Miles Jacobs is a child."

"He's twenty-four! That's the same age as Wes."

"And I'm twenty-seven. Too old to be dealing with immature men who don't know what they want." I blow my hair out of my face. "I need an older man."

"You just need someone who's the opposite of who you usually go for."

"Well, usually I fall for assholes."

"Shouldn't be too hard, then," she teases.

We sip our beverages and look around at the stadium. The crowd is beginning to fill in, and I'm hit with a wave of nostalgia as I think back on playing here to a roaring crowd.

I'm a great lacrosse player. I know that deep in the marrow of my bones. The Creator gifted me not just with the game, but with the skill and discipline to play it well. Competing as a Division I college athlete remains the highlight of my life. My drive and confidence took a nosedive after graduation, however, and I'm still picking up the pieces.

"Actually," I begin hesitantly, "I'm kind of talking to someone new."

Genny spins around so fast she nearly drops her cup. "Excuse me?"

I'm almost certainly going to regret this.

I flick a piece of fuzz from my t-shirt to look chill. "Just something casual."

"You're talking to a new guy, and you didn't tell us!" Her voice jumps an octave.

"It's really new," I say.

She huffs. "Kenzie's going to kill you for keeping secrets. Well, tell me all about him!"

I stab a clump of ice with my straw. "He's, uh–"

"Not a lacrosse player, right? Those are on your Avoid list."

I scratch the back of my head. "Actually..."

"Chelsea John!" Her jaw drops.

"It was an accident," I say sheepishly.

"How do you accidentally—You know what? *I'm* going to kill you, because you're over here chatting up some rando player, when you *could've* been seeing Wes!"

I cough into my hand. "I can't date Wes."

"Why not?" she asks with exasperation. "I've been telling you for months that he's a total catch."

"He's too young," I say, "and he's too close to our friend group. If we dated and it ended badly, it would create a lot of stress and drama for everyone."

"*If* it ended badly," Genny says pointedly. "I can't imagine Wes turning into a jerk because of a breakup."

I grumble and sip from my straw.

"He's only a few years younger than you, and he's *so good*, Chels. I wish you'd give him a chance."

"Too risky."

She sighs. "Fine. So what's your new guy's name?"

"Uh—" I hadn't anticipated needing to come up with a name for him. "I'd rather not say."

She narrows her eyes at me. "Why?"

"Because I don't want you and Kenzie launching an internal investigation into his life starting from kindergarten."

"Instead, we'll be shaking you down for details. Got it."

I chuckle.

"So, a mystery man who plays lacrosse." She continues to glare at me. "Can we give him an alias to solidify his mysterious nature?"

I think for a few seconds. "The Bear."

"The Bear?" she splutters.

"Yes."

"Why The Bear?"

I shrug. "That's up to you to figure out, Detective."

"Is this a clan thing? Is he Native?"

As usual, my worst-laid plans blow up in my face.

"I've dated plenty of non-Native guys. Consider the nickname open-ended."

"You are infuriating."

I chuckle.

"How long has this been going on?" Genny asks.

"About six weeks or so."

She mutters and pulls out her phone. "I'm telling Kenzie on you."

A horrifying thought occurs to me. "Could you not tell Zeke for now?"

She eyes me suspiciously. "Why?"

I shrug and attempt to look unbothered. "I'd just rather not deal with his judging me."

"Zeke's not judgmental."

"Maybe that's the wrong word, but he'd be weird about it. Protective and macho."

She laughs. "You might be right about that. He thinks of you as a sister."

The players jog onto the field for warmups, and we cheer at their arrival. Zeke and Wes find each other after a minute and pass the ball in front of the net before Wes winds up and shoots at the goalie.

"It's weird to see Wes with a long pole," I say. Some defenders and midfielders in men's field lacrosse carry six-foot sticks, a big change from the indoor game. *Damn, he looks good with it, too.*

"Isn't it?" Genny says. "He's a badass. You'll see him out there whacking guys and swinging that thing around all game. We're lucky he had his short stick with him that day we played together."

"Mmm hmm." I admire his form as he winds up and cranks another shot into the net. "Might've been fun, though."

She glances over at me with an eyebrow raised. "Glutton for punishment?"

If Wes is involved? Hell. Yeah.

"Something like that," I mutter.

The game is electric. It's clear these two teams do not like each other, based on the unnecessary pushes, penalties, and audible trash talking.

Shortly after halftime, Zeke gets laid out on a dirty hit at midfield. He was scooping up the ball when another player rammed into him from behind, sending his large frame crumpling to the ground with an audible *crack* of equipment.

The refs don't call the obvious penalty, and Havoc fans loudly express their disapproval with boos and shouts as play continues.

Genny grabs my knee and squeezes as Zeke is slow to get up, clearly in pain.

"He'll be all right. He's got a thick sku—oh, shit."

My voice fades as Wes launches himself at the player who leveled Zeke, shoving him backward. Two other Havoc players run over to back him up, and pretty soon it's a full-on melee. Jerseys are grabbed, gloves are shoved in faces, and creative insults are yelled.

"Oh boy," I say as Wes loses his helmet in the scuffle. He doesn't back down, even though he's probably five inches shorter than the nearest opponent. He's standing up for his injured teammate, and unfortunately, it's extremely hot.

"He's back on his feet," Genny says with relief as Zeke is helped up by another player. He fist bumps Wes as he walks by the penalty box on his way to the Havoc's sideline.

Wes is an absolute menace for the remainder of the game. He aggressively retrieves ground balls, foils potential goal scorers, and breaks up plays. My jaw hits the floor at one point when he leaps, swinging his stick up and over the player he's defending.

He dislodges the ball and sends it rolling towards a Havoc player.

"Holy heck," I exclaim.

"I told you," Genny says. "He's a different person with that long pole."

"I thought he was a nice guy." *Do I need to re-evaluate everything I know about him?*

We both wince as Wes slashes across his opponent's body.

"I felt that one."

The game is drawing to a close, and the Havoc are up by one. It would be huge to get a goal right now and put the game away, but unfortunately the team is stuck in their own end.

"Get it out of there!" Genny yells, her legs bouncing nervously.

The goaltender makes a save, but the ball rebounds back to the other team. The shot clock resets, so now they have a fresh thirty seconds to try again.

The offense cycles through some passes, raising the pressure on the Havoc defense as they move closer to the net. I can't see the game clock, but I know it's close to the final whistle.

One of the attackmen hesitates with the ball in his stick, his eyes wild as he looks around. *I wonder if he's a rookie?*

Wes likely has the same thought, and he slides in from his position to double-team the offensive player. The attackman quickly winds up to throw the ball away, but Wes anticipates his move and slashes to knock the ball loose. He kicks it over to a nearby midfielder, who scoops it up and makes a fast break down the field.

The fans jump to their feet in celebration of the turnover.

"Go! Go! Go!" Genny and I scream.

Wes doesn't miss a beat, catching a pass from the middie and barreling across the field. The Havoc attackmen spread out into formation near the goal, each of them covered by defenders. Zeke is to the right of the net, his favorite spot.

"He's going to pass it to Zeke for the goal," I say to Genny.

Wes comes in hot, and a defender moves up to cover him, leaving Zeke undefended. *Bad call, bro.*

I grin, knowing what's coming next.

Wes winds up as though he's going to shoot, but instead passes over the defender. Zeke grabs the ball and spins around in one movement, leaping to shoot high over the goalie's shoulder.

A satisfying *ping* rings out as the ball sails into the net and rattles the goal posts.

The crowd explodes with cheers. There's only five seconds left on the game clock, and the Havoc are going to win.

Wes bounces on his feet and shimmies his shoulders in celebration. He's quickly swallowed up by Zeke and their teammates as they joyfully pile on each other. I bite my lip so hard I wince, because he is *so damn cute* I can't stand it.

Genny squeals and pulls me in for a hug. "What a play!"

My insides are a mess. Nothing is hotter to me than watching a talented man kick ass at the Creator's Game. I flip through mental images of what it would be like to wait for Wes after games and get pulled in for sweaty kisses. It would be so easy to give in to the easy dynamic we've fallen into together. To be with him.

Until it wasn't. Until it ended in tears and resentment and losing more of myself to a man. Again.

I liked Wes more than I wanted to admit, but I couldn't do that to myself again. No one else would protect me and fight for me, so it had to be me. I had to put myself first.

The teams finish with their handshakes and bro hugs after the game, and the players begin to disperse. Most head to the locker room, but Zeke and Wes jog towards the audience.

Zeke pushes his lacrosse stick through the fencing at the front of the bleachers and deposits it at Genny's feet. He grabs a railing and hauls himself up until he's close to her. "Hey, baby."

She smiles widely and cradles his face, pulling him in for a kiss.

Damn. That's hot.

I look away from their embrace, acutely feeling the lack of a hunky man to pull himself up to me for a kiss.

My gaze catches on Wes, and ironically, the hunky man is *right there*. But I can't.

His eyes sparkle. "You want a kiss, too? I'll climb up there for you."

I roll my eyes. "In your dreams."

"Abso-fucking-lutely." He plants the end of his stick into the ground and leans on it. His hair is drenched in sweat, and his eye black is streaking down his cheeks, but dammit, he looks good enough to eat.

Zeke and Genny are still nose to nose, chatting quietly in a world of their own.

I clear my throat. "You looked good out there, Rookie. I like you with the long pole."

He raises an eyebrow, and I cringe at my unintentional innuendo.

"I'm impressed you noticed from all the way up there."

This man.

"I didn't mean—"

He chuckles. "I know you didn't. The long pole is my superpower, honestly. I'm a different player with it. I miss having one in the indoor game."

"I could tell. I've never seen you play that aggressively."

"Does that do it for you?" His eyes sparkle.

Heat rises in my cheeks. I look out onto the field, searching for something to fixate on besides his hazel eyes. "I always thought it would be fun to play with one. You get to whack at people all game."

"You can borrow mine if you'd like," Wes says. "I'll sacrifice my body for your amusement."

"Are you saying you'd like me to handle your long pole?"

He barks out a sharp laugh, and it triggers my own fit of giggles.

"*That* one was on purpose," he says with a grin.

"You're a quick study."

He smiles at me while shaking his head. "You're something else."

I shrug and look away in an attempt at nonchalance. I turn to find Genny watching with an amused smile playing on her lips.

Zeke jumps back down onto the field. "You two should come to lunch with us," he says.

Wes catches my eye, and I smile. "We seem to keep meeting this way," I say.

Genny tilts her head. "What do you mean?"

"I ran into Chelsea at the Oneida Cultural Center a few weeks ago, and weaseled my way into dinner with her and a friend." Wes hasn't taken his eyes off me, and it's going to create a problem.

"I can't shake this guy," I say with a smile, "but I can't stay. I have to head into work." I'm not sure whether I'm disappointed or relieved to have an excuse to avoid spending more time with him.

Wes' face falls, but he recovers quickly. "Ah, that's too bad. Another time, then."

I tuck a strand of hair behind my ear. "Yeah. Another time."

He watches me for a few seconds before setting his stick on the ground. "Let me give you a quick hug goodbye."

"Oh, I—" I look around, trying to find a way onto the field, but the nearest entrance is several sections over.

"Don't worry, I'm coming up." He contemplates the distance between himself and the bleachers.

"Need a boost?" Zeke quips.

"*No.* I got it." Wes jumps and grabs the bottom railing.

"You don't have to—" I start to say.

He lifts his bodyweight until he's close enough to swing a leg onto the platform. He pulls himself the rest of the way up and smiles at my surprise.

"I may not be tall, but I do a lot of pull-ups." He grins and envelops me in a sweaty hug.

I exhale, my nails digging into his back. "You're disgusting."

He chuckles against my ear, and the vibrations rumble through my core. "Well, if you'd stuck around, I would have showered for you."

He's objectively gross, but my body has not gotten the message. It's too busy going into overdrive at his nearness.

"I'll see you sometime soon?" My voice comes out as a whisper. "I'm playing in Canada for the next month, so things will be busy."

"I'll be traveling with my team, too. I wish I could catch one of your games." He gives me one last squeeze and jumps down to the field.

I attempt to settle my breathing. "You both had a great game today. Incredible effort, especially at the end."

"Thanks, Chels." Zeke runs a hand through his wet hair. "You want to hit up the showers and get out of here?" he asks Wes.

"Let's do it. See you ladies soon." Wes' eyes twinkle as he glances at me, and I'm *really* going to need him to cut that out.

"Um, were you *flirting* with Wes?" Genny elbows me as we head back to our seats to gather our things.

Shit. "No. We're just friends."

"I always joke with my friends about wanting to *handle their long poles*." She fixes me with a pointed stare, and I laugh. "And since when have you been friends? You've only met him a couple of times before this, right?"

The first rule of Spicy Book Club is you do not talk about Spicy Book Club.

I ignore her question. "He's cute, OK? But I can't hop back into a relationship. I don't trust myself to make good decisions about men."

"Well, I hope Wes knows that," she says, "because he looks at you like you're the last bottle of water in the desert."

The feeling is mutual.

Chapter 10

On^stase'
Green Corn / August

Wes

It's midnight, and I'm knee-deep in the latest book club installment: a small town romance involving jam making. My schedule has been so busy with travel, lacrosse, and personal training clients that it's been weeks since I've been able to read. I desperately wanted to catch one of Chelsea's WMSL games, but I've been playing across the country every weekend. I haven't seen her in a month, and I'm close to inventing an excuse to visit the Oneida rez again.

My mind wanders as I think back to seeing her at my game in July. I was disappointed she couldn't stay longer, but her presence was such a treat I couldn't be too down about it.

Zeke, Genny, and I grabbed lunch at a diner afterwards. A fully loaded hamburger was calling my name after burning all my fuel on the field.

"Zeke, could you do me a huge favor?" Genny asked with a sweet smile. "I forgot my wallet in my car. Would you mind grabbing it from me?"

He waved her off. "I'm paying."

"Please? I don't want it sitting out."

He lowered his menu to the tabletop. "You're lucky you're cute. Gimme your keys."

Genny spun to face me as soon as he left. "Hey, so..."

I looked up at her with a raised eyebrow. "What's up?"

She stabbed at the ice in her cup with a straw. "You'd mentioned months ago that you were trying to get Chelsea's number. Did you ever talk her into that?"

I smiled. "I did. We've talked a few times."

Her face lit up. "Really? That's great!"

"Why do you ask?"

"Well—" Genny bit her lip. "I don't want to overstep, but I really think the two of you are perfect for each other."

"Yeah?"

"Yeah." She took a sip of her water. "But Chels is—She's been hurt in the past, and the idea of a genuinely nice guy is foreign to her."

"I had a feeling."

"Are you two—?"

"We're not dating, if that's what you're asking."

She sighed. "Are you still interested in her?"

"I'm not interested in anyone *but* her, to be honest."

Genny grinned. "See, I knew I liked you."

The door dinged as Zeke came back inside and walked towards us.

Her eyes darted to him and back to me. "Just be patient with Chelsea, if you can. She has a lot of misconceptions about herself and what relationships should be like. Her last ex was a real piece of work."

"How so?"

Zeke dumped Genny's keys on the table with a clatter. "Are you sure you left it in the car? I looked everywhere and couldn't find it."

She dug through her purse and produced her wallet with a sheepish smile. "Oops. I guess I looked right past it earlier. Sorry, babe."

My phone buzzes, so I set my Kindle down and smile at the notification that just came through.

> **Chelsea:** Hey Rookie. You up?

> **Me:** I'm not a rookie anymore, you know

> **Chelsea:** What would you like me to call you, then?

> **Me:** You can call me whatever you want. What's up?

> **Chelsea:** Are you alone?

My stomach tightens. *This can only be good.*

> **Me:** Who would I be with?

> **Chelsea:** I dunno. You could have a girl over or something

> **Me:** You're the only girl I want to have over

My phone screen lights up with her name and picture. It's a regular phone call, not our usual video chat we use for book club.

I swipe to answer. "Well, hi there, gorgeous."

"Hey," her voice is breathy, and my dick leaps to life. She sounds as though she just woke up, and my mind goes into overdrive picturing her tangled up in her sheets with tousled hair and rumpled clothes.

"What can I do for you?" I settle back against my headboard, one arm propped behind my head.

I hear her adjust her position with a soft sigh. "I fell asleep reading in bed, and I—" She pauses, and my heart beats loudly with each passing second. "I had a really good dream."

"About the book?"

"About you."

I suck in a breath. *This is unexpected.*

"Were you knocking me on my ass while scoring on me again?"

"No. You were here. With me."

I'm playing a million different scenarios for how to proceed, terrified of guessing wrong.

"Chels, are you—" I swallow. "Was I—"

"You were touching me, and it felt *so good*."

A low rumble emerges from my chest before I can stop it. "Do you want to tell me about it?" I take off my glasses and set them on top of my Kindle.

"I don't know." She gives a half-hearted chuckle. "I've never told anyone about a dream like this."

"Use your words, baby. Please. I want to know everything."

"Do you really?"

"This is my most anticipated audiobook of the year. Fire it up."

Chelsea giggles, and I'm about to lose my mind with frustration at being apart from her.

"You showed up in my room after a game. You said you'd been thinking about me all day and couldn't wait any longer to see me."

"I can understand the sentiment," I murmur. "What else?"

"You climbed into bed and started kissing me." She hesitates. "You kissed down my neck and ran your hands over me."

I close my eyes and try to summon self-restraint. "Did you like how I kissed you?"

"Yes," she answers with a soft whine.

I'm mentally calculating how long it would take to drive to her if I went 30mph over the speed limit on the Thruway.

At the risk of sounding like a 90s phone sex operator, I ask, "What were you wearing?"

"A sleep set, the same one I'm wearing now. A navy blue tank top with matching shorts."

I can instantly picture her beneath me, and I'm in trouble.

"I bet your body feels amazing under that fabric."

"I wish you were here," she breathes, her voice catching. "I haven't seen you in so long."

My breathing picks up. "I know it's late, but I can't leave knowing you're thinking about me."

"Then stay. Please."

"Well, since you asked so nicely," I groan, wrapping my palm around myself through my sweatpants. "*Fuck*, Chels." I drop my head back with desire and frustration. "Can I see you?"

"No, just voice," she insists. "Will you—" She pauses to take a breath. "Will you talk dirty to me?"

Fuck me. I didn't anticipate a wet dream coming to life tonight.

"Anything you want, baby." I exhale shakily, struggling to stay focused. "Tell me what else I did in your dream that you liked, and I'll take it from there, OK?"

She swallows. "You had your fingers inside of me, and you made me come so hard."

"Did I use my mouth on you?"

"No, but I wish you had."

I groan. "Dream Me is an idiot. I'm going to need you to get those pretty nipples hard for me, OK? I'm not there to do it myself."

"They already are." Chelsea gasps slightly before moaning a few seconds later. "But it feels really good to pretend you're the one touching them."

The girl of my dreams is touching herself and imagining it's me. *This is unreal.*

"Are you going to listen to what I tell you to do?" I ask, my voice gravelly.

She swallows. "Yes."

"That's a good fucking girl."

The moan I'm rewarded with shakes me to the core. Chelsea is a badass in her daily life, but my girl wants to let go and get taken care of after dark. I'm happy to oblige her.

I'm painfully hard at the image of her squeezing her perfect breasts at my command, nipples aching to be touched. "I would have those nipples in my mouth if I were there," I growl. "That tank top would be pushed up so my lips could be everywhere."

She groans. "You turn me on so much."

"The feeling is mutual. Tell me how wet you are for me."

She's starting to whimper, and I'm having to make a conscious effort not to finish myself off before she gets hers. "I'm really wet."

I bite my lip and groan. "I bet you are. I want you to use your fingers and imagine that's my tongue instead." Her needy noises are pushing me closer to the edge. "I would take my time licking every inch of you if I were there. I want those gorgeous legs wrapped around me and shaking."

"Wes, please." Her voice is desperate.

"Are you going to come for me, Chels?" I breathe unevenly. "Slip two fingers inside and fuck yourself for me. I want you to come on my fingers just like in your dream."

"Wes..."

"Yeah, baby?"

"I'm so close..."

"I know you are. And my name is going to sound so fucking sweet when you scream it."

Her voice shudders as she works herself into a frenzy, near tears with need.

"God, I love hearing you beg for me," I pant, my release just as close. "Come for me, Chels. I want to hear you lose control."

She falls over the edge, and I just barely have enough time to grab some tissues off my nightstand. She cries out my name, and I am absolutely fucking gone.

"Oh my God," she wheezes, trying to catch her breath after a minute.

"I was about to get in my car and drive three hours to make sure you got off," I breathe heavily, feeling dizzy from the intensity of my own climax.

"Wes?"

"Yeah?"

"Thank you."

"Any fucking time." I exhale. "In fact, please call me whenever you need to get off and I'll spring into action like Batman."

She laughs deeply and slowly, sounding sleepy and satisfied. I hum with masculine pride.

"I wouldn't have guessed you had such a filthy mouth under that nice guy exterior."

I laugh. "You told me to talk dirty to you."

"Yeah, but I didn't realize you'd be so good at it."

"Want me to do it more often?"

She giggles. "Don't threaten me with a good time."

I shake my head. "How are you so damn perfect?"

"All because I enjoy a man talking me through it over the phone?"

"Just admit you're the perfect woman and I'll let you go."

"Stop it." I can hear the smile in her voice.

We sit in silence for a few seconds.

"Chels?"

"Yeah?"

I pause. "Thank you for trusting me. For being vulnerable with me."

She groans. "Don't get sappy."

I smile. "All right, all right. Good night."

"Night, Wes."

Chapter 11

Yey^thókwas
Harvest / September

Chelsea

I t's one of the biggest days of my lacrosse career, and I'm trying my hardest not to feel sick to my stomach.

The Haudenosaunee have been competing in international lacrosse events since the 1980s. We field our own teams of Indigenous men and women, separate from the American and Canadian national teams. And today I'm trying out for them.

Later this month, the Haudenosaunee women will compete at the World Lacrosse Box Championships in Utica, NY, only a thirty-minute drive from where I live. This event only happens every four years, so it's a big deal. Men have been playing in this championship for years, but it will be a historic first for the women.

Genny: Good luck today, Chels! You're going to kill it at tryouts

Kenzie: Sending good medicine your way!

Me: Thanks, gals. I want to puke from nerves. It's been years since I tried out for the national team.

Kenzie: You just took a little time off to become even more deadly. You're back and better than ever!

My mind wanders as I pull on my gear in a bustling locker room on Six Nations Reserve in Ontario. After I graduated college, I let myself believe there wasn't a place for my style of lacrosse. I play fast, rough, and smart, which doesn't always translate into scoring flashy goals. But I cause turnovers, draw penalties, and feed goalscorers the ball. I'm a valuable player on any team, but sometimes I catch myself questioning my worth if I'm only looking at my stat line.

I hear my phone vibrate as I'm fastening my rib pads.

The Bear: Give 'em hell today. I'm cheering you on from across the border

Me: *Ya:wʌ́.* I need all the hype I can get

The Bear: Let me know how it goes. And if you need a little stress relief when you get home, just send up the Bat Signal

Me: I've created a monster

The Bear: *angel emoji*

Wes and I have been flirting our heads off since our surprise phone sex, and I'm enjoying the hell out of it. I debated calling after my steamy dream last month. We'd agreed to flirt, but it was a clear step forward in whatever our relationship was turning into. I told myself that it didn't have to mean anything serious. And now I'm in a good mood all the time because he's getting me off damn near every day, so this feels like a win to me.

He's getting scary good at knowing exactly what to say, and when to say it, to bring me to the edge faster and harder than I ever have in the past. *I can only imagine how good it would be in-person.*

And that's my wake-up call to come back to reality. Wes needs to stay firmly in the Friends With Phone Sex Benefits category so I can focus on hopefully competing for my nation on the international stage. I grab my stick and head for the floor.

"Chelsea! I'm so happy to see you here!"

I gasp in delight as Lauren Powless, my former teammate at Albany, comes running up to me as I enter from the bench.

"Lo! Oh my gosh!" We embrace, and I squeeze her tightly. "This is the best surprise."

Her dark eyes are misty. "I'm sorry I didn't keep up with you after graduation. Life got crazy and, well, you know."

"Don't worry about it. I didn't reach out enough either." I start stretching against the boards, and she joins me. "What have you been up to?"

Lauren looks down at the floor. "Well, I had a baby."

My eyes widen. "Shut up."

"It's true." She bends her knee and pulls up her lower leg, stretching out her quads. "It wasn't planned, and my life has completely changed."

"Well, *yeah*, of course it would. You have a baby!" I grip her shoulder, and she finally looks over. "I'm so happy for you."

She presses her lips together. "I'm kind of struggling with being happy for myself, to be honest."

I pull her back to me for a quick hug. "Want to grab a bite to eat and catch up after this?"

She smiles. "I'd like that."

"Great. Now let's go show these coaches they can't live without us."

Lauren and I both made it through the initial round of cuts and the final scrimmage. It was a blast to play with her again. Our experience as teammates allowed us to anticipate each other's movements and pull off some creative plays. Hopefully, that helps us stand out to the coaching staff as they make their final decisions. There are only a handful of spots remaining on the roster, and a bunch of very talented players competing for them.

"Wanna get Indian tacos at Maracle's?" Lauren suggests as we leave the arena.

I practically melt. "Oh my God, *yes*! An Indian taco would fix me right now."

Thirty minutes later, I'm moaning loudly as I bite into my overstuffed fry bread. "This is so good."

"You should charge people for that kind of reaction," she teases.

"I'm so hungry." I take another large bite. "I was too nervous to eat much before tryouts."

"I had a few bites of my kid's breakfast before running out the door," Lauren says. "We're not doing a very good job of fueling these old lady bodies, are we?"

"We're not." I chuckle. "So, tell me about your life. Are you still living on the Onondaga Nation?"

She shakes her head. "No, I live here on Six Nations now. My son's dad is here, and we split custody."

"I'm sorry it didn't work out with him. That has to be really hard."

"It is, but it's better than staying with him." She sticks out her tongue. "I should never have messed around with him in the first place. Not one of my finer decisions in life."

I raise my plastic cup of Cherry Pepsi to clink against hers. "I'm right there with you. My dating history is full of regret, as well."

"At least I got a cute kid out of it." She smiles fondly. "But it means I haven't played much since college. It's been really, really hard getting back into lacrosse shape after pregnancy. Plus, I have so much less time between work and a little one."

"I shouldn't complain about my time off from lacrosse, then. I only have myself to worry about!"

"It's really fucking hard to come back, no matter the reason," she says. "What came up for you? I never would have imagined you'd stop playing after college. You were always a dominant player on the field."

I lick a bit of sour cream off my thumb. "I self-sabotaged, if I'm being honest. I live so far from the indoor leagues in Ontario, and there weren't enough women near me to get a practice group going. It felt too hard to keep up with it, and then I started thinking I wasn't good enough to bother putting the time in."

Lauren raises an eyebrow. "If Chelsea John doesn't feel confident in her abilities, then what hope is there for the rest of us?"

I roll my eyes. "Please."

"I'm serious, Chels. You're incredibly skilled, and you've always known it. What happened?"

I knew what had happened. Life happened, but then *Brock* happened.

I stab at the ice in my cup with a straw. "It wasn't just one thing. I just...lost my way."

"Then you need the game's medicine more than ever." She squeezes my hand. "We both do."

Chapter 12

Wes

A small cardboard box bounces off my head and clatters to the kitchen floor.

"*Ow.*" I whip around. "What the hell, man?"

"I've been trying to get your attention, and you're off in outer space." Sawyer grins. "Could you give me a hand with this bookcase?"

I regretfully pull myself from the memory of Chelsea telling me, in great detail, what she'd do if she were with me last night. *She is so fucking se—*

"I lost you again, bro," Sawyer calls from the living room. "What's going on with you?"

"Sorry. Just tired, I guess." I grab one end of the world's heaviest bookcase and haul it to the other side of the room. "Where the heck did this thing come from?" I ask with a groan once we set it down.

"No idea. Some player must've brought it years ago and didn't want to take this monstrosity when he moved out." He collapses onto the couch with a grin. "But now we have room to play mini sticks in here."

I chuckle and rip open a nearby box, grabbing books from inside and beginning to organize them on the shelf. "You've never sounded more Canadian. I can't imagine ownership wants us putting holes in the wall when someone dives after a ball."

"We live in the team house now. It's our duty to provide the party."

Years ago, some Outlaws alumni bought a rowhouse in Buffalo that current players can affordably rent. It's been occupied for a while, but two players moved out in the offseason, and it became available. Sawyer and I were the first to request (read: beg, in my case) the space, and I couldn't be happier to move out of my crumbling apartment on the outskirts of town.

"This is going to be a very different season for me." I smile. "Last year I had Zeke close by to train with, but otherwise I spent a lot of time alone." I slide the last book into place. "It'll be nice to have more of a community."

"You're probably going to regret that." Sawyer launches himself off the couch and heads for the fridge. "I have a feeling you're going to get sick of me real quick."

He hands me a root beer on the way back. "It takes a lot to get under my skin. You're safe." I clink my bottle against his and settle in.

He takes a swig. "You ready for the World Games in a couple weeks?"

I perk up. "Yeah, I can't wait. Ten days of lacrosse and hanging out with my buddies."

My phone buzzes, and I pull it from my pocket.

Chelsea: Rosters just dropped. No national team for me this time

Chelsea: *sad trombone GIF*

I swear under my breath.

"Everything OK?" Sawyer asks, propping his feet on a stack of moving boxes.

My fingers fly across the screen to type out a quick response before setting the phone down.

Me: I'm sorry, Chels. They're going to kick themselves for missing out on you.

"Yeah. Just a friend."

Chelsea: I'll still come to watch some of the games, though.

Warmth blooms in my chest at the thought of seeing her again soon. I have no idea what to expect now that we're talking nonstop and having spicy phone time, but damn, I can't wait to find out.

"I wish I could play with you, Jamie, and Zeke," Sawyer says. "Team Canada is not nearly as much fun. Bunch of lame white guys."

Sawyer's not Native, but his family has lived with his stepdad on Six Nations Reserve since he was a teen. He's part of the Haudenosaunee community, but not eligible to play for the national team.

"You'll be our archnemesis there." I grin. "Maybe this is finally the year the Haudenosaunee take down the Evil Empire in Canada for the gold medal."

He tosses a pillow at me and I bat it away with a laugh.

"If you're nice, maybe I'll be a mole on the other side."

"Finally, you're good for something."

Another pillow sails my way, and I sprint to the other side of the room.

Chapter 13

Chelsea

I'm trying not to be down in the dumps about not making the national team, but I am *really* down in the dumps.

"Want to go out after this?" Jess asks, her brow furrowed as she watches me aimlessly re-arrange the reading area at Shako:wi. "We could play some slots at the casino, grab dinner, whatever you want."

"I kind of just want to have an early night, if you don't mind." I sit back against the legs of a leather chair near the bookcase. "I'm not feeling up for going out."

She counts the money in the cash register but keeps her eyes on me. "I'm worried about you. You haven't been yourself."

I shrug. "I'm not even sure what 'being myself' looks like anymore, Jess. I feel lost."

She shuts the cash drawer and sits in the chair across from me. "What's going on? You've been shutting me out lately. I know you've got a thunderstorm going on inside you, and I want to listen."

Tears prick at the corners of my eyes. "I didn't mean to shut you out. I'm sorry."

Jess drops to the ground and scoots next to me. "I didn't mean it like that. I've noticed you're down, and you haven't talked much. You do that when you're beating yourself up about something."

I lay my head on her shoulder. "I've been trying to restart my life for the past nine months, but it feels like nothing is catching. I'm stuck."

"You played in the WMSL this past summer and had a great season. You tried out for the Haudenosaunee Nationals for the first time in years. You're damn good at your job here, and your beadwork has been selling well."

I sigh. "I'm too old for these to be the highlights of my life. I want to be doing something meaningful that I really love. I want to play more lacrosse. I want to have a real path forward, not just be doing random things to make ends meet."

"I understand. I'm happy enough with my life the way it is now, even working two jobs, but I'm content to be here with friends and family. You've always seemed made for something more." She looks over at me. "Have you considered leaving the rez? You'd have more opportunities if you moved, as much as I'd hate not to have you around."

"I have, but I've never been able to go through with it," I say quietly. "I love our people, and living in our traditional homelands is such a privilege."

"It is, but it can also be an albatross if it keeps you from being who the Creator made you to be. You can still be connected to your community and advocate for the Oneida people from somewhere else." She gives me a squeeze around the shoulders. "Have you considered moving back to Cattaraugus? You'd be close to jobs and lacrosse in Buffalo, plus you'd get to see your dad more often."

A tiny light flickers in my heart. "That does sound really nice, and I've thought about it. I'd be sad to leave you, of course, and Shako:wi. I know it's just a part-time job, but I've cherished my work here."

We sit in silence for a few seconds. Smoke wafts over from the smudge bowl near the door, and I deeply inhale the medicines.

"You know what I just remembered?" Jess says. "The Buffalo History Museum has a gallery for Haudenosaunee history and cultural items. I always forget about it because it's a small part of the museum, but my mom knows the woman who runs it."

"Really? How have I never heard of this?"

"It flies under the radar, but it's really cool that it's a part of an actual museum, and not just a cultural center tucked away on a reservation." She gets to her feet as the door chimes. "Do you want me to have my mom reach out to the director? She's her best friend's daughter."

"That would be amazing. Thanks so much, Jess." She helps me up, and we approach the entrance to greet our visitors.

We're locking the doors at closing time when my phone rings.

"You sure you don't want to go out?" Jess asks.

"I'm sure. One sec, let me answer this." I slide my finger across the screen. "Hello?"

"Is this Chelsea John?" a friendly male voice asks.

"It is."

"Hi Chelsea. This is Randy Bissell from the Haudenosaunee Nationals."

My stomach drops. "Hi Coach. How are you?"

He chuckles. "I've been better, but I'm hopeful you can help me with that."

Jess tilts her head. "Who is it?" she mouths.

I hold my index finger up. "What can I do for you?"

"I just lost one of my forwards to injury, so I'm in a bad spot for the World Games next week." I can hear the grin in his voice, and I tamp down the hope springing to life within me. "Would you be willing to join the team and give us a shot at winning our very first medal?"

My eyes widen, and Jess covers her mouth.

I bounce up and down before gathering myself. "I'd be honored, Coach. What do you need from me?"

Coach Bissell runs through the upcoming timeline, practice schedule, and carpool opportunities. The tournament starts soon, so things are moving fast. We wrap up, and I say goodbye with as much calm and tact as I can manage before screaming in the parking lot.

"A roster spot opened up, and they want me!"

Jessica grabs me and we jump around together. "Oh my God. I'm so happy for you, Chels! This is the break you needed!"

I fear my face will hurt for days after smiling this hard. "I can't believe it. How is this possible?"

"Hard work and a bit of luck." She squeezes me hard. "Not so lucky for the girl who got hurt, I suppose."

"I know. I feel bad." I open my messages to send a text to Lauren, who made the initial roster a few weeks ago.

"We are absolutely going out tonight, woman. We need to celebrate!"

"OK, OK. You win." I grin and send the message. "Do you mind driving? I have a million people to text."

"All right, passenger princess. Let's go!"

My phone blows up as my family and friends write back.

> **Lauren:** NO WAY! This is the best news! We get to play together again!

"Let's hit the casino," Jess says. "I can use my employee discount at one of the restaurants."

"Sounds good."

> **Mackenzie:** WHAT?! You made the team?!

> **Genny:** You did it, Chels!! This is incredible! I'm so proud of you.

My phone dings again as we exit the car.

Lake'niha: Congratulations, Chelsea! I can't wait to see you play for Team Haudenosaunee. *Kunolúkhwa.*

Me: Love you, too, Dad. I'll let you know once I know our game schedule.

Jess runs inside to see which restaurant has seating while I wait for her near the slot machines. I pull up my message thread with Wes for the tenth time tonight, my fingers hesitating over the keyboard.

He was the first person I thought to text, which freaked me out, so I messaged Lauren instead. I had a sentence typed out before I deleted it and wrote to the girls group chat. I've gone back and forth on what to say, and now I haven't said anything.

I jump when a message from him pops up on the screen, as though I summoned him.

The Bear: How was your day? Anything exciting going on at Shako:wi?

What if...

Jess comes over, smoothing the front of her patterned dress. "We're good to go. Ready for dinner and drinks?"

I toss off a quick message before putting my phone away. "Heck yeah!"

Me: Pretty quiet day. Grabbing dinner with Jess now. How about you?

Chapter 14

Wes

"This place is huge." I look around in awe at the sprawling sports complex in Utica, where we'll spend our next ten days competing against the world's best box lacrosse teams. "How many playing surfaces are here?"

"Four, I think," Jamie says as we approach the team check-in tables. "They're all connected, but it's easy to get turned around. Make sure you always travel with a buddy." He winks at me.

We complete our registration and receive some tournament swag: a t-shirt, lanyard, and hat.

"The game schedule is online if you want to see when the other teams play," the woman at the desk says, her beaded earrings swinging. "All the rosters are on the website as well."

"Fantastic. Thanks, Rebecca." Jamie flashes her a smile, and she blushes.

"Do you know her?" Zeke asks as we make our way to the Team Haudenosaunee meeting area.

"No," Jamie says, "I just read her name tag."

"You're making the aunties swoon, Jammer," I tease.

He laughs. "My attention to detail brings all the girls to the yard. I hope you're watching, nephew."

Our first game isn't until 8pm, but we have a team meeting, lunch, practice, and the Opening Ceremony before that. The three of us carpooled from Buffalo early this morning, so it is a jam-packed day from start to finish.

I drove, so I haven't had a chance to check in with Chelsea yet. I'm feeling mixed emotions about this coming week and a half: so much excitement to be here competing with the Haudenosaunee, but also guilt and sadness that she isn't here living out her dream, as well.

> **Me:** Wish you were here

> **Chelsea:** Me too. Looking forward to seeing you

> **Me:** Are you still thinking of coming for Sunday's game?

> **Chelsea:** I'll definitely be there on Sunday

> **Me:** I'm really looking forward to seeing you

> **Chelsea:** Same

Our team meeting ran long. In addition to game strategy for tonight, the staff needed to distribute uniforms, team shirts, and regalia for tonight's Opening Ceremony.

"I was hoping we could catch the end of the Haudenosaunee women's game, but we just missed it," Zeke says as we walk past the multipurpose center where the game was held.

"Let's make sure we get the whole team together to watch the next one. It's important to support our sisters," Jamie insists.

The last of the Haudenosaunee players are trickling off the floor as we pass. I smile at the sight of long braids and ponytails poking out from beneath box lacrosse helmets. I notice one woman with caramel-colored highlights in her hair, and my mind wanders to Chelsea.

"We should get some lunch before practice," Jamie says. "Does everyone have a plan to eat and get back in time?"

"Yes, Dad." Zeke grins. "Genny's just about here, and we're going to a restaurant she used to frequent with Chelsea."

My heart thumps painfully. *Dammit. I miss her.* It's been two and a half months since I've seen her, and I'm going crazy.

"I'm meeting up with my parents and kid. Wes, do you have anyone to eat with?"

I shrug. "Not yet, but I don't mind eating alone. It gives me a chance to catch up on my book."

"You should see if Sawyer's available. He's usually desperate for decent company by this point in the day."

"OK, I will." I pull out my phone and send him a quick text. "What time do we need to be back for practice?"

"No later than two."

"I'll be there."

> **Me:** Lunch plans?

> **Sawyer:** YES PLEASE.

We meet at a restaurant down the street from the arena. Tons of other teams have the same idea, based on the amount of international gear I see. Team Jamaica is seated before us, and players from Team Australia wander by. The hostess seats us next to a group from Team England.

"How's it going over on the Death Star?" I say, handing our menus off to the waitress after she's taken our orders.

Sawyer chugs some ice water. "Fine. The Storm Trooper maneuvers are pretty boring, but sometimes they let me play with the lightsabers."

"You know all the guys on Team Canada pretty well, don't you?"

"Yeah. I played in juniors with a lot of them, plus on national teams over the years." He stirs the water with his straw. "They're fine. I just enjoy playing with the Native guys more."

"Why's that? Besides the fact that we're cooler."

"The way you think about the game is so different. It's not about individual stats or even beating the other team." He settles back into the booth. "It's about putting your best on display, being a good teammate, and entertaining the Creator. There's more room for creativity and less rigidity in playmaking."

I smile. "It's pretty awesome getting to play that way as a team. It feels like backyard ball, and I feel more like *me*."

Sawyer nods. "I know what you mean. I picked up some of that style playing in Six Nations for so long. I want to unleash that more this season."

"Me too. I held myself back a lot last year since I was so focused on making the starting roster."

"You've gotta help me pull off a hidden ball trick this season." His eyes sparkle. "I've never been able to sell it."

"I'll see what I can do. Sneakiness has never been my best feature."

We chat amiably about our upcoming games. Canada will be playing the Haudenosaunee on Sunday, one of the most anticipated matchups of the round-robin portion of the games.

A hostess walks towards us, followed by a group of women.

"What are your plans for toni—"

It can't be.

My voice trails off as I catch sight of Chelsea. She walks through the room with a gaggle of players from the Haudenosaunee women's team, wearing an official team t-shirt that hugs every one of her curves.

Her eyes lock onto mine, and that little minx *smirks*.

I open my mouth, but no words emerge. My body is frozen at the unexpected delight of seeing the woman I obsess over at every waking moment. Time slows to a crawl as she passes by our table. Her smoky vanilla scent overtakes my nostrils, and my stomach clenches in response.

"Hello! Earth to Wes." Sawyer waves his hand in front of my face, and I jump in surprise.

"Sorry, man. I drifted off for a second. What's up?" I say, wrenching my eyes away from Chelsea and back to my teammate.

His mouth twitches upward. "You drifted *way* off." He loudly sips his water and gestures with his chin. "Who's that?"

I swallow nervously. "Who?"

Sawyer waggles his eyebrows. "I know that look. Who's the girl?"

"There's no girl."

"You're telling me you weren't just drooling over that Indigenous knockout over there?"

I shrug. "I mean, sure, she's pretty."

"Want me to get her number for you?"

I close my eyes in exasperation. *Oh, I've got her number.*

"I know a few of the women at her table. Let's go say hi." Sawyer's eyes sparkle as he pushes back his chair.

"No, no, let's not do—"

He's already striding away, so I scramble to catch up.

"Can we not do this?" I hiss at him as we approach the group.

"You need to live a little," he says without slowing down. "Kimmy, Amanda, how are you ladies doing?"

Chelsea looks up at Sawyer before moving her eyes over to me. That damn smirk plays at the corners of her mouth again.

Oh, she wants to play this game? I'll play.

Sawyer grabs a chair from an empty table and slides it over, spinning it around and sitting backwards.

"Nice to see you all again. Gabby, how's your cousin?"

Gabby grins. "She's great. I make her hate-watch all your games with me."

Sawyer roars with laughter. "Excellent. Her hatred of me fuels my best goals."

I loiter awkwardly at the end of the table next to Chelsea, mentally willing Sawyer to hurry the heck up.

"Hey, stranger," she says to me, not taking her eyes off Sawyer.

"Hey, yourself." I take advantage of everyone watching Sawyer animatedly tell a story and lean down until my mouth is next to her ear. "You are in so much trouble right now."

"Why's that?"

"For lying to me." I smile at the sight of goosebumps spreading across her forearms. "You told me you wouldn't be here."

"There was a last-minute injury, and I got the call."

I'm so damn proud of her. She's worked her ass off to get a spot here.

"You still could've told me." I move an inch closer. "I'll have to find something to do with you."

"Oh, please, go easy on me." She glances up, mirth sparkling in her eyes.

"Not a chance."

She gulps down some water, and I smirk.

"I'm glad you're here." I whisper.

"Me too."

Sawyer is wrapping up his story, and I make a show of checking my watch. "I need to head back for practice, unfortunately."

"Same here." Sawyer gets to his feet and returns his chair. "Do you ladies all know Wes? He plays for the Haudenosaunee."

The group shakes their heads.

"Hi Wes, I'm Lauren." The woman sitting next to Chelsea holds out her hand. "I'm Onondaga. Can't believe I haven't met you before."

I return her handshake. "I'm Oneida from Wisconsin, so I didn't come up through the junior leagues around here."

Lauren brightens. "You're Oneida? So is Chelsea." She elbows her teammate.

Chelsea glances up at me, and I'm surprised to see her cheeks turning pink. "We've met," she says.

Lauren frowns at her, and I take the opportunity to make my exit.

"It's a pleasure to meet you all. The men's team is planning to be at your game tomorrow."

"I'll come too," Sawyer says. "I know the coach's family." He winks at Gabby, and she smiles.

"I'll let Uncle Randy know," she says.

"How do you always know *everyone*?" I ask on our walk back to the sports complex.

Sawyer shrugs. "I like people. And it comes in handy to know the right person when you're trying to get a chance somewhere.

Speaking of which," he says pointedly, "what's the story with you and Chelsea? I assumed you didn't know her."

I smother a smile. "We've hung out. She's a friend of Zeke and Genny's."

"And you like her," he states.

"No." I glance up to find him looking at me. "Maybe a little."

"I knew it!" He slaps me on the back. "We need to make sure the two of you see each other here. You're stuck together for the next ten days, so make the most of it."

Chapter 15

Chelsea

I nervously bounce back and forth on moccasin feet. Team Haudenosaunee is lined up for the Opening Ceremony, and we have a long time to wait. Our contingent will be one of the last to walk out, and my nervous energy is off the charts.

"This is the fun part," Lauren says with a grin. "Let loose and enjoy yourself."

I fidget with my white tunic decorated with purple and gold ribbons. "How can you be so calm?" I ask. "This is big. First ever women's indoor team at this level."

She throws an arm around my shoulders. "And we're so lucky to be part of it. There will be plenty of time for nerves, but tonight's not one of them."

We won our first game against Hong Kong earlier today, and it was surreal to play the game of my ancestors with players from the other side of the world. I feel so grateful to be part of this piece of women's history, but it's hard to fight my inner mean girl who tells me I shouldn't be here. That I didn't earn my place.

Everyone else has been playing together for years. You're just here because someone got injured.

I shake my head to clear away the intrusive thoughts. "Is your family coming tonight?" I ask Lauren.

"Yeah, my parents are here with my sisters and my son." Her smile could power a small village with its megawattage. "Look how cute he is in his *gasdó•wä•*'." She pulls up a photo on her phone, and I gasp.

"Oh, my goodness. He's beautiful, Lo!" I coo over the dark-haired toddler in a tiny headdress and ribbon shirt. "Look at him!"

"Do you have anyone here for you tonight?" she asks.

I nod. "My parents are here. Seated far apart from each other, hopefully." I grin ruefully. "Jess and Genny, too. They're longtime friends of mine."

"I think I remember them," Lauren says. "Genny played too, right?"

"Yeah. We played together in high school, but she didn't play in college. She was too busy with her teaching degree."

Someone in the back starts loudly playing hip hop music from their phone. Lauren shimmies her shoulders into mine and bumps into me until I laugh.

"You need to lighten up, Chels. This is the first long break I've had from mom responsibilities, and I need you to have fun with me."

I smile. "I can do that."

Wes appears at my elbow, decked out in a purple ribbon shirt and team shorts. He looks eye-meltingly gorgeous.

"Well, hey," he says, handing me a small Haudenosaunee flag from the three in his hand. "You're missing some patriotic cheer."

I smile and wave it around a bit. "Thanks. I'm just feeling nervous."

"Nervous? This is the easy part."

"That's what I told her," Lauren says. "She's being silly. Nice to see you again, Wes." She nods at him, and he smiles.

"You too, Lauren. Do you two know each other well?"

"We were teammates at Albany. We tore up the midfield together."

Wes raises an eyebrow. "How did I not know you played middie, too?" he asks me.

"I prefer to remain mysterious," I say.

His laughter fills the waiting area and mingles with the ringing of Lauren's phone.

"My mom wants to video chat, I'll be right back," she says, ducking off into a quiet corner.

"Are you still mad at me?" I ask Wes, a smile tugging at the corners of my lips.

"It's impossible to be mad at you," he says. "I might punish you for keeping secrets, though." He pauses. "If you're into that kind of thing, which I know you are."

I kick his ankle and clear my throat loudly, looking around us for eavesdroppers.

He chuckles. "It was the best surprise."

I fiddle with my purple floral earrings. "It *was* pretty great to see the look on your face when you saw me at lunch."

"You got me good, I have to admit."

Our fingers brush as he takes a step closer.

"You look beautiful," he leans over and whispers in my ear. "I can't focus on anything else."

I fight back a smile. "Thank you. You look pretty handsome yourself."

"It's really not fair."

"What's that?"

"That you have to be so smart, talented, funny, *and* hot. How's any other woman supposed to measure up?"

I place my open hand on my cheek to cover the blush that has erupted. "Stop it."

"It's an honor to be here with you." He smiles at me warmly.

"Same. Now get out of here before people start asking questions."

He grins and turns his head away. "I see how it is. But you'll be blowing up my phone in a couple of hours."

I bite my cheek to hold back a grin. *He's right, and he knows it.*

The Opening Ceremony turns out to be magical. The Haudenosaunee process out to loud cheers as we are honored as the originators of lacrosse. It feels amazing to wave our flag and to be dressed in our finest clothing and jewelry.

A Mohawk elder gives the Thanksgiving Address to open the ceremony. It's an ancient speech of gratitude for the natural world. Depending on who is speaking, it can last a few minutes or a few hours.

"We give thanks to the Stars who are spread across the sky like jewelry. We see them in the night, helping the Moon to light the darkness and bringing dew to the gardens and growing things. When we travel at night, they guide us home. With our minds gathered together as one, we send greetings and thanks to the Stars. Now our minds are one."

Wes catches my eye mid-address and gives me a smile that warms me down to my toes. I picture the Great Bear constellation hidden under his ribbon shirt and try to re-focus.

"Now we turn our thoughts to the Creator, or Great Spirit, and send greetings and thanks for all the gifts of Creation. Everything we need to live a good life is here on this Mother Earth. For all the love that is still around us, we gather our minds together as one and send our choicest words of greetings and thanks to the Creator. Now our minds are one."

It's the perfect way to celebrate this historic occasion before digging deep in search of a medal.

Wes winks at me as he heads to the locker room, and I feel like a teenager with a crush.

"You seem happy," Genny says when we meet up in the stands following the ceremony. We're staying to watch the men's game against England.

"I am," I say. "Making the team really lifted my spirits."

"*And*," Jess chimes in from the other side of me, "she has an interview coming up with the Buffalo History Museum."

Genny's eyes widen. "What is this? You haven't mentioned anything to me about Buffalo!"

"I didn't mean to keep it from you," I say, settling more comfortably into my seat. "It all happened really fast and at the same time as making the roster, so it kind of slipped my mind."

"Well, spill it!" Genny insists, clapping her hands in anticipation.

I fill her in on Jess' family connection with the gallery director, and my thoughts about moving strategically to put myself closer to job and lacrosse opportunities.

"Well, selfishly I'd love to see you come to Buffalo so you could be closer to me, but it's also inspiring to see you finding your own path and making shit happen," Genny says with a smile.

"We'll see. Everything is still very much up in the air, but I think I really want this."

The teams come out for warmups while we talk, and we exchange waves with Zeke and Wes on the floor.

"Are you still talking to The Bear?" Genny asks.

I'm suddenly rethinking all my life choices. This conversation topic may break containment to a different, and more dangerous, participant.

"Um..." I stall for time, praying my roommate didn't hear her.

"Who's The Bear?" Jess asks.

Dammit.

Genny shrugs. "Some guy Chelsea's been talking to lately. She's given me no information, except that it's casual and he plays lacrosse."

Jess blinks. "The only guy she's been talking to lately is—"

I shoot her pleading daggers with my eyes.

Her own eyes widen in shock.

"Who?" Genny leans forward. "Who has she been talking to?"

"Uh—" Jess looks at me and then back at Genny. "I guess it must be The Bear. She hasn't given me a name."

Genny huffs. "Dammit. I was really hoping you had some insight."

"Mmm. She really doesn't tell me much these days." Jess side-eyes me, and I exhale with relief.

"Thank you," I whisper.

"Really? *The Bear?*" she hisses. "That's pretty on the nose."

"I know it's ridiculous, but it's the first thing I came up with when she asked." I glance over at Genny, who's typing out a message on her phone. "Can we talk about this later?"

"Oh, you bet we're talking about this later."

"I'm going to run to the bathroom before the game starts. Anyone else need to go?" Genny asks.

"Nope, I'm good," I say, and Jess concurs.

Once Genny leaves, I swing back around. "Nothing has happened with Wes, I swear. We've just been talking."

"About spicy books," Jess points out.

I cringe. "Yes. But nothing has *happened*." I'm not being entirely truthful, but this is the panic talking. "I don't even know why I mentioned anything to Genny about it. It's like I got possessed by an oversharing spirit and *oops*, there I go." I take a breath. "He's just a friend."

My leg bounces up and down as I wait for Jess' response. I'm afraid of losing her friendship over a failed relationship with her newly discovered cousin, and my heart is in my throat as she silently looks onto the turf.

"You really like him. That's why you couldn't help telling Genny."

I swallow. "I don't want to really like him."

"Why not? He's a nice guy, and you two seem into each other."

"I've never seen dating within a friend group end well. The Zeke and Genny stuff was hard on our friends for *years* until recently. And I have so much more I want to accomplish before inviting a man back into my life." I fiddle with my ribbon skirt.

She looks over at me with a soft smile. "I don't care if you date my cousin. I think it's awesome, to be honest. So don't let that stop you from following your heart."

I squeeze her knee. "I don't know what I want to do. My head is a mess about this. I need more time to get my career on track, and men complicate everything. I want to figure things out without other people telling me how they think I should feel."

Jess nods. "I completely understand. Consider me a vault."

"Thank you, Jess. I wasn't sure how you'd respond," I say, relief washing over me.

"No problem. But if you hurt him, I'll kick your ass." She fixes me with a pointed look. "I'd tell him the same thing about you."

I laugh and pull her to me for a sideways hug. "I'll do my best."

Chapter 16

Wes

C oach runs us through a tough practice on the second day. We got our first win last night, but the real test will be our game against Canada tomorrow. Most of our team has played together in the past, but there are some new guys and room to improve our cohesiveness.

Sweat drips from my hair as we head to the locker room. I'm looking forward to a shower and watching some other games, including Chelsea and the Haudenosaunee women in a couple of hours.

"Would you be willing to re-string my stick?" Jamie asks as we exit the practice rink. "I meant to do it before we left town but didn't have a chance."

"Sure. Do you have the stringing kit with you?"

"Yeah. I want to make sure everything's in good shape for tomorrow's game." He presses his fist into the netting. "My shots are coming off funny."

"I can do it this afternoon, if you'd like," I offer. My high school coach taught me how to string, and I've enjoyed it ever since. It's relaxing to work with my hands and bring a stick back to life.

A shower and fresh clothes have me feeling like a new man. Zeke's off spending time with Genny, so Jamie and I wander the interconnected arenas in search of a game to watch. We settle on the U.S. Virgin Islands versus Italy, grabbing a couple of seats in the back.

I reach for Jamie's stick. "Do you have that kit with you?"

"Yeah. One sec." He digs around in his bag and produces a stack of mesh, shooting strings, and hockey laces.

"Thanks, man." I rub my hands together, downright giddy at the opportunity to string.

Jamie chuckles. "You really like doing this? I don't have the patience for it."

"I really do. It's a chance to turn my brain off and forget about life for a little while." I unzip my bag and pull out a small pair of scissors I keep tucked away for these types of occasions.

He exhales. "I could use more of that. But stringing just frustrates me and makes me swear a lot, so I don't think that's the medicine I need."

I snip the strings attaching the old mesh to the stick. "Probably not. How about an elder hobby like knitting?"

He elbows me, and I chortle.

"Watch out for sharp objects, bro," I say, snapping my scissors towards him.

We watch the game as I begin attaching the topstring to the sidewalls of the white plastic head. So much of stringing is about keeping tension and being precise, and soon I'm lost in the process.

A whiff of soap and warm vanilla hits my nostrils, and I lift my head.

Chelsea plops down in the seat next to me. "*Shekólih.*"

A grin spreads across my face. "*Shekólih.*"

She's wearing a pair of gray shorts and a purple Team Haudenosaunee hoodie. Her damp hair is pulled into a high ponytail, her pink lips shining with the barest hint of gloss.

I stare at her a little too long, and she raises an eyebrow at me. My smile grows.

"Jamie Montour. It's nice to meet you." Jamie leans across me with his hand extended.

Chelsea chuckles and returns his handshake. "I know who you are. *Everyone* knows who you are."

He smiles warmly. "Well, I know who *you* are, Chelsea."

She freezes. "You do?"

"Of course. I followed your college career at Albany. You're a hell of a player."

She blinks. "Jamie Montour, lacrosse prodigy of my youth, watched me play college ball?"

"Absolutely. I like to keep track of the up-and-coming Haudenosaunee stars."

"I'm blown away."

I chuckle as I weave with purple string. "She kicked my ass when we played together." I'm struggling to keep my eyes off her. She's so close, but I can't touch her. I don't know if she'd even *want* me to.

Jamie laughs. "I would have loved to see that. How do you two know each other?"

"She grew up with Zeke and Genny," I reply.

Chelsea's knee ever-so-slightly nudges against mine, and I lose track of the knot between my fingers.

"Those are good people to have in your corner." Jamie looks across the small arena. "Hey, I'm going to say hi to some players I know from Team Canada. I'll catch up with you later."

"See ya, Jammer."

Silence hangs between me and Chelsea as I restart the section I'd been working on before she touched me and blew my focus to smithereens. For once I'm at a loss for words around her. How do you strike up a conversation with the woman who doesn't want to date you but *does* call you for spicy time? Especially when you are very much hoping she changes her mind about that whole staying single thing?

"You're the team stringer?" she asks, staring straight ahead at the game action.

"I am."

I continue pinching mesh and tightening string as quiet falls between us once more.

"So, you must know how to tie really good knots."

I smother a laugh. I've read enough of her books to know that's an appealing concept to her. "I do." I pull to maintain tension as I work. "I'd be happy to show you sometime."

She exhales, and it's mixed with a throaty groan.

I cannot control my grin, but I keep my eyes trained on the stick in my hands.

"You're going to be a real problem for me," Chelsea mutters.

"I sure hope so." I press my bare knee against hers and hear her sharp intake of breath. "Can I take you out sometime while we're here?"

She hesitates. "I don't know if I'm ready for that."

"We'll walk down the street and I'll buy you a book and a coffee."

She fiddles with the end of her ponytail. "You drive a hard bargain, but I should probably stick with the single life for now."

"You don't sound very single when you're begging me to—"

"*Wes!*" she hisses and kicks my foot.

I chuckle quietly and try again. "I know you like me. How about *two* books and a coffee?"

"You couldn't handle me." She's teasing, but I sense a note of seriousness behind her tone.

"Baby, I would *love* to handle—*ow!*"

She kicks me again.

"Will you stop?" Her eyes sparkle, and that damn flush is back in her cheeks. It makes me want to find all the ways I can make her blush and start a collection.

"I'll stop, I promise." I expected her continued resistance, but the disappointment aches nonetheless. "You're the one who came over here, I'd like to point out."

She huffs and doesn't reply.

We watch the game for a few minutes in companionable silence. I see Jamie walking back towards us as the whistle sounds for halftime.

"For what it's worth," Chelsea begins, "if anyone could convince me to give up my vow of celibacy, it would be you."

My stomach flips hopefully. "That's good to know."

She leans over as Jamie approaches, and her warm breath on my ear causes me to shiver. "I'll see you later, Rookie."

Chapter 17

Chelsea

"W e're going out tonight, girl. I hope you're ready!"
Lauren calls from the hotel bathroom.

I groan. My body's not used to playing games on
back-to-back days, and my legs and shoulders are aching with a
quiet soreness. We played England this afternoon and eked out
a win, but it was hard fought. Their defense is physical, and I
wound up taking just as many bruising checks as I usually dish
out.

"How are you so fresh after that game?" I ask from my bed. I
haven't managed much more than a few trips to the bathroom
and flipping the pages of my book since we got back to our
shared room.

"This is my first free night in *years*. It's giving me energy."

The opening notes of "Freebird" play from her phone, and I
laugh.

"All right, all right. I'll pop some anti-inflammatories and see
what kind of outfit I can put together." I swing my stiff legs off

the side of the bed. "Do you want me to invite anyone out with us?"

"Sure! The more the merrier."

I inch towards my suitcase for ibuprofen and down a couple of pills. I crawl back onto the mattress, tucking one knee under my chest and stretching the other leg long into a pigeon pose.

"You OK out there?" Lauren asks with a laugh as I moan in the delicious ecstasy of stretching out sore muscles.

"Yeah, just trying not to die." I lower to my forearms and pull together an on-the-fly group chat as my inner thigh releases.

> **Me:** Hey party people! Anyone want to come out with me and Lauren tonight? I can show you the best nightlife Utica has to offer

> **Genny:** Yes! We'll come!

> **Zeke:** I'm pretty beat, but I guess I'm coming out if Genny is :)

> **Genny:** Want me to add Sawyer and Jamie, too?

> **Me:** Sure, go for it

Wes: Sawyer is a good time guy and will absolutely go out if he's not already. Jamie's probably asleep

Zeke: I wish I were Jamie

Sawyer Lane has been added to the chat

Jamie Montour has been added to the chat

Genny: Sawyer, Jamie, want to go out for drinks and fun tonight?

Sawyer: YES. Why didn't you ask me sooner?

Sawyer: Who else is coming?

Jamie: I'm half asleep, but you all go have fun without me

Wes: Called it

Me: You coming, Wes?

Wes: I'm going to skip this one. I want to get a good night's sleep before we take on the Axis of Canadian Evil tomorrow.

Sawyer: Hey! I heard that

I frown and switch legs. Wes is usually game for anything, especially if I'm the one asking.

"Any takers?" Lauren strolls into the room looking like a supermodel in a little black dress and her mahogany hair loose around her shoulders.

"Hot damn," I say. "You look amazing. How have you had a baby?"

She waves me off. "Oh please. Keep telling me how gorgeous I look." Her dark eyes twinkle, and I grin.

"Do you need earrings? I travel with a million pairs."

"*Yes.* Can I see what you have?"

"There's a fabric pouch on top of the dresser. Help yourself." I switch over to my texts with Wes.

Me: Everything OK? It's not like you to skip out on a good time.

The Bear: Yeah, I'm just tired after the past two days.

> **Me:** Do you need anything? I could bring you whatever

> **The Bear:** That's a dangerous offer

> **Me:** Why?

> **The Bear:** Because what I really need is you

"So, what's going on between you and Wes?"

My head snaps up at Lauren's question. She's slipping the backs onto a large pair of gold salmon ghosts from an Indigenous-owned company in the Pacific Northwest.

"Oh hell. You look *hot*," I say. "Those earrings are perfect with your dress."

"Thanks! Now answer my question." She raises her eyebrow at me.

"I'm not sure what you mean." I toss my phone to the side and start slowly untangling my legs out of the deep stretch.

"Girl, I'm not blind. He was making you blush and giggle at lunch yesterday when you thought no one was watching, but then you went cold as soon as I said something." She digs in her purse for lip gloss. "Then he came over to say hi before the Opening Ceremony, and I *know* he wasn't there to see me."

I shrug. "Like I said, we know each other. He plays in the NLL with Genny's boyfriend, so we've hung out a couple of times. That's all."

"I don't buy it, but whatever you say."

I force out a laugh. "What? He's a nice guy, and we get along."

"Mmm hmm. I'm keeping an eye on you, John."

I'm putting on a smiling face for my friends as we hop to a few bars, but my thoughts are caught in a whirlpool of Wes.

Because what I really need is you.

His response to my text earlier shook me. I'd tried to reply a dozen times in the past few hours, but only managed to stare at the blank reply box.

I'd been playing with his emotions for months, and I knew it. He'd been upfront with me about his interest since the day we met, and I couldn't seem to stop giving him mixed signals. *No, I won't give you my phone number, but I will accept your follow request on social media. No, I won't go out with you, but I will talk to you every day. No, I won't let you kiss me after we spent hours flirting and laughing together, but I will beg you to talk dirty to me.*

He'd given me the space I'd asked for, and only responded to my initiations. And yet I kept throwing up walls as soon as he got too close.

"Are you having fun?" Lauren asks, throwing her arm around me. Her drink sloshes dangerously close to the edge of her glass.

"Absolutely." I smile with all my teeth and hope she doesn't notice that I'm faking it.

"He's cute." She gestures towards Sawyer, who's deep in an animated conversation with Zeke and Genny. "What's his deal?"

I shrug. "I don't really know him, to be honest. He's always struck me as a bit of a playboy, but I haven't spent time with him to know if that's true."

She giggles. "Gabby Bissell says he's a friend of her family, and her cousin can't *stand* him. I'm dying to know why."

"You don't need that drama tonight, Lo," I caution.

She sighs. "You're probably right. But damn, it's been a long time since I've gotten laid, and he looks *good*."

Genny shimmies over, her wineglass in hand. "How's it going over here? Everyone letting loose a little?"

"I am, but Chelsea's a wet blanket." Lauren takes a sip of her drink.

"Hey!" I protest.

"You don't have a game tomorrow, right?" Genny asks. "So you can have a drink or two?"

I sigh. "No, just practice tomorrow. I know I'm going to wake up sore, so I've been focused on hydrating instead."

"You fit right in with the boys. Big game tomorrow, so they're sticking to water." Genny waggles her fingers at Zeke, and he lights up with a smile. "We probably won't stick around much longer. I can tell Zeke's fading. He's staying at the hotel with me tonight."

My ears perk up. "Not with the team?"

"No, I convinced him to sneak out." She giggles. "Hopefully, poor Wes isn't too lonely without his roommate. I'm surprised he didn't want to come out tonight."

"Yeah, me too."

Wes is alone in his room tonight.

No, Chelsea. This would be a bad idea. Don't even think about it.

Lauren wanders over to chat with Sawyer and Zeke, and it feels like an opportunity to make a bad decision.

"Think I should check on him when I get back to the hotel? He seemed off."

Chelsea John! Stop it right now!

Genny brightens. "That's a great idea. I've been feeling a little guilty about stealing Zeke away the night before the Canada game. Would you mind?"

"Not at all. What's their room number?"

Thirty minutes later, Zeke and Genny are saying their goodbyes, and I start yawning.

"Don't tell me you're tired," Lauren says.

"I'm really hurting after today's game. Did you want to head back soon?"

She pouts. "No."

"I can stay out a bit later," Sawyer offers. "I'm not drinking, so I'll make sure she gets back safely."

I frown. This wasn't part of my plan.

"No offense, Sawyer, but we barely know you," I say.

"Chels," Lauren hisses and smacks my arm.

"No, no, I get it. I'm glad you're looking out for each other." He smiles warmly.

"She'll be safe with Sawyer," Genny reassures me as she shrugs on her coat. "I trust him one hundred percent."

"See? I'm a Boy Scout," Sawyer puffs out his chest.

"Please don't make me have to kick your ass tomorrow, bro," Zeke says.

"On the floor or off?" Sawyer grins.

"Off. I'm definitely kicking your ass *on* the floor tomorrow."

"Will you share your location with me?" I say quietly to Lauren.

"I will, but you're being crazy." She takes out her phone and taps around. "Done."

"Thanks. Just be safe, OK?"

"I promise." She squeezes my hand. "I'm a mom with free time, but I'm not reckless."

We hug and I head out, my heels clacking on the sidewalk as I walk quickly back to the hotel.

I missed Wes tonight. I can't deny the joy he's brought to my life since we reconnected five months ago. I've never had a man so unabashedly crazy about me. I'm used to men who play games, and who see themselves as the prize. At worst, I've felt trapped in toxic situationships with men who barely appeared to even like me. Wes hasn't given me a single hint that he would be like that. But I couldn't seem to put down the walls I'd built around my heart after Brock.

I buzz into my hotel room and emerge a minute later. My heart pounds as I get in the elevator and watch the floor numbers change.

This is the worst idea I've ever had. Or maybe the best.
Fuck it, it's fine.

Chapter 18

Wes

I set my book down with a frustrated huff. It's 11pm and I'm grumpy.

I would wait forever for Chelsea if that's what she needs, but I underestimated how much harder it would be when I'm physically around her every day.

Watching her play earlier today was a revelation. I knew she was good based on our pickup game with Zeke and Genny, but seeing her trip up some of the world's best players was exhilarating. Her ability to read the defense and set up plays in transition was impressive, and I was going to need to pick her brain about her strategies for my own game. Watching her physicality as she pushed around a very good English team was such a turn-on.

Our spicy phone time is fun, but I want to kiss her after games and hold her hand when we're with friends. I want to buy her dinner and listen to her stories about Shako:wi and the beadwork pieces she has in progress. I want to lay her down in my bed and feel how her body responds to my touch. I want to give her the world, but I can't. Her friendship has been a light in my life, and I'm afraid to jeopardize it, but I want more.

I should've gone out with her and our crew tonight, but the thought of pretending she was just a friend for another few hours felt like too much. It has been a nonstop struggle since we arrived in Utica, and I knew it would leave me frustrated before another long day of lacrosse and seeing her tomorrow.

But then she hadn't responded to my text. *Did I push her too far?* It wasn't like her to leave me on read, and I had felt too vulnerable to follow up.

It's late, and I need to get a full night's rest for tomorrow's game. I drop my phone on the bed and head to the bathroom to take my contacts out. I'm splashing water on my face when I hear a knock.

What the heck? Zeke's off at Genny's hotel for the night, but maybe he forgot something? I dry off with a towel and approach the door. A look through the peephole sends my stomach flipping end over end.

Chelsea's on the other side, bundled up in a coat with her dark, silky hair piled on top of her head. I open the door and pull her inside quickly, checking the hallway for anyone who may have seen us.

I close the door behind her and she presses her back against it, her eyes heated and locked on mine. "Room service," she purrs, untying one of the knots in her belted coat.

"*Fuck,*" I breathe, drinking in the sight of her. "What are you doing here?"

My eyes follow the bob in her throat as she swallows. "I need you, too."

I groan and reach for her, my hands cupping her face to bring her closer.

She puts a finger to my lips. "Rule #1: no kissing."

"Dammit, Chels." My mouth is halfway to hers, so I pivot to her neck, kissing behind her ear and down the caramel column of her skin. Her breathing picks up as I move lower. Her coat impedes my progress, so I blindly fumble with the last knot in her belt. "What else?"

"Rule #2." The belt loosens and her coat falls open. "You need to keep it in your pants."

"Ho.ly. Fucking. Shit." I pull back the edges of the coat to find she's only wearing a black lace bra and panties. Her body is absolutely incredible. I run my hands tentatively down the curves of her waist. "Am I dreaming?" I ask, my eyes going everywhere all at once.

"I need you," she repeats in a whisper. "Please touch me, Wes."

I gather her hands in mine and pin them above her head. Her soft gasp sends lust spiraling through my veins as I begin trailing kisses down her sternum and along the swells of her breasts. My head is foggy as she squirms against me.

"Where?" I rasp. "Where do you want me to touch you?"

"Everywhere," she says. "Please."

I gently part her legs with my knee and press against her. "This is so much better than the phone."

She nods and licks her parted lips.

I'm desperate to kiss her, but turn my attention to her breasts instead. I run my thumb over the peak of her nipple and groan with need as she whimpers under my touch. I bend my head and graze my teeth ever so slightly over the thin lace covering her. "You want me to touch you here?"

She wiggles with impatience. "Yes."

My fingers wind a lazy course down her ribs and across her stomach before brushing against the top of her panties. "Do you want me to touch you here, too?"

She arches her back to get closer to my bare chest. "*Yes.*"

"Fuck, Chels." I bury my face in her neck. "This doesn't feel real. I don't want to scare you off."

She breathes heavily and glances up at her hands still caught in mine against the door. "I came to accept my punishment. For lying to you yesterday."

I rest my forehead against hers, trying to slow my racing heart. "You are so fucking hot," I whisper.

She smirks and rolls her hips against mine. It detonates the bomb inside of me, blowing my hesitation to smithereens.

I fall to my knees, grabbing her ass with both hands and pulling her forward. "Baby, I don't want to punish you." I trail kisses along the edges of her panties, nipping the fabric with my teeth. "I want to worship you."

Her knees start to shake, and I hold up her weight with one hand while swiping my other thumb beneath the lace.

"You feel so fucking good," I growl, kissing her through the sheer material, "and you're already so fucking wet for me."

She's whimpering my name, her hands tangling in my hair as I get lost between her legs.

I peel her panties down, desperate to taste her. I gently lift one foot at a time, careful not to catch the fabric in her heels. "These are sexy," I say, brushing a kiss against each calf before I set her legs back down. "Keep them on."

Chelsea looks down at me, her eyes heavy with desire, and I have never felt more powerful than on my knees in front of this woman.

I kiss my way up her inner thigh, teasing her with my beard as I come close to where she wants me. My breath skates over her as I switch sides, and she bucks away from the door towards me.

"Not yet, baby." I'm going to take my time enjoying her, no matter how much she begs.

"Wes," she pleads, "I won't be able to stand for much longer."

Her legs are trembling, and she winces when I squeeze her backside. "Are you sore from your game?"

"Yeah."

"You played hard." I bring my hands to her and softly lick her. Her moans fill the room and intermingle with mine. "You need someone to take care of you tonight."

"Yes, please." She lifts her leg and runs her foot down my side.

I catch it and bring it over my shoulder, sinking into her with my fingers and tongue as she clutches the door handle for balance. Her head drops back with pleasure as I suck on her clit. It's absolute heaven, and I never want to come up for air.

I love this position, but I'm about to lose her to the floor at the rate her hamstrings are quaking.

I get to my feet, intent on pushing her coat off her shoulders. I toss it aside and press her tightly against the door. "Hang on to me, OK?"

She circles my neck with her arms, and I lift her hips. She yips in surprise before wrapping her legs around my waist and gripping tightly.

"I told you I could pick you up," I say, carrying her towards the bed.

She chuckles against my neck. "You're doing an excellent imitation of a book boyfriend right now."

"I'm just getting started."

She pulls back to look at me, and her lips are so close to mine.

"Are you sure I can't kiss you?" I ask breathlessly.

She shakes her head. "No kissing. Not yet."

"You drive a hard bargain, but I like a challenge."

My dick is straining against my sweatpants, but I can deal with that later. Right now all I want is this woman coming on my tongue.

I toss her onto the bed and she grins, grabbing for me as I sweep my phone and book off the edge. I grip her hips and pull her onto me as I lie down.

"You set the rules," I growl, straddling her legs on either side of my chest, "but I get to decide your punishment."

Her hair is falling out of its messy bun as she struggles to stay upright. "This doesn't feel like punishment." She lifts an eyebrow at me and I smack her right ass cheek in response. "Hey!"

"That's because you're not begging me to let you come yet."

She groans, and I pull her forward even closer to the headboard behind me.

"Sit on my face, Chels."

She hesitates, looking uncertain for the first time since I've known her.

I smack her ass again and she squirms. I'm so fucking hard and desperate to have her back against my mouth.

"I don't want to crush you." She bites her lip.

I look at her with exasperation. "Are you kidding?"

"I'm not exactly small." She tries to scoot back, and I drag her to my mouth.

"Sit. The fuck. *Down*."

"Wes, I—*oh!*" She protests until I get my tongue on her and then grips the headboard like a life raft.

"All the way down, baby. Just like that." I'm swallowed up by her as she finally sits down fully, my head between her quivering thighs and my mouth full of her.

I can barely hear underneath her as my pulse thunders in my ears, but I can make out her moaning my name as she grinds against me. *Sky World is calling me home*.

She rides me like that until her hips start to press harder and I know she's getting close. I lift her off me a few inches, and she cries out in frustration.

"Not yet, baby." I chuckle.

"You fucking assho—"

I lower her again, licking her long and slow. I know I won't be able to deny her for too long, so I want to make the most of my time with her like this. Each time, I let her get a little closer to the edge before pushing her away again. She cries and curses until I bring her back.

"Are you going to lie to me like that again?" I ask, rubbing her clit with my thumb.

"No," she chokes out, her body shaking with desperation.

"And who does this perfect body belong to?"

She's breathing heavily, and I hold my breath, praying I didn't push her too far.

"You," she moans, tugging on my hair with one hand while the other stays braced against the headboard.

Holy fucking smokes.

I press two fingers into her while I groan around her clit.

She moans so loudly that I'm certain someone next door is going to file a complaint with the hotel.

"Oh my God, Wes," she begs. "Please get inside me. I need you."

It takes every ounce of my willpower not to throw her down and nail her to the mattress.

"Another time," I rasp, curling my fingers into her and rubbing against a spot that I know will send her over the edge. "Just as soon as you're ready."

She comes undone, shaking and crying with the intensity of her climax. She digs her fingers deeper into my hair, hanging on for dear life as I maintain the pace of my fingers and mouth.

I pride myself on being a good lover, but I don't think I've ever made a woman come this hard. The fact that it's Chelsea sends my ego to the moon.

Her tremors begin to slow, and I pull my fingers away. My arms encircle her hips so I can catch her on the inevitable collapse. She melts into me, and I roll her onto her back. I hold her close and pull the blanket around her.

"Holy fucking shit," she gasps.

I chuckle against her neck. "That about sums it up, yeah."

We lay together in silence for a few minutes while she comes back to earth.

I kiss her forehead. "Let me get you some water. I'll be right back."

She mumbles gibberish, and I internally preen. I grab a water bottle from the fridge and grin when I notice her panties on the floor nearby.

"I don't think I can move the rest of the night," she mumbles as I crack open the water.

"Then stay here. I'll sneak you out in the morning."

"Can't. Lauren's coming back soon."

"Dammit."

She props herself up on her forearm and chugs water. "Thank you," she says once she's finished.

"You're welcome."

She blushes. "No, I mean, thank you. For *that*."

A grin spreads across my face. "I'm just happy to be here. Thank *you* for showing up on my doorstep." I shake my head in disbelief. "I can't believe you want *me*." I nuzzle her neck. "Do you want to go again?"

She barks out a laugh. "I love your enthusiasm, but there's no way my body is going to let me do that again tonight."

"I've told you how I feel about challenges."

She smiles with a glint in her eye. "You're the one who needs a first round." She traces her fingers down my chest to the waistband of my sweats.

I swallow. "I'm keeping it in my pants, as instructed."

One finger slowly voyages southward, and I hold back a groan as she runs it down my length.

"I can still have fun with you if it stays there. Besides," she says, gently wrapping her hand around me, "rules are meant to be broken."

Every hormone-crazed cell in my body screams at me to let her, but I bite my cheek and thread my fingers with hers. "Don't worry about me. Tonight was for you."

Chelsea whines and looks me up and down like a piece of meat. *Am I into being objectified by her? Hell yes.*

"There will be other times. I hope." I raise her hand to my lips for a kiss. "I don't want to move too fast for you. This was a lot."

She closes her eyes, and my nerves kick in.

I rub my thumb against her lower lip, and her lids flutter open. Her eyes swim with emotion before she quickly composes herself.

"I suppose you've earned the right to take me out for a book and coffee."

I laugh and cup her cheek with my hand. "Well, it's about fucking time."

Chapter 19

Chelsea

I get back to my hotel room just before Lauren. I somehow manage to throw on an oversized t-shirt and wash my makeup off before I hear voices on the other side of the door. I dive under the covers just as she comes in.

"You're alive!" I say with a hasty smile.

She chuckles. "The rumors of my death and dismemberment have been greatly exaggerated." She pulls her heels off and throws them into the closet before working on her earrings. "Sawyer was a perfect gentleman, much to my disappointment."

I raise an eyebrow. "Oh?"

She grabs some pajamas from her bag and heads to the bathroom. "I flirted, but he behaved himself. It's probably for the best." I hear the water running as she washes her face. "I don't need any distractions here."

"That's the spirit. Boys suck."

Lauren pads back into the room. "What have you been up to since you left the bar?"

The best freaking orgasm of my life.

I shrug and reach for my book. "Nothing much. Just reading in bed."

She falls asleep soon after, and I pull my phone off the nightstand. The glow lights up my face as I type out a message.

Me: My skin smells like you and I can't sleep

The Bear: God, that's hot

The Bear: Sneak out and come back here. I'll tire you out again

Me: You need to get some rest

The Bear: Then stop texting me, gosh

Me: Good night, Rookie

The Bear: Good night, beautiful

Two days later, the skies are cloudy, but my heart feels light with anticipation. I'm waiting for Wes at a bookstore a half mile from the arena. I pull my trench coat more tightly around me to ward off the chill, grateful that I dressed warmly in jeans and a sweater.

My God, that man worshipped me the other night. I couldn't stop thinking about how his mouth was hot and desperate against me, as though he couldn't get enough. There was no faking the way he'd stared at me, his eyes heavy with desire and astonishment when I showed up at his door. I've always enjoyed sex, but usually spent the time hoping the guy wouldn't look too closely at my body. Wes couldn't *stop* looking, and it tapped into a confidence I didn't know I had. It was a turn-on of epic proportions.

Our Spicy Book Club chats and steamy phone calls suggested Wes knew what he was doing in the bedroom, but the reality was beyond my wildest dreams. His hands were determined and confident, like he already knew just how I liked to be touched. *I suppose he did take notes.*

The thought of him paying attention to my offhand comments so he could learn what would drive me crazy in bed makes me squirm against the brick wall.

"Chels?"

My eyes, which I hadn't realized had fluttered closed, flew open to find Wes smiling at me. My breath catches.

"Hey. Sorry, I got distracted."

His eyes run over me like liquid velvet. "I know the feeling."

I couldn't remember the last time a man had looked at me with such naked desire.

I smooth invisible wrinkles from my coat. "You look like you want to eat me."

"That's because I do." He steps closer and leans in. "And I like how you taste."

My brain short-circuits.

I freeze, and he chuckles, sneaking a quick kiss along the side of my neck. "Sorry, I shouldn't sexually harass you on the first date." He places a hand on my waist and gently nudges me inside. "Let's go get you a book."

The bookstore is an explosion of color and coziness, with overstuffed chairs tucked in reading nooks nestled between bookcases. A small café is situated in the back, featuring beverage and snack options. It smells like books and uninterrupted reading time, and my stomach flips happily in response.

"Come find me when you're ready," Wes says as I wander towards the fiction section.

"Sounds good."

I leisurely browse the shelves, picking up the occasional book to read the back blurb or flip through the pages. It feels like a warm hug, having a few hours off from team activities and spending them in the company of books. Not to mention the cute guy.

I select something from the Romance section and go in search of Wes, finding him in U.S. History.

"Hey." I plant a kiss on his shoulder as I come up behind him.

He turns around with a grin, winding his arm around my waist and pulling me to his side.

An unreasonable panic flashes through me at the intimacy, and I stiffen in his arms.

"Too much?" he asks, loosening his grip. "You kissed me, so I thought I was safe."

I sigh. "I know. I'm sorry." I look down at the ugly store carpeting but step closer to him. "I'm having a hard time following my own rules around you."

He palms my lower back and nuzzles against my neck, his beard tickling my skin. "Then maybe we should break them."

"I don't think I'm ready for that yet." I glance up at him.

"Let's check out and get some coffee," he says. "I probably shouldn't be alone in a dark corner with you, because all I'm thinking about is pinning you against a bookshelf."

I groan and place my book in his outstretched hand. "We've really made things hard for ourselves with all the sexy texts and phone calls. Don't even say it." I point my finger at him as he opens his mouth to make a lewd play on my words.

He grins, and we head to the cashier.

The store café has several round tables with vibrant velvet chairs. I curl up in one as Wes sets our drinks down.

"So, tell me about your book," he asks as we settle in.

I slide the colorful paperback across to him. "It's a lacrosse romance," I say with a smile. "I've never seen one before."

He turns it over. "Sounds like an untapped market. Maybe we should write one about us."

"What did you pick out?" I gesture towards his book.

"It's a history of the Oneida Nation during the American Revolution." He slides it to me, and I page through a few sections. "My mom told us a bit about this growing up, but there's so much I never learned."

"The Oneida were America's first allies," I say with a wry smile. "Look how well that turned out for us."

"No kidding." He leans forward to look at some of the photos. "There's so much history in New York I missed out on."

I cluck my tongue. "I wish you all were still with us on the traditional homelands. There's something missing without you here."

We sip our drinks in silence. I glance up to find Wes looking at me.

"I can't stop thinking about you," he says quietly.

"Me either." I inhale deeply. "Wes, I—"

"I'll wait for you as long as you need," he interjects. "I'm crazy about you, Chels."

My heart thumps painfully. These are words I've longed to hear from a partner, but they also scare me. I don't feel ready to hear them. I don't feel *worthy* of hearing them.

I lick my lips, which suddenly feel dry. "I don't want you to have to wait for someone. You're too good for me."

He scoffs. "Be serious. You're the most incredible woman I've ever met."

"You may think that, but you're still inexperienced."

He chokes on his coffee. "Inexperienced?!"

I huff. "You know what I mean."

"You didn't have any complaints the other night."

"Wesley."

He grins over his coffee cup. "Using my government name now? I like it."

"I'm serious." I sip my tea. "You're young, and there are women out there who would trip over themselves to be yours."

"First of all," he says, leaning forward on his elbows, "you're only three years older than me. Secondly, you and I go together like corn, beans, and squash. We complement each other perfectly, and you know it."

The rookie tells no lies, unfortunately.

I grumble in response.

"Lastly, I don't want anyone else." His hand reaches over to cover mine. "I want *you*, Chels. That's it. If I have to wait for you to feel safe and comfortable being in a relationship again, then so be it. I'm not going anywhere."

I swallow. I don't want to hurt him, but I'm also scared as hell to realize I'm falling hard for him. This was *not* part of the plan.

"I wish you would stop being so darn likable," I say with a dramatic sigh. "Cut it out."

He smiles and rubs soft circles over the back of my hand. "Sorry. You're stuck with me. I'm determined to outlast you on this."

I watch his thumb trace over my skin, marveling at his sweetness while also flashing back to the decidedly spicy things he can do with that thumb.

"You are a big fucking problem for me, Harrison."

He brings my hand to his lips for a quick kiss. "Good." I don't pull away, and he takes the opportunity to graze his teeth over my knuckles.

I suck in a breath, and he raises his eyes to mine. "You're a big fucking problem for me, too." His breath skates across my skin as he tenderly dusts kisses down my fingers. "I hope you'll let me stick around for a while."

Chapter 20

Wes

The Haudenosaunee women are in a battle with Team Canada.

It was always going to be tough to beat them, as Canadian teams are typically the best in the world at box lacrosse. Today is no different. Our women are keeping it close, but are still behind by a pair of goals late in the fourth quarter.

"They're getting beat in their own end," Jamie says. "The defense needs to toughen up and get the ball out of there and to their playmakers."

"Losing Chelsea really hurt," Zeke adds. "She's their most physical player."

My stomach has been in knots since she took a hard hit into the boards just before halftime. She hasn't gone to the locker room, which suggests a less severe injury, but she hasn't left the bench since.

"She was reading their defense well before she went out," Sawyer chimes in from the row in front of us. "I wish we had her on the Outlaws."

I smile at my teammates' praise. She really is an incredible player, and with each game I can see her confidence growing. She's looking looser on the floor, which has led to creativity in her passing and shooting. She set up a beautiful goal for Lauren in the first period that had tied the game at the time.

"You think she'd want to put up with *you*?" the woman sitting next to Sawyer says without her eyes leaving the floor. "You're insufferable."

Jamie covers his mouth to suppress his laughter, and Zeke kicks him in the ankle.

Sawyer has been getting destroyed by this girl all game, and it's amusing the shit out of us.

"I love when you hit me with the SAT words, Princess," Sawyer replies. "I'll have to write that one down."

"I'm going to move to a different section."

"Don't waste your time. I'll just follow you over there." Sawyer bends forward and cringes as two players collide at midfield. "I only get to enjoy your delightful presence a few times per year, and I wouldn't want to miss out."

"What's their deal?" I whisper to Jamie, who always knows everything about everybody.

"Sienna Bissell. Her uncle is Randy Bissell," he says.

My eyes widen. "*The* Randy Bissell? Hall of Fame player for the Outlaws?"

"That's the one," Jamie continues. "He's the Haudenosaunee women's coach. Her dad and Sawyer's stepfather are close friends, so she and Sawyer have spent a lot of time together. She has zero tolerance for his bullshit."

"I mean, us too," Zeke says with a grin.

Jamie chuckles. "She gets under his skin like no one else. I bring popcorn anytime those two are near each other."

I watch as Sawyer leans over to whisper something in her ear, and Sienna rolls her eyes.

"Why is he sitting with her then?" I ask.

"Because he fucking loves it." Jamie grins.

"Mmm hmm. I'm picking up what you're putting down, Jammer."

Team Canada scores and puts the game away with less than ten seconds remaining. It'll be the first loss for the Haudenosaunee in pool play, which is impressive.

"We should wait for the team by the locker room," Jamie says. "Hype them up."

"Good idea. We've got time before practice," Zeke agrees.

I'm desperate to see Chelsea and find out the extent of her injury, and I accidentally jump out of my seat so fast the bottom flies up with a bang.

Jamie raises an eyebrow at me and stands up at a more leisurely pace. "Sienna, did you want to come with us?"

Sawyer gets to his feet and holds a hand out to her. She ignores him and rises on her own.

"Sure, I can stay for a few minutes. I was hoping to see my cousin and my uncle, anyway."

"What are you up to, Lanes?" Jamie asks.

Sawyer runs a hand through his brown hair. "I've got practice soon, so I need to bounce, unfortunately." He watches as Sienna climbs the steps to join our group in the row behind him. "Say hi to your family for me."

"I will." She adjusts her leather purse strap. "They like you, for some reason."

His cocky grin reappears. "At least someone in that family has taste."

"We'll catch up with you later." I nod in his direction.

"Tell the ladies they played a hell of a game," he says. "They're going to be a menace in the elimination rounds."

Chapter 21

Chelsea

The loss to Canada is gut-wrenching because we had a real chance.

We had momentum in the first half. Our defense was finishing checks and keeping them away from the ball. The goalscorers got into position and had quality shots on goal, including several that went in. This was the best game I've played since college, and I know I could've helped put us over the top in the final quarter if I hadn't gotten hurt.

Tears of frustration sting my eyes in the shower, and I blink them away.

My right shoulder hit the boards funny on a body check. It seems to be a bruise and muscular pain, rather than a break or tear, but the pain is debilitating and I couldn't keep playing. Coach Bissell let me stay on the bench with an ice pack in case things improved, but I didn't see another minute on the floor. Watching from the sidelines as the game slipped away was a helpless and infuriating feeling.

"How's the shoulder?" Lauren asks as we get dressed.

"Painful," I say with a cringe.

She gives me a worried look and pulls a hoodie over her head. "Maybe you should go back to the hotel room. Take a hot bath and relax."

"John!" Coach yells from across the locker room. He crooks his finger when I turn to look his way.

I make my way to him, my shoulder throbbing with every step.

"How's it feeling?" he asks.

I bite my lip. "I've been better. But I'm sure it'll be fine in time for tomorrow's game."

He fixes me with a serious look. "We're not rushing you back. We need you once we get to the elimination games later in the week."

I hide a smile. *The team needs me.* "Yes, Coach."

"Check in with Paige on your way out. She wants to get you into a sling for now until we know what we're dealing with. Take the rest of the day off. Full rest, and we'll check in tomorrow morning."

A groan nearly leaves my lips, but I catch it in time. "Will do."

By the time the team trainer gets me into a sling and on a dose of painkillers, the locker room is empty. I grab my stick and my backpack, throwing it onto my good shoulder before walking out. I'm three steps out the door when I hear a voice that makes my blood run cold.

"Well, this is a surprise."

I turn and see a slow smile creep across Brock's face.

What. Is. He. Doing. Here?

I could kick myself for being surprised, because of course he was at the World Games. I saw him playing in the men's Haudenosaunee versus Canada game, but I'd managed to distract myself by watching with Genny and Lauren. I'd kept my eyes on the players I knew and scowled anytime he showed up in my field of view. But what is he doing *here*, hanging around outside the locker room long after everyone has left?

My core starts to tremble, and I tighten my grip on my stick. "Fuck off, Brock."

He leans against the wall outside the locker room. "Never thought I'd see you here. Did someone get hurt, and the team was desperate?"

This asshole always knew how to hit me where it hurts most. I pretend I don't hear him and keep walking. I see Wes and some of the men's team at the end of the hallway, so I head in their direction.

Brock steps into my path. "What's the hurry? I'd love to catch up now that I know you're here."

"No thanks." I pray he doesn't hear my voice shaking.

"You seeing anyone? Let me buy you a drink tonight."

"No. Please excuse me." I try to step around him, but he stays in front of me. "Brock, please. I just want to get to my friends," I insist.

"There you are." Wes appears with a wide smile, but I can see the concern in his eyes. "We've been waiting for you. Hell of a game." He slings an arm carefully around my shoulders and squarely faces Brock.

Brock looks Wes up and down with a scowl. "Do you mind? We were talking."

"I do mind, actually, because she doesn't want to talk to you."

I'm shaking like a leaf under Wes' arm, and he squeezes my uninjured shoulder in response.

Brock ignores him. "Another white guy, Chels? I figured you had enough after me."

Wes tenses and my head spins. I'm torn between screaming in rage and letting loose the hot tears threatening behind my eyes.

"We good here?" Jamie pushes past Brock and claps Wes on the shoulder.

"Jesus. All this firepower for some no-name player?" Brock scoffs.

Jamie cranes his neck as though he's checking for the name on the back of Brock's jersey. "I don't know who *you* are, man, but she's been playing at an elite level for almost a decade."

Brock's eye twitches. "You know me, Jammer."

"Don't call me Jammer, because I don't know who the hell you are. If I've met you, then you were wholly unremarkable."

Brock barks out a laugh. "Whatever, man. Not sure what a guy like you is doing defending her. She's beneath you."

I'm still shaking but desperately trying to hide it. My eyes dart around in search of an exit route. I need to get out of here now before I embarrass myself.

Wes steps between me and Brock. "We're done here," he growls. "You need to move."

Brock shakes his head. "She must have the two of you pussy-whipped. It's a shame she's not worth it."

Bam!

Brock's body slams into the wall when Wes grabs him by the collar. I gasp softly, fear coiling in my stomach.

"Go. The fuck. Away." Wes says coldly.

Jamie wraps a hand around my upper arm and tugs me closer to him. "Stay back," he says quietly.

Brock opens his mouth in retort but falls silent as Zeke approaches from behind Wes. His broad frame towers over them.

"Get out of here, man. Let's go." Zeke places a firm hand on Brock's shoulder and yanks him down the hallway.

Brock glares at the rest of us before trying unsuccessfully to shake Zeke's grip. "I got it. Back off."

Zeke follows behind him as he walks away, making sure he actually leaves.

The sound of my labored breathing fills my ears. I bite my cheek and rapidly blink away the tears threatening to spill from my eyes.

Wes approaches, and all I want is to melt into his arms and cry. He reaches for me, but Zeke gets there first and pulls me into a hug, trying to avoid my sling.

"You OK, Chels?" he asks.

"She's not OK," Wes says quietly.

"I'll be fine," I reply, my voice muffled by Zeke's chest. "I just need a few minutes."

"Do you want to go back to the hotel for a bit?" Wes asks.

I nod, and Zeke releases me. "I'm supposed to be resting today, anyway."

"I'll walk you back in case you cross paths with that asshole," Zeke offers.

"Thanks." I smile weakly. "I appreciate that."

"You've got everything you need? We can head over now," Zeke says.

"Yeah. Thanks, guys. For everything." I look over to Wes and Jamie. "You didn't have to do that. You barely know me." My voice trails off as guilt and shame wash over me.

"You're one of us," Jamie says. "*Onkwehón:we* stick together. You think we're going to let some white boy get under your skin?"

"Don't let Sawyer hear you say that," Zeke jokes.

I smile and catch Wes' eye. He's looking at me with sadness and worry in his gaze.

"Sawyer would never, because he knows he'd get his ass beat the next time he went home to Six Nations," Jamie says.

I want to stay with Wes, but Zeke slings my bag over his shoulder and gestures across the arena. "Ready?"

"Yep." I look back at Wes one last time as we walk by.

"Call me," he mouths silently.

Chapter 22

Wes

I'm going to lay out that piece of trash the next time we play.

I noticed him hanging around the locker room after the game, but figured he was waiting for a straggler from Team Canada. Chelsea was the last player to emerge, likely delayed by her injury treatment, so I have to think he was waiting for her specifically.

My jaw is so tight it hurts as I watch her depart with Zeke. It's taking every ounce of my control not to run after them and pull her into my arms. I was worried enough about her being hurt, and now I'm beside myself with rage about this creep who clearly has a past with her.

"She'll be OK," Jamie says. "Zeke will get her back safe, and then she can rest."

My hands clench. "Do you know that guy?"

"I know who he is, but I don't know much about him beyond his stats. He's been on the Canadian roster in the past, and he plays in the NLL. Sawyer would have more insight."

"Can we kick his ass next game?"

"Fuck yes."

"I knew I could count on you."

Jamie checks his watch. "We've got a couple of hours before practice if you need to run errands or anything."

My eyes slide over to him. "Errands?"

He shrugs and refuses to meet my gaze. "I don't know what you get up to in your free time. You might want to replenish your snack supply or buy Utica knick knacks."

I watch him for a few seconds as he leisurely drinks from his water bottle.

"I'll see you at practice?" Jamie says.

I smile. "I'll see you there."

I know exactly what I want to do for the next two hours.

🌲   🌲   🌲

Me: What's Chelsea's room number? The team trainer came out with a bottle of painkillers after you left. I can drop them off on my way to lunch

Zeke: Oh yeah, she needs those. Appreciate it. She's in room 608

Thirty minutes later, I'm knocking on her door, my arms laden with plastic bags. No response.

Shit. Maybe she fell asleep? I knock again. Nothing.

> **Me:** Hey gorgeous. If you're awake, I'm at your door.

I hear feet hit the floor. I hear her sigh of relief before she opens the door.

"I'm so glad it's you." Chelsea reaches out and pulls me inside by my collar. "I thought it might be someone else."

I swear. "I didn't think of that, I'm sorry." I hold up the white bags in my hands. "I brought you supplies."

She beckons me inside, and I set the bags on top of the desk. I unload the items, narrating as I go. "Spicy Italian sandwich for lunch. No lettuce. Cherry Pepsi. Ibuprofen, because I wasn't sure if you had any. Zip-lock bags so you can make ice packs with the hotel ice. Epsom salts. Water. And I sent you a code for an audiobook, since it'll be hard to turn pages with one hand."

I look up to find her eyes shiny with tears. Panic rises in my throat. "I'm sorry, I overstepped. I shouldn't have—"

She wraps her good arm around my neck, and my words die off. Her fingers thread through my hair until she's cradling the back of my head.

My breathing stops. I'm afraid to move.

"You did all this for me?" she whispers.

I nod, lost in the depths of her chocolate eyes. "I knew you'd be stuck here for a few hours without Lauren, and would need to take care of your body so you can heal."

She gazes at me, searching for something in my face. "Stay still."

I haven't moved a muscle since she touched me. "OK."

Her hand moves to my jaw, brushing against my cheek with her thumb. Her breathing is shallow as she gently tugs me down towards her until my forehead rests against hers. Our lips are millimeters apart, so close I feel her breath shuddering against my beard.

Chelsea swallows, and her hand trembles slightly. "You know my favorite sandwich? And what I like to drink?"

I'm definitely not getting enough oxygen into my lungs, but I nod. "I noticed at dinner with Jess."

Her eyes flutter closed, and if I lean forward the tiniest bit...

Her lips brush against my cheek before traveling to the corner of my mouth. A half-starved sigh escapes me as she kisses along my jawline.

"Thank you," she says, her eyes opening to look deeply into mine. "You're so good to me."

"I told you I would be." I tentatively raise my arms to wrap around her. "You're easy to take care of."

She continues touching my face, the pads of her fingers running over my skin and lips.

I swallow and draw circles on her back with my hand. "Why don't you eat and I'll run you an Epsom salt bath?"

Chelsea wrinkles her nose. "A hotel bathtub is not the most relaxing place."

"I know, but your shoulder will thank you for the magnesium infusion."

She frowns, and I gently push her down into the desk chair.

"Sit. Eat." I unwrap her sandwich and twist open the bottle of Pepsi. "When are you due for your next dose of painkillers?"

She takes a large bite of the sub and moans so enthusiastically my dick twitches. "This is amazing. I've been craving one of these."

I smile and kiss her forehead. "Good."

Her teeth catch a stray piece of provolone cheese, and I'm going to need a moment. "I can take more ibuprofen in an hour."

I take the cap off the bottle of medication so she won't need to struggle with it later. "Enjoy that, and I'll be right back."

The bathtub here isn't exactly a spa-like environment, but it'll have to do. I fill it with hot water and Epsom salts, stirring with my hand to be sure the rough crystals dissolve. I glance at the various skincare and makeup products on the sink as I wait for the water to rise, smiling as I imagine her washing her face at night or applying lip gloss in the mornings. *What I wouldn't give to see a similar spread taking over my bathroom counter.*

I turn the faucet off and head back into the bedroom. Chelsea is sipping her drink and leaning back in the chair with a blissful expression on her face.

"That was amazing, thank you," she says dreamily.

I don't think I satisfied her half as well the other night, but I'm glad she's fed and happy. "Glad to be of service. You should get in the tub, and I'll make you an ice pack."

"You're very bossy." Her eyes dance with mirth.

"You like that?"

"In certain rooms more than others." She takes a final swig from the bottle and comes to her feet.

She takes two steps before I carefully scoop her into my arms, avoiding her injured shoulder.

"Hey! My legs aren't broken."

"This is what I've wanted to do since you came out of the locker room, so humor me." I navigate to the bathroom with the utmost care, avoiding sharp edges and randomly strewn shoes on the floor.

Chelsea rests her head on my shoulder. "It *is* kind of nice to get the full princess treatment."

"That's what you'll get anytime you're with me." I gently set her down near the tub. "Here you go, my queen."

"Thanks." She breathes in some steam. "Ooh, you got the lavender scented salts?"

"Of course I did. I'm not a barbarian."

She examines the milky water. "I suppose I should get in now."

"Right. I'm going to go get ice. Let me know if you need anything."

"You wish."

I chuckle. "Not right now. This isn't the time."

"Well then, shoo. Outta here, Rookie."

I clean up the trash from Chelsea's lunch and go in search of the room's ice bucket. It takes me a minute to find it tucked inside the fridge. I'm placing a plastic bag inside the container when I hear Chelsea call my name.

I knock on the bathroom door. "You OK?"

She's silent for a few seconds before speaking. "I, uh—I'm having a problem."

"What's wrong?"

"I need your help."

"Do you want me to come in?"

"Yeah."

I slowly open the door. "What's up?"

She has one arm out of her t-shirt, her cheeks are pink, and her forehead is beaded with sweat. "I can't get this off without straightening my arm, and it really, really hurts to straighten it right now."

I take a moment to consider our options. "Well, let's get you out of this sling first."

"I tried, but it hurt, and I chickened out."

"Let me give it a shot." I fiddle with the adjustable strap on her upper back. "Your pain meds are probably starting to wear off."

"Probably." She hisses when the strap loosens and her forearm lowers. I catch her arm and hold it carefully in place as I finish pulling the straps free from her body.

"Can you keep your arm bent while I pull off the sling?"

She nods and cradles the limb.

I cautiously tug the sleeve off her forearm, pausing every few seconds so she can adjust her grip.

"Doing OK?"

"Yeah. You can pull it the rest of the way off."

"OK, tough guy." I give a final tug and toss the sling to the floor. "Now comes the hard part."

She bites her lip. "I think I need you to pull the shirt over my head while I hold my arm in place."

"If you wanted me to take your clothes off, all you had to do was ask. No need for all these theatrics."

She steps on my toes, and I laugh.

"I can do that. And I promise I won't look."

Chelsea huffs. "Please. Nothing you haven't already seen."

"I haven't seen all of you yet." I run my thumb against her cheek. "And I don't want you to feel uncomfortable."

"It's OK." Her voice is soft and low. "I feel safe around you."

"I'm glad." Her shirt bunches in my hands around her waist. "Think of me as a doctor. Ready?"

She nods, her opposite hand supporting her arm. "Ready."

I pull her Team Haudenosaunee t-shirt up and over the back of her head. I ease it over her injured shoulder and past her elbow.

"Let me see your hand."

I thread my fingers through hers to hold the arm in place while I tug the shirt the rest of the way off.

"Piece of cake," I say, folding the shirt and setting it on the counter. She's standing in front of me in a gray sports bra, and I frown. "Do you need to get this off, too?"

Chelsea laughs throatily. "It would be much worse trying to wrestle this off once it's wet, believe me."

I swallow, my eyes running down her torso.

"I thought you liked a challenge." I look up to find her watching me with a raised eyebrow.

"All right, John. Let's give this a shot." I draw in a shaky breath and spread my hands wide at the base of her ribs. "Tell me if I'm hurting you, and I'll stop."

I run my hands up the back of her bra and hook my thumbs over the edges, slowly peeling the tight fabric over her breasts. I keep my eyes on hers as I continue to roll the garment up, my fingers brushing against the sides of her curves.

"Sorry," I whisper. "I'm trying not to touch you."

Longing swims in her eyes. "No problem."

The devil on my shoulder tells me to back her up against the wall and kiss down her neck. My fingers ache to know whether her nipples are stiff with desire or pliable in the warm air. Instead, I clear my throat.

"Do you think you could pull your good arm through?"

She licks her lips and nods.

I fist the fabric and pull until she gets her arm free.

"This fucking thing is so tight. How is this comfortable?" I pull the sports bra over her head before it can strangle her.

Her laughter is low in her throat and fans the liquid heat taking over my veins. "It's not. No woman likes these things."

Without intending to, I take a step forward and bump her against the wall.

"Sorry," I breathe.

Her breasts brush against my chest and answer my question: her nipples are hard.

She releases a barely audible moan, and I bite my cheek to suppress a whimper.

"You can't make those kinds of noises, baby," I plead. "I'm hanging on for dear life over here."

"I thought you were a medical professional?" Her hips roll into mine, and my nails scrape her back.

"Chelsea."

She closes her eyes and inhales deeply. "Let's finish this."

Her bra is hanging off the crook of her elbow at this point, so it's easy to pull loose and toss to the floor. Eyes trained to the ceiling, I feel around for a towel and hold it up in front of her.

"Do you need a hand getting in the tub?" I desperately need to get out of this hot room and away from this hot woman before I do something I'll regret.

She peels off her shorts, kicking them into the corner before wrapping the towel around herself. "I should be all right. There's a handrail I can use."

"Good. Just let me know. I'll get that ice now."

I busy myself with odds and ends while she soaks in the tub. I fill up the ice bucket, put her water in the fridge, set out her next dose of pain pills, and arrange a bunch of pillows against her headboard so she can sit propped up.

"Wes," she calls.

"Yeah?"

"Could you bring me something to wear? There should be a big t-shirt and a pair of underwear near the top of my suitcase."

I suck in some air. "Are you trying to kill me?"

Her chuckle echoes off the bathroom wall. Water splashes as she gets out of the tub.

I peek into the suitcase closest to her bed, hoping it's hers and not Lauren's. The first shirt I pull out is from the Oneida Community Center, so this feels like the right bag. My fingers brush against a pair of black cotton panties, and I'll spend the rest of the day knowing she's wearing only those under her clothes.

A wall of steam emerges as she cracks open the door. "Here you go." I hand the items to her.

"Thanks." She closes the door. "Could you help me get the sling back on once I'm dressed?"

"Of course."

I lean against the doorframe, trying not to picture her dropping the towel and getting into her clothes. A few minutes later she re-emerges, and I'm pretty sure my tongue falls out of my mouth and rolls across the room at the sight of her.

The t-shirt hits the tops of her thighs, giving me an eyeful of creamy bronze skin that is going to haunt my dreams for the foreseeable future.

I grab the sling from the counter and begin pulling it onto her forearm. She watches me as I maneuver the straps around her shoulder and back. Her long wet hair tangles in the apparatus, and I try to gently move it out of the way.

"Sorry," she says, clawing at it with her good arm. "I couldn't pull it back with one hand."

"Want me to braid it for you?" I ask.

She pauses. "You know how?"

I shrug. "I braided my sister's hair all the time. It's easy."

She nods. "That would be nice to get it out of my face, thank you." She directs me to her supplies by the sink, and I gently brush out her tangles.

"No one's braided my hair for me in years," she says quietly.

I divide her curtain of hair into three sections. "Does it feel nice?"

"It does. You're very gentle."

I softly kiss the side of her neck as I weave the wet pieces together. "You deserve to be taken care of." My fingers work slowly, trying not to tug too hard or miss any strands. "Who was that guy harassing you earlier?"

Chelsea tenses up, as I expected her to. I dust more kisses against the shell of her ear, and she relaxes slightly. "Someone I used to date."

"I take it things ended badly?"

She waits a few breaths before responding. "He was never as interested in me as I thought I was in him. But his ego bruises easily."

So he's an absolute idiot on top of being an asshole, got it.

"Is it all right if we don't talk about it now?" she asks before I can form another sentence. "I don't want to think about him anymore today."

I tie off the end of the braid and reach for the sling straps once more. "Fine by me. But I'm ready to listen if you want to talk another time."

She leans against me as I tighten the straps until her sling is properly aligned. The weight of her against my chest feels like a warm hug, and I wrap my arms around her from behind.

"You ready to get tucked into bed with an audiobook while I head off to practice?"

"Yes, please. I feel like I could fall asleep standing up."

"Can't have that." I bend down and swoop her up into my arms again.

"You're spoiling me," she murmurs as I lay her back against her pillows and pull up the blankets.

"Get used to it." I cup her cheek as her eyes flutter shut. She's not going to last long enough for an audiobook. "Text me later and let me know how you're doing, OK?"

"I promise." Her voice trails off.

My heart swells painfully in my chest as I pull her hotel room door closed behind me, desperately wishing I could stay.

Chapter 23

Chelsea

The past week has been brutal, but it's paying off in the most magical way.

I missed the next two games, including the quarterfinals against Ireland, but was finally back on the floor for the semis. The American team is always a tough opponent, and they played nearly perfectly that day. We played hard and kept it close, but ultimately lost by four goals.

There wasn't time to feel too badly about ourselves, because today we play for a bronze medal against Australia. Hearing the Haudenosaunee national anthem at the start of games is an incredible honor, but especially in this environment.

Everything breaks our way: Our goaltender plays lights out, limiting the Aussies to five goals; balls bounce the way we want them to; and our passes connect crisply. I score two goals in the second half, assisted by Gabby and Lauren. The game is *fun* from start to finish, and I'm emotional at the thought of this life-changing experience coming to an end.

Joy builds in my chest as the game clock winds down. Tears spill from my eyes when the final horn sounds, and we all drop our sticks and gloves to pile on our goalie in celebration. We won by ten goals, an impressive achievement.

"It has been a dream come true to play here with you," Lauren says, her voice thick with sentiment as she hugs me tightly.

"Same. I'm so glad you're back in my life." I tap her on the helmet with a wide smile.

The bronze is heavy around my neck as we finish the medal ceremony and our families and friends join us on the floor. I wrap my palm around it, running my thumb over the etched grooves as my parents find me in the crowd.

Genny, Mackenzie, and Jess join us after a few minutes, followed shortly by the men's team. My face hurts from smiling, and I'm having a hard time remembering a happier moment in my life.

Wes grabs me and swings me around off my feet. "I'm so incredibly proud of you and happy for you," he says, his eyes shining.

"Thank you," I manage to respond before I'm pulled into a photo with some teammates.

I'm not able to make my way back to him anytime soon, as there's no shortage of people to talk to, interviews to give, and photographers to pose for. I eventually feel a hand on my shoulder and spin around to find Zeke.

"I know you're busy. Just wanted to let you know we're heading out." He bends low to give me a hug. "We've got our game in the morning, and Coach will kill us if we're out much later."

In the chaos of tonight, I'd forgotten the men were playing Canada tomorrow for the gold.

"Yeah, of course. Go get some sleep." I look for Wes, but he's caught up in conversation nearby with Jess. My chest aches at the lack of time spent with him today, and we're all going home tomorrow afternoon.

So much has happened over the past ten days that my brain hasn't processed this coming to an end. I've been floating in a bubble of lacrosse, friends, and Wes, and that's about to pop. Tomorrow I'll have to say goodbye, and I'm not ready.

I can't shake the heaviness in my stomach as we trek back to the hotel. A group of younger players decide to go out for drinks, but Lauren and I beg off due to exhaustion.

We drop our mountain of gear on the floor and collapse into our beds once we get back to the hotel.

"I don't want to pack," Lauren whines.

"Me either." I stretch out into a starfish.

She rolls onto her side. "I should probably run to the store before it closes. I wanted to get some snacks and water for the road. Do you need anything?"

"No, I'm good. Home is practically next door for me."

She hauls herself out of bed. "OK, I'm going before I can talk myself out of it. I won't be long."

I groan. "I should start packing while you're gone. This sucks. Where are our personal assistants?"

She grins and pulls on her coat. "Right? They should hand them out during the medal ceremony."

The door clicks closed, and I'm consumed with the desire to see Wes.

He's probably asleep.

I likely wouldn't have a chance to give him a proper goodbye tomorrow.

He has a huge game in the morning. He doesn't need distractions tonight.

Our time together this week has felt *easy.* He's sweet, gentle, and full of light. My heart feels like it's breaking at the thought of being apart from him again for who knows how long.

> **Me:** You still up?

> **The Bear:** In bed, but yeah.

I don't even put on shoes before I'm grabbing my key and flying out the door.

Every second it takes to get to his room is too long. I pull out my phone in the elevator and send him another text.

> **Me:** What are you up to?

> **The Bear:** Not much. Just reading. What's up with you?

> **Me:** Where's Zeke?

The Bear: In the shower...why?

Me: Open your door

I sprint down the hall to his room as he peeks out. He's shirtless and wearing wire-rimmed glasses.

"Everything O–" He stops short as I push him inside.

"Is Zeke still in the shower?" I ask, my hands running up his bare chest.

Wes nods, his eyes searching mine.

Thank you, Creator.

I press him against the wall and twist my shaking hands into his tousled hair. It's slightly damp, as though he'd recently showered.

"Chels," he exhales. "What do you need?"

"You," I whisper, unable to wait another instant.

I hungrily pull his mouth down to mine and lose all sense of time and space as the feel of him envelops me. He smells like Dove soap, and he tastes like heaven.

I gasp as his tongue parts my lips. His arms surround me and draw me flush against his warm skin. I feel like I'm burning up from the inside.

We're desperate for each other, our hands and tongues intermingling as we give in to ten months of yearning. His teeth catch my bottom lip, and I moan.

We went much further than this last week, but kissing him feels so much more intimate. I want to swallow him whole. My skin heats everywhere he touches. His hands frame my face while he kisses me deeply before tracing down my neck and shoulders.

Our heavy breathing floods my ears until the sound of the shower curtain opening wrenches me back to reality.

Crap. Zeke.

I stumble backwards. "I have to go."

"No, wai—" Wes reaches for me, his chest heaving and his cheeks flushed, but I pull open the room door and rush outside.

I walk quickly towards the elevator and try to catch my breath. It's physically painful to be separated from him right now.

"Chelsea!"

I turn to see Wes chasing me down the hallway.

"What are you doing?" I ask breathlessly, taking in his appearance. He's still wearing a pair of sweatpants and nothing else.

"Do you seriously think I'm going to let you leave after that?" He grasps my upper arm and tugs me into the ice machine alcove. He nudges me into the far corner and presses my back into the wall, his mouth immediately back on mine.

"Wes," I moan, my hands roaming over the broad expanse of his skin.

"I need more of you," he whispers against my lips.

My heart feels like it will burst with emotion. I didn't expect to fall this hard for him, although I should have. The signs were there from the beginning; I just ignored them.

I claw at his chest, wishing he were wearing a shirt I could use to pull him even closer. "You realize you're half naked, right?"

"I don't care." He wraps a hand in the hair at the nape of my neck and gently tugs. "And I didn't think you'd mind."

I groan at the sensation.

"OK, wait." I pull back to look at him. "You wear glasses?"

He blinks in confusion. "What?"

"You're wearing glasses. And they're all fogged up." I bite my lip and adjust them on his face.

He smiles. "I take my contacts out at night."

"They're sexy. You should wear them more often."

"Maybe you should come over at bedtime more often."

I tug him back to my mouth. "Don't tempt me."

We make out until the ice machine hums to life and scares the living daylights out of me.

He chuckles and lifts my chin with his thumb. "What changed tonight?" He brushes his lips across mine. "Rule #1 went out the window."

A flicker of fear flares in my stomach. Showing vulnerability has always been a weakness of mine.

"I couldn't bear the thought of leaving tomorrow and not knowing when I'd see you again." I swallow. "I've been telling myself this is just a bit of fun between us, but I'm realizing it's more than that. And that freaks me out."

"It feels like more to me, too." He scans my eyes. "Your ex from last week...has he said those types of things to you before?"

I look away. "He has."

"Then you know he's a coward who gets off on making other people feel small."

I nod and rest my cheek against his chest.

"None of what he said is true," Wes murmurs against my hair. "He doesn't know ball, and he wouldn't know a good woman if she punched him in his stupid face. Which I absolutely hope you do at some point."

I smile. "I shouldn't be bothered by it. He's always been like that."

Wes tenses.

"I'm going to help you rewrite every story he's told you about yourself, Chels." He traces along my jaw. "You deserve to believe how magnificent you are in every way."

My insides liquefy as he kisses me softly and wraps me in his arms.

"In the meantime, I'm planning to knock him on his ass when we play tomorrow."

I giggle and relax into his embrace. "Thank you."

"Anytime, baby."

He holds me for a minute, and I close my eyes in contentment.

"So, I've been thinking." I fidget with his chest hair. "What if we give this a shot?"

"Give what a shot?"

"Us."

He kisses me deeply. "Are you sure?"

"I'm sure about *you*," I respond truthfully, "but I'm not ready to open up to our friends yet. I wish I was, but I'm not there."

"Do I embarrass you?" His eyes twinkle.

I shake my head. "Not at all. But I've been so vocal about staying single and focused on my goals, and I feel a bit silly about going back on that."

"I don't see it that way, but I understand if you do. I won't stand in your way." He peppers kisses along my jaw until I giggle. "We'll go slow."

"Thanks for being patient with me. I know I'm not easy."

"I disagree." He kisses me on the forehead. "But we should get you back to your room."

"You too." I run my fingers through his hair.

"You go first. I need a minute."

I raise an eyebrow at him and glance down at the front of his sweats.

"Don't give me that look. This is your fault in the first place."

"Sorry." I brush a kiss against his lips. "I'm going to miss you, Rookie."

"Let's find time to see each other in the next few weeks, OK?" He tucks a stray piece of hair behind my ear. "Training camp doesn't start for another month, so I can come to you."

"Make sure you pack your slutty little glasses."

"I can wear them during the daytime for you, if you'd like."

"I hope you're ready for how much action you're about to see."

He cradles my jaw for a kiss. "I've been training for this. Bring it on."

Chapter 24

Yutékhway^he'

Storing Food / October

Chelsea

Today's the day, and I feel like a live wire.

I drove to Cattaraugus last night and crashed on Mackenzie and Genny's couch. I was up with the birds to review my notes about the Buffalo History Museum's exhibits and pace around the house until my friends woke up.

"You're up early," Genny says as she emerges from her bedroom. She's dressed in athletic clothes and wearing headphones.

"I hope I didn't wake you."

"Nah. I'm always up this early to run before work." She pulls me to her for a hug. "You're going to knock their socks off today, Chels. You know your stuff about Haudenosaunee history, and you're fantastic at sharing it with others."

I squeeze her back. "Thank you. I hope that comes through. The idea of an interview makes me nauseous."

"I can't wait to hear how it goes." She beams at me. "Will you be here when I get back?"

I nod. "The interview's not until 10, so I have a few more hours to feel sick to my stomach."

"I'll quiz you when I finish my run, how's that?"

I smile and wave her off before returning to my pacing.

Several hours later, I approach the museum and smooth my gray pencil skirt. I don't feel like myself in this corporate outfit, but I'd rather be overdressed than underdressed. I check my makeup and hair in my phone camera, smiling at my beaded strawberry earrings. *You can take the girl out of the rez, but she still loves big earrings.*

My palms are sweaty as I open the front door. My black pumps *tap, tap, tap* on the linoleum floor while I walk towards the welcome desk.

"Hi, good morning." I hope no one notices the quiver in my voice. "I'm here to meet with Natalie Shenandoah."

The staffer checks some nearby papers. "Chelsea, right? I'll let her know you're here."

I thumb through a museum brochure while I wait. My insides tap dance with excitement at all the wonderful local artifacts contained here. I could easily spend a full day, or more, studying everything.

"Chelsea! I'm so glad to meet you." A smiling and statuesque woman with long brown hair comes around the corner.

"Thank you so much for meeting with me, Natalie," I say, extending my hand to her. I feel like a gorilla in a cheap suit acting so formally with another Native, but I'm not sure how else to behave. I take note of her black slacks and forest green sweater, grateful I decided to dress up.

"Of course! I'm so glad you reached out, and please call me Nat. As soon as I heard your background, I knew I had to talk to you." She gestures around the room. "Would you like to see the Native American Gallery?"

"I would love to."

The gallery is stunning. It contains similar artifacts and themes as Shako:wi, but on a grander scale. There's a replica longhouse entrance, furs, and large oil paintings of historic Haudenosaunee leaders. I prefer Shako:wi's bright and interactive space, but I can't deny this place *feels* like a museum.

"This is wonderful." I peer inside a display case at an old corn husk doll. "I admit, I didn't know that Buffalo had a dedicated exhibit for the Haudenosaunee like this."

"A lot of people don't," Natalie says. "One of my goals for the next five years is to better advertise what's here, especially for all the Haudenosaunee people that live in the Buffalo-Niagara region. This shouldn't just be a place for non-Natives."

"You could consider collaborating with the local cultural centers and museums for events, maybe even exhibit cross-overs. I bet most nations would be amenable to it."

She smiles. "That's a fantastic idea. Can I borrow that?"

I laugh. "Go right ahead. I know Shako:wi would love the opportunity to partner with you, for one."

"You lived in Cattaraugus for a few years, too, right?" she asks.

"Yes. I lived with my dad during high school, and I'm back and forth between there and the Oneida reservation all the time."

"If you took a job here, you'd need to move away from your community," she says seriously. "Is that something you're comfortable with?"

I nod. "I'm feeling ready for that. I lived in Albany while I was in college, and it gave me some space to spread my wings a bit. It was challenging, but it helped me grow."

"I know what you mean." She walks beside me as I wander down the final row of artifacts. "I feel the same way about living here now. I get home as often as I can, but there's a wonderful Native community in Western New York. That helps."

I follow Natalie to her office, tucked away in a hallway behind the exhibits. She gestures for me to sit, and I plop down into a leather chair with as much ladylike grace as I can muster.

"I really like you, Chelsea."

I smile through the knot forming in my throat. *I really like you, but...?*

"Your degree in Indigenous Studies, in addition to your time at Shako:wi and lived experiences as a Native woman, makes you a highly desirable candidate." Natalie clears her throat. "I can't believe that sentence just came out of my mouth. I've acclimated way too much to corporate speak."

I laugh with relief. To be honest, her formality is making me sweat.

"What I mean to say is, you'd be perfect for a role here, and I very much want to offer you one."

"But?" My stomach turns.

"But," she says with a grimace, "the Museum is reeling from some funding cuts, and we're under a lot of pressure to keep hiring to a minimum. I'd love to see you as a curator here, but I'm afraid that's not possible right now."

I swallow painfully. My heels are tight, and I'm more than ready to get out of here and kick them off. "I understand."

"Here's what I *can* do." She leans forward conspiratorially. "I can offer you a lower-level position. I hate to do that because, quite frankly, it's insulting to you. But it gets your foot in the door and allows us to potentially promote you to a better-paying position down the road."

My heart leaps with hope. "I would be interested in that."

"The pay would stink. I'm so sorry. But it should be more than what you're making at Shako:wi."

I nod enthusiastically. "I can make that work."

"Yeah?"

"Yeah!"

Natalie smiles broadly. "We'd be so lucky to have you. Feel free to take a few days to think it over, too. It's a big decision."

I *tap, tap, tap* across the tile floors and slide back into my car. I check in all directions around me before pumping my fists and shaking my hair with joy.

Chapter 25

Wes

I bend at the waist, gasping for breath. "You're killing me, man. Can we give the sprints a rest?"

Sawyer and I have been training together at a facility downtown, and today he's kicking my ass.

"Not if you expect to come flying down the floor to score goals in transition this season, my friend." He's out of breath, but not nearly as winded as I am.

"What have you been doing all summer? You weren't this fast before."

"Running. A lot of running." He signals for a water break, and I gratefully drag myself across the room to my water bottle.

"Any particular reason?" I ask after a long gulp.

He winces. "Nothing better to do, I guess. And it gives me time to think."

"About?"

He shrugs. "Life. Goals for the season. My date last weekend."

My ears perk up. "Was it good?"

He blows out a dramatic exhale. "No. Not even a little bit."

"That's too bad. Onto the next?"

He fidgets with his heart rate monitor. "I guess. Slim pickings on the dating market right now, which I assume you've noticed."

I squirt some water into my mouth. "What about Sienna Bissell?"

Sawyer lifts his head. "What about her?"

"You two have...*chemistry*."

He laughs sharply. "Yeah, we go together like bleach and ammonia. She'd rather jump over Niagara Falls than go out with me."

My smartwatch vibrates, and I glance down to see Chelsea's name. I fumble my bottle in my rush to tap and open her message.

> **Chelsea:** Any chance you're free for lunch? I'm downtown.

"Thanks." Sawyer hands me my fallen water bottle, and I rush to my gym bag. "I just need to reply to a message. I'll be right back for more torture."

"Hot date, I hope." He leans against the wall.

> **Me:** I can be ready in thirty. Just tell me where to meet you.

210

"Do you mind if I beg off early? I forgot I'm meeting someone for lunch."

He raises his eyebrows. "It *is* a hot date!"

I clear my throat and start throwing the rest of my stuff into the bag. "Just a friend I haven't seen in a while. I'll see you at home later?"

"Mmm hmm." He watches me suspiciously as I hustle out of the facility.

The gym is just a few blocks from the team house, and I jog the whole way home. *My body is going to make me pay for this tomorrow.* I throw open the front door and kick it closed as I pull my sweaty t-shirt over my head. I'm going to take the world's fastest shower, and then go wherever Chelsea tells me.

A few minutes later, I'm throwing on jeans and a sweater while checking my messages.

Chelsea: Joe's Deli

Me: Sounds good. See you in ten minutes.

I pocket my phone and head towards the door before skidding to a stop. I hustle back to my room, pick up a bottle of cologne I probably haven't used since college, and give myself a spritz.

Nine minutes later, I'm parking down the street from the restaurant. I check my hair and smooth my beard in the rearview mirror before hopping out of the car.

I force myself to walk at the pace of what I hope is an unhurried stroll. I scan the sidewalk for her but come up empty. I'm rolling up to the deli when a woman in business attire turns around to face me.

I'm positive that I react like one of those cartoon characters whose jaws drop and tongues roll out of their mouths when they see a beautiful woman. It sure feels like I develop heart eyes.

"Hey!" Chelsea smirks and pulls me to her for a quick hug. "You OK? You might want to take a breath."

"You—" I stammer, taking in the sight of her. "Who *are* you?"

She's wearing a form-fitting skirt that hits at her knees, and it's the sexiest thing I've ever seen. Her black sweater is modest, but all I want to do is tug the neckline down ever so slightly so I can admire the hint of cleavage there.

"Eyes up here, Rookie," she teases, tipping my chin up with her pointer finger.

"You can't seriously expect me to calmly order a sandwich with you in these conditions." My hands wander to her waist as I look her up and down. "*Fuck*, Chels. What's with the sexy secretary look?"

"You look pretty delectable yourself." She gives me a once-over, and heat blooms in my veins. "I really like this sweater." Her hand fists the fabric as she leans forward ever so slightly and breathes deeply. "And your cologne."

"Change of plans. Come home with me," I beg. "Or let me drive you somewhere and we can make out in a field or something."

She giggles. "Not a chance. I desperately need food and to give you an update. Let's go inside."

I grab her hand and pull her back into my arms. I hold her close for a few seconds, my hand tangling in her loose hair. "I've missed you."

She relaxes. "I've missed you, too."

I regretfully pull back and sigh dramatically. "OK. Let's get you some food."

We grab a table tucked away in the back and settle in with our sandwiches.

"How's that silver medal feeling?" Chelsea asks between bites.

"Heavy. Sawyer's been insufferable about his gold."

"That tracks." She chuckles. "You'll get him next time. Silver for the Haudenosaunee men is an incredible achievement."

"So, tell me why you're mysteriously in downtown Buffalo on a Tuesday afternoon dressed like you're about to fuel my fantasies for the next six months." I brush my sneaker against her calf, and she shoots me an amused look.

"You've got a gaggle of fangirls who keep peeking around the corner here every few minutes."

I pause in the middle of chewing. "Seriously?"

"Seriously." She smirks. "They think you're cute."

"You're crazy."

She shrugs. "We'll see."

I take a swig of water. "Well?"

"Oh, right." She holds up a finger before swallowing a bite. "I had an interview this morning."

I set down my sandwich, an insistent smile pulling at the corners of my mouth. "You did? Where?"

"At the Buffalo History Museum. They have a Native American gallery, and Jess has a friend of an auntie who knows one of the directors."

"That sounds perfect for you."

She tucks some hair behind her ear. "It's a full-time job, with a lot more visitors than Shako:wi. It could open up some new doors for me."

I reach across the table and place my hand over hers.

"Are my girlfriends watching?"

She presses her lips together. "No."

"Good." I raise her hand to my mouth for a quick kiss. "Continue."

She huffs, but I see her smother a smile. "So, I met with Natalie today. She showed me around, and then we talked for a bit."

I lean forward. "And?"

She's losing the battle against a smile. "I got the job."

"You got the job!" I jump out of my seat and pull her up out of hers. I lift her off her feet and twirl her in a circle until she pleads for me to stop.

I tenderly brush the hair out of her eyes. "I'm so proud of you, Chels."

Her cheeks flush. "Thanks. Well, I should say I got *a* job. It's entry level for now while the museum is dealing with funding cuts, but then I can hopefully start earning more."

"This is amazing news." We sit back down, but I've lost my appetite from excitement. "Does this mean you'll be moving here?"

"Yes. I have to figure out a place to live, but worst-case scenario, I crash on Genny's couch for a while. Nothing I haven't done before."

I frown. "I never thought I'd say this, but I wish I were still in my old apartment. You could've stayed with me."

She waves me off. "Not necessary. I'll work something out."

I lean back in my chair, staring at her with unbridled adoration. "So, you're going to be dressing like this every day for work?"

She giggles. "Probably. Although I'm going to need to go shopping if that's the case. I had to borrow this skirt from Genny, and it's too small."

"I'm not going to survive this, Chels. How am I going to be out in public with you looking like an absolute smokeshow?"

She rolls her eyes. "Stop it."

"I have never been more serious."

"Excuse me? Are you Wes Harrison?"

Chelsea catches my eye and raises an eyebrow. I slowly turn to find two young women watching me with wide eyes, shifting back and forth on their feet. College students, I would guess, based on their Buff State sweatshirts.

"I am. Hi." I smile awkwardly.

Chelsea kicks me under the table, and I ignore her.

"Hi. We're huge Outlaws fans. Would you mind giving us your autograph?" the blonde woman asks.

"Absolutely. I'd be happy to."

She hands me a small notebook with shaking hands. "Thank you so much. We really appreciate it."

I scribble an encouraging message and my signature on a page, feeling profoundly silly but also elated at being recognized in public for the first time.

The brunette clears her throat. "Are you two on a date?"

I open my mouth to respond, but Chelsea beats me to it.

"Oh no. Just a couple of friends having lunch." She smiles.

I glance at her with narrowed eyes.

"Oh, that's nice," the other woman responds. "Would you be interested in getting a drink sometime?"

Goddammit.

I finish my autograph and hand the notebook back to her. "I appreciate you asking, but I'm seeing someone at the moment."

Her face falls. "Oh. Of course you are. Well, thank you so much for this."

"We hope you have a great season!" the blonde chimes in, tucking her hand in the crook of her friend's elbow.

I wave politely as they leave before spinning to look at Chelsea. "Don't."

She smugly sips her water. "I didn't say anything."

I pick at my sandwich.

"How does it feel to be a Buffalo sports heartthrob?"

I choke with laughter on my next bite. "Are you jealous?"

"Not at all." She bites her lower lip. "Why would I be jealous when I have something they don't?"

"Does that turn you on?"

"Let's go find that field to make out in."

"Say less."

Chapter 26

Chelsea

"**P**romise you won't forget about me while you're living in the big city?"

I close the trunk of my car with a *thunk* to find Jess watching me with glassy eyes.

"Oh, Jess." I reach for her, and we hug tightly. "I'm going to miss you so much. You're a dream roommate and co-worker."

She pats my back. "I'm so happy for you, Chels. Big things are on the horizon for you." She pulls back with a sniff. "I'm just sad for myself. It'll be lonely around here without you."

"I'll be back to visit," I promise. "My mom won't let me off the hook that easily."

She gives me a watery smile. "Keep me posted on how everything's going in Buffalo, OK?"

"I will. And I'll text you when I get in later."

"Thanks." She follows me around to the driver's side door. "Oh, by the way, how are things going with Wes?"

I duck my head on the pretense of looking for my keys. "Uh, good. He's good."

She doesn't say anything, and I'm forced to look up. My Grand Canyon-sized smile gives away all my secrets.

Jess widens her eyes. "You *really* like him."

I cover my face. "I like him so much it's sickening."

She laughs. "And he's good to you? I don't need to yell at him?"

I shake my head. "He's so good I have a hard time believing it's real. I'm waiting for the other shoe to drop."

She peels my fingers away from my eyes. "Just enjoy it. I haven't seen you this happy in years. You'll get to know each other so much more now that you'll live nearby."

"Thanks, Jess." I squeeze her hands. "Your support means a lot."

She smiles. "Now get out of here. Thruway traffic waits for no one."

"I thought you didn't have a lot of stuff?"

Zeke looks around at the mountains of boxes piled high in the living room.

Genny smiles sheepishly. "It didn't seem like much until I started packing."

Mackenzie pats him on the shoulder as she walks by. "Hope you planned for an arm workout today."

He blows a lock of dark hair out of his eyes as he surveys the landscape.

Genny lays her head on his chest and smiles sweetly up at him. "Thank you, my love."

His face relaxes as he wraps his arms around her. "No problem. I'm thrilled you're moving in."

"Are you sure about this, Gen?" I ask, biting my lip. "I feel bad making you move out of your place."

"You're not making me do anything." She stands on her tiptoes to give her boyfriend a kiss. "Zeke's been dropping hints for months, so it's the perfect time."

He gazes down at her in adoration. "You're actually doing me a favor, Chels. Thanks for upending your life for me."

I chuckle. "Happy to help. Want a hand loading boxes into your truck?"

"Yes, please. I'll be here all day otherwise."

Mackenzie swings back through on her way to the kitchen. "Where are all your buff friends?"

He gives Genny one last kiss. "Wes and Sawyer are helping Sawyer's mom with some house projects today. I guess his stepdad hurt his shoulder pretty badly the other day, so he's out of commission."

"Oh geez, that's too bad." I already knew this from Wes, who felt bad he couldn't help with my move today.

"When do you start work?" Zeke asks as we carry boxes out to the driveway.

I set my box down with a grunt. "What does she have in there—bricks?"

He chuckles. "I don't know, but I'm glad my brothers can help me bring these up to my place on the other end."

"I start on Monday."

"Just a couple of days away! Are you excited?"

I grin. "I'm so excited. This feels like a fresh start."

He throws an arm over my shoulders and gives me a side squeeze. "I know what that's like. Hopefully, the move will be as good for you as it was for me last year."

The Bear: All moved in?

Me: Yep. Zeke and Genny left a little while ago. Mackenzie and I are watching old episodes of Love Island soon.

The Bear: Nice. I'm sorry I couldn't be there to help. I really wanted to

Me: No worries, we had it covered

Me: Not sure how we're ever going to see each other without these pesky roommates around, however

The Bear: Should I start poisoning Sawyer's pre-workout drinks?

Me: Maybe

The Bear: Speaking of which, would you want to join us at the gym sometime? It would be fun to train together

Me: Sure. Let me know your schedule and I'll see what I can manage around work

"Chels!" Mackenzie calls from the living room. "It's starting!"

"Coming!"

Me: Love Island calls. I'll catch up with you tomorrow

The Bear: Good night, beautiful. I'm so thankful you're closer

Chapter 27

Tehut^nuhela:túhe'

Giving Thanks / November

Wes

C helsea has been in Buffalo for nearly two weeks, and I
have yet to see her.

It's not for lack of trying. She works all day and has a forty-five minute commute in both directions. Anytime she happens to have a few minutes after work, I've been scheduled with personal training clients. Outlaws training camp started the first weekend of November, so I haven't been around on Saturdays and Sundays. One day I contemplated waiting on the hood of her car at lunchtime in case she left for a sandwich, but that felt borderline stalkerish. And not in a cute way.

Today is the day, however. I moved my evening clients to a different day and talked Sawyer into practicing later than usual.

Me: You still good to meet up at 5:30?

Chelsea: Yeah, just getting my stuff together now. Send me the address when you have a chance.

Sawyer and I carve out at least two sessions per week for pickup lacrosse in a small indoor facility. Other local Outlaws often join us, but tonight it'll just be us and Chelsea.

"Did anything wind up happening with you two?" Sawyer asks as we pass back and forth to each other.

"Who?" I toss the ball behind my back.

He catches it and flings it back one-handed. "You and Chelsea. You seemed awfully sweet on her in Utica."

I bungle the catch, and the ball skitters into the corner. "We're friends. That's why I invited her out tonight."

"Mmm hmm." He grabs the ball once I send it back over to him. "Just like you're friends with that cute blonde at the gym that keeps hitting on you?"

I scoff. "Hailey's nice, but I'm not interested. She's more your type, anyway."

"Ouch, dude." He laughs and sends me a bounce pass. "What's that supposed to mean?"

"I've seen you out with plenty of blondes, is all. Brunettes, too. You're a popular guy."

"Don't forget the redheads." He tosses the ball under one leg with a wink.

The door opens with a bang, and Chelsea bursts in. She's wearing a dark green wrap dress and heels, her hair pulled up into a clip and threatening to spill over the top.

"Sorry I'm late," she says, rushing across the turf with an equipment bag slung over her shoulder. "Let me just change and I'll be right out."

"Take your time! No rush." Sawyer smiles warmly at her as she makes a beeline for the restrooms.

I'm too busy openly gawking at how drop-dead gorgeous she looks. It would take a quick tug on that fabric belt for the whole dress to fall open in my hands. *I wonder what she's wearing underne-*

"Wes."

I whip my head over to where Sawyer is looking at me in amusement.

"Yeah?"

"Just friends, eh?"

"Shut up," I mutter, scooping up a nearby ball and firing it into the net.

Chelsea is consistently outscrambling Sawyer, and it's pissing him off.

I watch with a smirk as he attempts to outrace her for a loose ball and winds up slipping on the turf.

"Thank you!" she says cheerfully as she scoops the ball next to where he fell.

"She's impossible," he announces, throwing his arms in the air.

"I told you." I lift her stick with mine and manage to knock the ball out. "Now get off your ass and help me."

Her laughter echoes off the walls, and I feel lighter than I have in weeks.

An hour later we're all exhausted. I slide to the ground while gulping from my water bottle.

"OK, we definitely need you to join us regularly," Sawyer says, gasping for breath. "You challenge me way more than Wes does."

"Hey!"

He grins.

Chelsea chuckles. "Thanks for inviting me. This is exactly why I wanted to move here, to have more opportunities to play outside of my summer league."

"Let's make it a weekly thing. Can you make it happen, Wes?" he asks.

"I should be able to." I catch her eye and smile.

She flops over onto her back. "Let me see how I feel in the morning, and I'll get back to you."

Sawyer laughs. "You're an adult with a real job, so just let us know if it's too much." He squirts water into his mouth. "Did you want to shower before you drive back to Cattaraugus? You could swing by our place before you head home. That's a long, sweaty drive otherwise."

My eyes slide over to his, but he ignores me.

She takes a long drag from her water bottle. "That's really nice of you, if you don't mind one more person to fight for hot water."

"Not at all. Come on over."

"Don't say I never look out for you, bro," Sawyer says as we refill our water bottles in the kitchen.

"It's not like I'm going to get in there with her." Water hits the wall in the bathroom, and I'm struggling to keep my mind from imagining Chelsea in its stream.

He runs a hand through his damp hair. "I mean, if you want to try, then be my guest."

I elbow him in the side.

"I'll get in once she's done, and that way you'll have a moment alone with her," he says, elbowing me back.

A wave of gratitude rushes over me. "Thanks, man. I appreciate it."

Chelsea emerges a few minutes later, back in her dress and with her wet hair pulled up. "Thanks, guys. I feel so much better."

"Don't mention it. Mind if I jump in next, Wes?" Sawyer asks with a wink.

"Go for it." I'm crawling out of my skin to touch her.

The second I hear the bathroom door click, I'm gathering her in my arms and pressing her against the wall.

"You smell horrendous," she mumbles against my lips.

"I'm genuinely sorry." I run my palm up the side of her neck, and she moans. "We should shower together next time."

My hands wander down her sides and fiddle with the tie at her waist.

"I have to know."

"What's that?"

"What you're wearing under this." I tug and she protests into my mouth. "I've been thinking about it since you walked in."

She bats my hand away. "Hold on."

I wrench myself away. "Sorry."

"I'm just listening for Sawyer." She pauses for a second before tracing her fingers down her v-shaped neckline and tugging slightly.

I'm practically drooling as she pulls the dress aside enough so I can see the edges of her beige cotton bra. A low rumble starts in my chest as she brings my hand to her cleavage and I run my thumb against her curves.

"Next time I wear this, I want you to take it off of me," she says, her eyes locked on mine.

My mouth is dry, so I nod silently.

She grins and pulls me to her for another kiss. "I need to go. The shower just turned off."

"OK." I press my lips to her neck. "Thank you."

"For what?"

"Coming out tonight. Spending time with me. Letting me maul you."

She snorts. "You're very easy to please."

The bathroom door opens, and I jump back from her as she adjusts her dress.

"Enjoy your shower," she says with a wink.

Chapter 28

Chelsea

My bedroom door creaks open.

"Are you alive?"

I grumble beneath my heavy comforter.

"I'm not sure. It could be a wild animal."

"Maybe she's a vampire," a second voice says. "I only see her at night anymore."

I throw a pillow in the vicinity of the door and hear it hit something solid.

"Shit. She always had good aim. Chels, is that really you?"

"Go away," I mumble. "It's too early."

"It's noon. We were about to call either an ambulance or an exorcist." Amusement laces Genny's voice.

I throw the blankets off my face. "It's noon?!"

"Yes, girl. I figured you needed the sleep, but this is entering narcolepsy territory," Mackenzie chimes in.

"Shit." I rub my eyes. "I turned off my alarm so I could sleep in, but this is way too late."

Genny vanishes into the kitchen and comes back with a steaming mug of coffee that she sets on my nightstand. "We come bearing gifts."

"*Nya:wëh*." I smile gratefully. "I was hoping to get to the gym today, if anyone wanted to come with me."

The bed dips as Genny sits on the edge. "I might. I ran this morning, but I need to lift at some point this weekend."

The hot, milky beverage hits like crack as I take my first sip. "I've barely had time to lift this month. This work schedule is brutal."

"Do you think it'll settle down soon?" Mackenzie asks.

I nod. "I'm probably putting in too many hours since I'm new and trying to impress Nat. I haven't been taking my lunch hour, and most days I'm leaving after five. But I'm going to waste away if I don't start eating more and making it to the gym."

My phone buzzes at the same time as Genny's. *Curious.*

She pulls hers out of her back pocket. "You've been able to train with Wes and Sawyer once a week though, right? I'm so glad that has worked out." Her eyes light up as she scans her device. "Zeke'll be home early from training camp today, so I may need to take a raincheck on that workout."

Interest officially piqued, I reach for my phone as well.

The Bear: Coach is giving us tomorrow off and letting us out early today. Want to come over tonight?

Me: What about Sawyer?

The Bear: He's going to Six Nations for the weekend. I'll be awfully lonely in the house by myself.

Sparks ignite in my belly. Aside from a few sweaty make-out sessions, I've barely seen Wes since my move. Coming to Buffalo was supposed to allow us to see more of each other, but instead I hardly get a chance to even catch up with him via text.

"No problem. Maybe I'll go see Jess today," I say, nonchalantly setting my phone down. "She has the day off, and I know she's been lonely."

"What about *me*?" Mackenzie protests. "I've barely seen you, and I live with you!"

Genny narrows her eyes at me. "You're going to drive three hours in the middle of the day to spend the night with a friend?"

Sweat prickles the back of my neck. "Yes?"

Mackenzie gasps. "Is it The Bear? Did he just invite you over?"

A warm flush creeps up my chest and into my cheeks. "What? No."

Genny crosses her arms.

I bite my lip. "OK, fine. Yes."

She opens her mouth to respond, but Mackenzie's squeal drowns her out.

"I am *all* in favor of you getting some action. You're working too hard and need to relax."

"Have you two hooked up before?" Genny asks.

I take a long sip from my mug. "A little bit. But not...everything."

Her eyebrow goes to the ceiling. "Where did you see him?"

"OK, Mom." Mackenzie bumps her sister with her hip. "Chels, you should go shower, and we'll help you pick out a cute outfit."

I smile gratefully at her. "I will. Just let me finish my coffee." I take another few gulps.

"I just don't want you to get hurt," Genny says softly. "You've been through the wringer this year." She pauses. "Zeke told me you saw Brock at the World Games."

I set my mug down with a grimace. "I did. I'm really glad Zeke was there to move him along."

She reaches over to squeeze my leg. "I can't believe he said those things to you. I wasn't sure how to bring it up, so I was waiting for you to mention it." She pauses. "The Bear isn't...Brock, right?"

Bile rises in my throat. "No. *No.*"

"I didn't think so, but I wanted to be sure." She fiddles with a loose thread on my blanket. "Did he talk to you like that while you two were still dating?"

Talking about Brock always triggers a panic in my chest, but I do my best to hold it at bay. "Yes."

Her eyes lock on mine, and Mackenzie comes over to sit next to me. "Why didn't you tell us? We knew he was an asshole, but not an abusive one."

"He only said what I was already thinking about myself. He has always played on my worst fears about how others perceive me, so I believed him."

My friends tackle me with hugs and encouragement.

"Don't you ever think those things again," Genny says with a sniff.

"Can the guys kick his ass?" Mackenzie suggests.

I squeeze them both. "Wes offered to, but Brock wound up getting scratched in the gold medal game, so he didn't play."

Genny pulls back with a grin. "Was he hurt? Or just not good enough?"

"No injuries reported."

We giggle with delight at my ex's well-earned misfortune.

"Oh, Wes," Genny sighs. "He's going to be so sad that you're fooling around with this other guy."

I'm realizing the hardest thing in the world is smothering my ear-to-ear smile whenever Wes is mentioned.

"I think he'll survive," I say, pulling myself out of our friend pile. "Let me jump in the shower and we can talk more after, OK?"

I walk up the steps to Wes' place carrying a bottle of whiskey and years of emotional baggage.

My hands shake as I adjust the strap of my oversized purse crammed with emergency supplies. I'm not sure if he wants me to stay overnight, so I threw in some spare clothes and toiletries just in case. This feels suspiciously like a *Very Important Date*, and the thought has me quaking in my black ankle boots.

I've never loved my body. I love what it can do, but outside of a lacrosse field I struggle to feel desirable. I always seem to have extra weight in places I don't want it, and wind up living in athletic clothes any chance I get. Mackenzie pulled together an outfit I would love to see on her or Genny, but I'm struggling to feel at peace with it for myself.

I knock on Wes' front door and brush the front of my cognac leather miniskirt while I wait. The November air is biting against my black nylons and thin striped sweater. I dress up for work, but couldn't remember the last time I'd done so for a man.

The jade green door opens, and my stomach drops to the floor.

Wes' eyes skate over my figure, drinking me in as I melt into a puddle in front of him. He's wearing a soft gray Henley with navy slacks, his hair damp and tousled.

"Hey."

"Hey." I thrust the whiskey at him. "I brought this for you."

He smiles and accepts it with a tremble in his hand. "*Ya:wᵴ'.*" He brushes a kiss against my cheek as he closes the door behind us.

"You OK?" I ask with concern.

"Yeah." He swallows. "I'm just nervous."

"Why?"

"Because I really like you."

I curl my index fingers in his belt loops and pull him closer to me. "If it helps, I really like you, too."

He threads a hand through my long hair. "It does help, thank you." He carefully kisses the corner of my mouth. "I don't want to mess up your lipstick."

He'll be covered in it soon if I have my way, but I keep that thought to myself.

"Can I come in?" I ask, an amused smile playing on my lips.

"Shit. Sorry." He places his hand on the small of my back and nudges me inside. "You look so beautiful, I got distracted."

I think if I have another six months of Wes losing his shit around me, it might cure my body image issues.

"Are you hungry?" he asks as we round the corner into the kitchen. "I have some meats and cheeses I could get out."

"I'm starving, if you don't mind." He pulls out a stool for me at the breakfast bar, and I hop on. "I feel like I haven't eaten in days."

He frowns. "That's not good. Let's get you fed." He pours me a small glass of the peanut butter-flavored whiskey I brought. "Have you tried this before?"

"I haven't." Our fingers brush as he slides it over to me. "I know you like it, but whiskey tastes like battery acid to me. Peanut butter flavor sounded more appealing."

"It's delicious. Really smooth. I think you'll be a fan." He smiles and opens the fridge.

I sip and watch as he brings small plates of sliced items to the counter and starts to assemble them together.

"That's 'a few things you could get out'?" I ask incredulously. "You've got a whole charcuterie board prepped here."

A flush creeps across his cheeks, and it's extremely charming. "I wasn't sure what you'd want."

"So desperate to please."

He glances up at me and I smile around my glass. He blows out a breath and shakes his head.

"Cat got your tongue, Rookie?"

He pushes the tray of food towards me.

"I'm throwing you flirting softballs here, Harrison. You've got nothing for me?"

The stool next to me scrapes across the floor as he pulls it out. He grabs my legs and drapes them over his lap, his hand wrapping around my mid-thigh.

"I can think of at least twenty filthy things I'd like to say in reply, but I'm attempting to romance you tonight." He rubs his thumb across my skin. "Now eat so I can make you beg to hear them all later."

True to his word, an hour later Wes whispers dirty nothings in my ear while I plead with him for more.

I straddle him on the couch, my skirt hiked up nearly to my waist. He tastes like whiskey and a crisp, starry night.

"I like how this tastes on your tongue," I say. "It's warm and sharp."

His hands wander beneath my sweater as I grind my hips against his. "Do you want to spend the night?" he asks breathlessly.

"Yes, please." I tug on his hair and enjoy how disheveled I've made him.

"Are you su—"

I cut him off with a rough kiss. "I've never been more sure of anything."

He moans into my mouth. "If you change your mind, just say the word."

"I will." My thighs squeeze his tightly. "Now please take me to bed."

"At your service."

I climb off his lap and smooth down my skirt.

"Come 'ere." Wes takes my hand and pulls me towards the kitchen. "I need to do something first."

I lean against the countertop as he refills his glass with ice and whiskey. He takes a short sip of his drink and kisses me.

I mumble unintelligently against his lips as his tongue meets mine.

He gathers my sweater in his hands and slowly drags it up my torso before tossing it aside.

I hiss at the cool air meeting my bare skin, and he envelops me in his arms.

"My God. You are so—" He kisses my neck. "Fucking—" His lips move down my chest before settling between my breasts. "Gorgeous."

"Do you want to go to your bedroom?" I ask, sliding my arms around his neck. I'm anxious to be out of the bright glare of the kitchen lights.

"In a minute." He unzips my leather skirt, and it puddles at my feet. "I have plans for you."

I shiver as he peels my black tights down my legs, getting to his knees and kissing each inch of exposed skin along the way. I grip the countertop behind me while he slowly pulls the nylons from each foot.

He makes a low rumble as he runs his hands across my dark blue panties and up to the matching bra. "You wore these for me?" he asks, peppering kisses along the lace as he stands back up.

I nod and wind my arms around his neck. "I'm all yours tonight."

He kisses me with a deep groan. "You can't say things like that to me."

"Like what?"

"Like you're mine. Because I'll start to believe it."

"Oh!" I gasp in surprise as he lifts me onto the kitchen counter. The granite is cold against my bare thighs, and my legs reflexively wrap around his waist.

"Lean back for me, baby." He dusts a kiss across my lips before gently pressing on my shoulders.

I place my hands behind me and brace myself. "Like this?"

He trails kisses down my abdomen. "Lower."

I bend my elbows and come down on my forearms. "Better?"

"Yes." He pulls my hips closer to him and begins kissing up my inner thigh.

"Wes," I breathe. "Don't you want to—"

"Nope." He skates his nails over my panties. "I want you right here. I've been dreaming about this since that night in Utica."

"Really?"

"Really."

I bite my lip and watch him take another sip of whiskey. He drags the lace to the side and lowers his mouth to me.

"Oh, my God."

His breath is warm, and the alcohol on his tongue lights me on fire.

"You like that?"

A desperate gasp comes from my throat. "How are you so good at this?"

He chuckles and takes another drink. "I take the time to study what I love."

A string of obscenities drops from my lips as I grind against him. He floods me with sensation until I can barely stand it before pausing to lift his glass. He repeats the pattern until I'm writhing on the counter. I hear ice clink as he lowers the cup once more.

This time his mouth is cold, and I yelp in surprise.

"Too much?" he asks.

The bite of the ice fades quickly. "No. I just didn't expect it."

"Noted."

His beard and his breath tease me as I squirm beneath him. I'm sinking lower on my bent arms as my limbs turn to jelly. His mouth and fingers are everywhere, and I quickly lose track of all thoughts and inhibitions.

I cry out as my climax rips through me.

"Oh, fuck yeah, baby," Wes groans against me. "You do wonders for my ego."

I'm shaking as he gathers my torso in his arms and pulls me to him. "You good?"

I bury my head in his neck. "I'm good. That was just really intense."

"Well then, you're in trouble because I'm just getting started with you," he murmurs in my ear.

I squeal with delight when he tosses me over his shoulder and heads towards the bedroom.

"Wait! We should—"

"I'll clean up later."

Chapter 29

Wes

I slide Chelsea down the front of my body. Her long hair falls into her face, and I smooth it out of the way.

"I want to show you something." I say, spinning her around so her back is against my chest.

I hold her facing the full-length mirror in my bedroom. She glances away, and I wrap my hand around her cheek so I can gently turn her face.

"Look at how beautiful you are," I say. "Do you see what I see?"

She squirms, and I hold her in place with my other arm. "Can we please not do this?"

"No, baby. This is necessary." I kiss down the side of her neck.

She huffs but stops fighting me.

I trace the line of her jaw with my thumb. "Look at your big, beautiful eyes. They were the first thing I noticed about you. They made me feel welcome and wanted, even when you were telling me to get lost."

She smiles, and I move my touch to her mouth.

"These lips." I run my thumb across the bottom, and her tongue darts out to lick it. I groan and tighten my grip on her chin. "They're pouty and soft. I dreamed about kissing them for months before you let me." I wrap her silky hair in my hand and gently pull her head back until I can kiss her.

She moans into my mouth. "Wes, please."

I ignore her. "Now look at this fucking gorgeous body." I hold the weight of a breast in my palm as I brush my finger against her nipple.

She squirms again, but I've still got a grip on her.

"What do you see when you look at yourself?" I ask.

She groans. "This is silly."

"It's not. You first, and then I'll go."

She tries to wiggle out of my arms, and I lightly pinch her nipple in response. She breathes in sharply and leans more deeply into my chest.

"Chelsea." My voice deepens in warning.

She swallows. "I hate looking at myself like this. I don't like my body."

It breaks my heart to hear her internal monologue. I'm even more determined to mend the wounds she'd borne in the years before I met her.

I release my hold on her so I can skim the feminine curves of her waist and hips. "I don't even have words for how much I love your body. Do you notice how I can never take my eyes off you?"

"Wes," she whispers.

"I waited months just hoping for a crumb of your attention. Then I learned as much about you as possible so I could try to impress you and convince you to keep me around as a friend." I comb her hair across one shoulder so I can press kisses down the side of her neck. "I'm head over heels for you and still can't believe you want me around. I feel like the luckiest man in the world that this absolute goddess lets me kiss her."

"I let you do a lot more than kiss me." She sniffs with a watery smile.

"Fuck yeah, you do."

I slip my fingers beneath her lace panties and slide two of them inside her.

Her head falls back against me once more as she moans.

"I can't wait to see you take more than just my fingers," I rumble in her ear, moving them in and out. I'm desperate to be inside her. "Look how gorgeous you are like this."

Her eyes flutter open and she watches me in the mirror, desire clouding her gaze.

"You want more?" I ask, and she nods.

I adjust my positioning so I can get deeper inside her, circling against her clit with my thumb. She's already clenching around my fingers, and I nip at her earlobe.

"Are you going to come again for me, baby?" I increase the pressure and she whines.

Suddenly, her hand reaches behind and my pace falters.

"Not until you do." Her breathing is heavy as I continue working her while she squeezes me. "You need to let me take care of you for once."

Her fingers move up and down my length, and my brain scrambles. "But I'm having so much fun."

Her free hand links with mine and drags it away. She spins in my arms and nudges me back until my calves hit the bed. "You're going to have even more fun when you're in the back of my throat."

I groan, and she presses me down to a seated position. "Jesus, Chels."

She grabs the bottom of my shirt and peels it up and over my head. "You think you're the only one who can talk dirty?"

Her hands are all over me, and I'm pretty certain my heart is about to beat out of my chest. "I'm not sure how much I can take. I've already got my dream girl practically naked in my bedroom."

She kisses me so hard I have to catch myself from falling backwards. "Stay here," she mumbles against my lips, pushing me back further onto my forearms, like I had her on the counter.

"Yes, ma'am."

She kisses down my neck and spreads her palms down my shoulders and arms.

"I haven't had a chance to really look at you yet." Her lips travel down my chest, her nails skating along the muscles in my abdomen as she gets to her knees. She swears. "Your body is insane. Do you live at the gym?"

I whimper as her tongue traces a long and lazy path from my lower stomach to the top of my boxer briefs.

"Chels." My voice is thick as I watch her unbuckle my belt.

"Yes?" She flicks open the button of my pants, and I'm so turned on I could detonate on the spot.

"I—"

She tugs the zipper down at a glacial pace, and I need to pull out some deep breathing exercises to get through it.

"It is really hot knowing I do this to you," she says, easing my pants over my hips and to the floor. She kisses up the length of me through my briefs, and I can feel her warm breath through the fabric.

"I'm not going to last long if you do this," I rasp, "and I need to get inside you."

"You will." She rakes down my thighs with a hum of appreciation. "Your legs are sinful."

I'm squirming under her touch. "Baby, please," I beg.

Chelsea looks up at me with a wicked grin. "Hold my hair, OK?"

My world tilts off its axis when she finally takes me into her mouth. I fall flat on my back until she grabs one of my hands and brings it closer. My limbs feel like they're caught in molasses as I push myself up and gather her hair in my grip. The way her throat vibrates around me in a moan nearly catapults me over the edge.

"Chelsea." My voice shakes. "You're playing with fire."

She chuckles and slows her pace.

She's too fucking good, and I have to desperately pull her off within a few minutes.

"Bed," I croak with the barest command of the English language.

She scrambles to her feet and kisses me roughly.

I wrap my arms around her and pull her on top of me. My hand slides up her back and unhooks her bra with a needy flourish.

"Do you have—?"

"Bedside table."

She tosses her bra to the side as she forages for the box of condoms. Even after what happened in Utica, buying them felt like operating on a wing and a prayer.

Chelsea John is in bed with me. I'm afraid that at any moment I'll wake up from this dream.

She rips one open with her teeth, and I fear I'll never recover from how goddamn hot she is. She rolls the condom onto me as I attempt to summon what's left of my self-control.

"Are you ready for me?" I ask, settling between her legs.

She pulls me closer and grinds against me. "What do you think?"

I reach between us and groan at how wet she is. "You liked having me in your mouth?"

I run my length against her, and she exhales deeply. "We're doing that again as soon as you're recovered."

"Woman of my dreams." I start to sink into her and bite my lip at her tightness. "You doing OK?"

Her legs are trembling as she wraps them around me. "A bit full of yourself, aren't you?"

"Baby, you're the one who's full of me right now."

She clenches around me as she moans and laughs at the same time. Sensing my opportunity, I shove a pillow under her hips and fully slide into her.

"What was it you said about wanting to get me off before you came again?"

Her eyes roll back as I thrust into her. "Don't you fucking dare."

"Oh, I dare." I rub my thumb against her, and she shakes like an earthquake.

"Wes—"

"Yeah, baby?" I run my teeth against her quivering lower lip. "I wish you could see what a good fucking job you're doing taking me deep like this."

She climaxes with a yell and a shudder that sends me careening over the edge right along with her. It feels like my soul exits my body as the waves of pleasure reverberate through me.

Chelsea gasps for breath as I start coming down to Earth.

I kiss her cheek and wipe away the damp hair stuck to her forehead. "Sorry I cheated."

"You are in so much trouble."

"Oh no. I'd better hydrate."

Chapter 30

Chelsea

A car horn blares and jolts me awake with a gasp.

I panic as I look around the unfamiliar room until I remember where I am. Living on reservations and a college campus has not prepared me for the sounds of a city.

I glance beside me to find an empty bed. The sheets are warm, so Wes must have recently gotten up. I swallow down the fear that he's gone and left me to deal with the emotional fallout of last night. *He wouldn't do that*, I assure myself.

I trust Wes more than I used to, but years of shitty men are hard to shake. Last night was incredible. Earth shattering. Transformative. Hot as hell. *But now what?* We've clearly veered into relationship territory, and I increasingly want to slam on the gas pedal.

My stomach flips as I pull on one of Wes' t-shirts, and the desire to kiss him good morning is overwhelming. His current book is on the bedside table, and I want to curl up with him and read together. I want to cook breakfast with him and watch CBS Sunday Morning with my legs in his lap and a cup of coffee nearby.

I'm getting attached, which is terrifying. I make terrible decisions when I'm invested in relationships because the guys have never matched my enthusiasm. Brock, for example, rarely spent the night in the year we were together. On the rare occasions he did, he was out the door at first light. The worse the man, the more effort I seemed to put into fixing things.

I hear clattering in the kitchen and crack open the bedroom door to investigate.

Wes is pulling two mugs from a cabinet as the delicious aroma of freshly brewed coffee wafts over. He's shirtless and wearing black sweats, his glasses, and some delightful bedhead.

"You wake up looking this good?" I say incredulously.

He turns to watch me pad into the kitchen. His hungry eyes skim my bare legs and stall out where the bottom of his Oneida Nation Pow Wow t-shirt barely covers my backside.

"Jesus, Chels." He quickly crosses the space between us and sweeps me into his arms. "I underestimated how sensational you would look in nothing but my shirt."

"If you were a little taller, the length would be less obscene on me."

"Genetics are finally working in my favor."

His kiss is full of unbridled passion. He grips my backside and backs me up into the handle of the dishwasher. I let out an *oomph,* and he breaks away.

"Sorry. I need to get better at controlling myself around you."
He pulls me against him and feathers a kiss across my forehead.
"Good morning."

"Good morning. And please don't change a thing."

"I'm going to take you back to bed if you keep looking at me
like that."

"Are you going for a sock trick in our orgasm competition?
You already cleared the hat trick overnight."

Wes groans and runs his hands underneath my shirt.

I giggle into his neck. "I need to get out of here before Sawyer
gets home."

"I'll barricade the door. I don't know when I'll get to see you
again."

"I'll see you Thursday at pickup lax."

"It's torture playing against you and not being able to brag to
Sawyer that I pulled the most badass girl in all of lacrosse."

I feel dizzy from his kiss, his touch, his words. He scoops me
up and walks towards the bedroom, and all I want is to sink into
the moment with this man who worships the ground I walk on.
I don't want to overthink what this is and what it isn't.

"What about our coffee? Won't it get cold?" I ask softly,
kicking my feet that are draped over his forearm.

"Depends on how long it takes us to get that sock trick."

Two weeks later we're still struggling to see each other with any
regularity, and it's about to get harder with the NLL season

starting. Living in Cattaraugus is cheap, but it adds almost two hours to my workday and limits my opportunities to have a social life. As much as I love rooming with Mackenzie, I wish I could afford to get a place closer to Buffalo. Of course, my availability to see Wes is further hampered by his living with Sawyer. We catch moments alone together when we can, but they've been few and far between.

Which is why I'm over the moon when Zeke invites us out for drinks after Outlaws practice on opening weekend. The team plays its first regular season game tomorrow evening, and is staying in a hotel together the night before. Genny, MacKenzie, and I make the drive into the city on Friday night, and my legs are bouncing with anticipation.

On a whim, I'd pulled on a form-fitting pair of jeans I hadn't worn since college, and paired them with a low-cut top. The thought of distracting Wes all night gave me an unfamiliar confidence.

"You look hot," Genny says with an appreciative smile as we walk into Cobblestone Bar.

"Thanks." I tuck some hair behind my ear and fidget with my earrings. I'm wearing the gold salmon ghosts I'd loaned to Lauren in Utica. "It's nice to go somewhere that isn't work, home, or the gym."

"Ladies." Sawyer stands when he sees us, brushing a quick kiss against Genny's cheek. He grins when he gets to me, bringing me in for a bro hug. "Chels."

"Lanes."

The guys reassemble to make room for us, and Wes slides into the booth next to me.

"It's really not fair to wear your glasses out tonight," I whisper as I reach across him for a cup of water.

"Says the woman with the gorgeous cleavage," he murmurs back.

I press my thigh against his and busy myself talking to Genny. He traces circles on my kneecap a few times, and it's a challenge not to cozy up and spend the evening talking to him.

Halfway through our second drink, I run my fingers up Wes' length under the table. He sucks in a quiet hiss.

"How's your new job, Chels?" Zeke asks.

"I love it. My boss is great, and I'm learning so much about exhibit curation." My fingertips skate across Wes' zipper.

He props his elbow on the table and bites his knuckles.

I ignore him.

"What did you study in college?" Sawyer inquires.

"I was an Indigenous Studies major, but we talked a lot about the ethics of Native artifacts in museums, for sure."

I wrap my hand around Wes with a squeeze that makes him groan loudly enough for people to notice.

"You OK, man?" Zeke asks, looking over with concern.

"I'm good," he grits out, reaching for his drink. "Just getting tired."

"We can head out soon," Zeke offers, throwing his arm around Genny and kissing the top of her head. "We've got practice in the morning."

Wes nods and pulls his phone out of his pocket. I see his fingers typing in my peripheral vision.

My phone vibrates on the table, and I chuckle under my breath. I purposely ignore it and take a long drag of my beer, eventually checking my messages with one hand.

> **The Bear:** If you keep that up, you're going to find yourself moaning against a bathroom stall in five minutes

Ho.ly. Fuck.

I set the glass bottle down with a *thunk*, my cheeks warm with arousal. I type back a quick response and try to hide behind my drink.

> **Me:** Don't threaten me with a good time

I feel Wes' phone buzz in his pocket and smile. Damn, it's fun to wind each other up in public.

"Is that The Bear?" Genny asks me, and my eyes fly over to hers in panic.

"Uh..."

"Who's The Bear?" Wes asks, genuinely puzzled.

Shit. How does this keep happening?

"Chelsea's secret situationship," Mackenzie answers. "They're constantly texting each other all kinds of filthy shit."

Wes turns and looks at me, amusement dancing in his eyes. "Oh, really?"

Sawyer lights up. "Chelsea! You've been holding out on us."

I close my eyes and pray to the Great Spirit for a sinkhole to swallow me.

"Who is he?" Zeke asks.

"She won't tell us," Genny responds with a pout. "Some lacrosse player."

"And she *doesn't* date lacrosse players," Mackenzie adds with a pointed look in my direction.

"Do we know him?" Zeke looks at Wes, who shrugs in an exaggerated fashion.

"Probably." Genny drums her fingers on the table. "But Chelsea's given us almost no clues."

Wes takes a sip of his whiskey. "That's a peculiar nickname, The Bear. Wonder what that's about."

I kick his shin, and he chuckles into his glass.

"Genny and I have a whole conspiracy theory chart trying to figure out who this guy is," Mackenzie huffs.

"I think he's The Bear because he's burly," Genny volunteers.

"Oooh, a burly man," Wes raises his eyebrows at me.

I glare in return.

"Or maybe he's a teddy bear," Mackenzie posits. "Gruff on the outside but cuddly on the inside."

I can feel Wes' body shaking with repressed laughter.

"I don't know, Chels," Zeke says with concern. "If he only wants to keep things secret with you, then he's probably not a great guy."

"But the sex is phenomenal," Mackenzie interjects, and my face flushes anew. "That's key!"

Someone kill me.

"Phenomenal?" Wes smirks, running his thumb over his bottom lip. "Seriously?"

My heart pounds in my chest as I raise my beer to my mouth. "Best sex of my life," I say plainly, taking a sip.

He stares back at me, biting his lip as our friends whoop with delight.

"I'm so jealous," Mackenzie sighs, her chin falling forward onto her palm. "I'm not enjoying being single again. Cover your ears, Zeke."

"Trust me, I've given my brother an earful," Zeke mutters.

Genny squeezes her sister's forearm with sympathy.

"Just be careful, Chels," Zeke cautions kindly, knocking his empty glass gently against my bottle. "Any guy worth his salt should be happy to tell the world that you're his."

I choke on my last sip of beer. "Who said anything about being *his?*"

Genny guffaws. "You're crazy, girl. Get this." She leans forward conspiratorially. "Chelsea always has a book in her hands, and The Bear has started reading her favorites so they can talk about them."

Wes is going to blow our cover because he is unabashedly grinning like an idiot.

"What do you like to read?" Sawyer asks.

They all look at me and I sigh with gusto. "Romance novels."

"Oh, shit," Wes laughs. "Is he taking notes?"

"Tons of notes," Mackenzie nods emphatically. "She's turning him into a Book Boyfriend."

"It's really hot," Genny sighs.

"How much do you *tell* them?" Wes asks me, his eyes dancing.

"Sadly, we do not get play-by-plays," Mackenzie laments. "But we get enough."

"My God," Wes chortles, draining the last of his whiskey. He's never going to let me live this down.

Zeke raises Genny's hand to his lips for a kiss. "Well, I don't know any lacrosse players who read romance, so this guy may be more into you than you think."

"You read a lot, don't you, Wes?"

Genny's question slices through the jovial air, causing me and Wes to freeze.

He clears his throat. "Yeah, I do. I like the classics. I'm reading *The Odyssey* right now."

Damn, that's hot. He hadn't told me that. I suppose we've been too busy texting each other fantasies inspired by our last Spicy Book Club read.

"Be on the lookout for other players sneaking peeks at their Kindles before games." Sawyer smiles.

Wes coughs. "I will."

We start wrapping up our bills, and my phone buzzes again.

The Bear: So, you're telling your friends about me?

Me: Not you. Your burly alter ego

The Bear: I wish you were coming home with me tonight

Me: Just snuggle with Zeke instead

The Bear: He's taken

"Well, Chels, best of luck to you and The Bear." Wes claps me on the shoulder before sliding out of the booth. "He's a lucky man," he says softly.

I notice Genny looking at him curiously. *Dammit.* I'm going to need to throw her off the scent in the coming days.

"Thanks," I reply, avoiding his eyes. "I appreciate that."

"Chels," Genny says slowly after the guys depart, "Wes still likes you."

"Well, of course he likes me," I say quickly. "We're friends."

"No, I mean," she leans forward, "I think he has a real, honest-to-God crush on you."

I bark out a surprised laugh. "We're too old to have crushes."

"Crushes don't have an age limit." She sips her water. "You two have chemistry. And I think that man is pining for you."

"I'm not sure where you're going with this."

"I'm just saying," she says. "Wes has a lot of the characteristics you like about The Bear, but you've never given him a chance."

"He's cute as hell," Mackenzie chimes in.

"He's kind," Genny adds.

"He's strong enough to throw you around," Mackenzie continues.

"He's smart, funny, loves to read," Genny is on a roll.

"Stop it, you two," I laugh.

"It's something to consider if things don't work out with The Bear," Genny insists. "Wes is a really good man, and I know he'd be interested."

Lying to my friends is becoming a weight that sits on my chest each day. For the first time, I briefly consider telling them. But then what? *Chels is back in yet another relationship that's going to crash and burn. Maybe he won't be as horrendous as Brock, but they all end the same way.*

I smile weakly. "I'll keep that in mind."

Chapter 31

Wahsu:tés

Long Nights / December

Chelsea

The Outlaws have the weekend off due to the impending holiday, and Sawyer's visiting his brother in Toronto. As a result, my ass has been happily parked in Wes' lap for the past twenty-four hours.

I sigh and snuggle deeper into his chest as we binge-watch the first season of *North of North*. My back is sore from shoveling out my driveway yesterday morning before work, and relaxing with Wes has been a much-needed break from life.

"Are you comfortable enough?" he asks, shifting slightly. "Do you need anything?"

I brush my fingers against his cheek. "This is perfect."

I'm close to dozing off in his arms when he clears his throat.

"Can I ask you something crazy?"

My eyes pop open. "What's that?"

He plays with the loose hair at the end of my braid. "I have a bye week coming up at the beginning of February. Most guys plan a big trip for that time."

"Nice. Where are you thinking of going?"

"I've been wanting to go to one of my favorite places: Door County, Wisconsin." He gently loosens the braid sections near my scalp, where he knows they get tight as my hair dries after a shower. "There are cabins on the lake, a winter market, hiking trails, stuff like that."

"Sounds romantic," I tease.

His eyes jump up to mine. "About that..."

"Oh. *Oh!*" I sit up. "Are you asking—?"

"I am. Would you like to come with me?" He swallows. "I'm not sure if you can take time off work yet."

"I'm not sure either. Let me talk to Nat about it on Monday."

"OK." He kisses me softly. "It's not a big deal if you can't, or if you'd rather not."

"A hot guy wants to whisk me away on a romantic vacation? Yeah, I'm going to make that happen."

"Who's the hot guy?" he says with a smile. "Must be The Bear."

I straddle his lap and lower myself firmly, loving the moan that rips from Wes' throat in response.

"The Bear is just sex." I bring my mouth down to his. "He doesn't do romance."

He pulls my hips against his, hands tightly gripping while his tongue dips between my lips. "What a stupid man, in that case, not to realize what he's got."

I prop one forearm against the back of the couch behind him as I grind on him. Our heavy breathing fills the room, and I suspect we may not make it to the bedroom.

A rustling sound pierces through my foggy senses, but I'm too far gone to react in time.

"Hey, Wes! I'm back earl—"

I jerk my head up and come face to face with a wide-eyed Sawyer walking through the front door.

"Oh! I was just—" I scramble to hop off of Wes but my legs get tangled in the process.

"I think I forgot something in my truck," Sawyer says and quickly disappears back behind the door.

"Oh my God," I groan as I collapse onto the couch. "I want to die."

"It's going to be OK," Wes assures me. "Sawyer won't say anything to anybody."

"Have you *met* Sawyer? He studied at the Auntie School of Gossip." I stand and begin anxiously fluttering around the living room. "I should go."

"Chels." He watches me pace back and forth.

"Maybe I'll sneak out the back and we'll just pretend it never happened?"

He smiles and grabs my waist as I pass, pulling me back down to the couch with him. "What if this is a good thing?"

I shake my head in disbelief. "Have you lost your mind?"

"If Sawyer knows, then we don't need to sneak around at my place anymore. We'll be able to see each other more often, and actually act like we're dating."

I search his eyes. "I don't know if I'm ready for this."

Wes wraps his arms around me and pulls me tightly to his chest. "You're in full fight-or-flight mode, killer."

I relax into his chest. My pulse is still racing, but I'm able to take some deep breaths.

"There's my girl." He gives me a squeeze. "How about I talk to Sawyer and see what we can work out?"

"Can I hide in your bedroom while you do that?"

"You can hide in my bedroom."

"Thank you."

I hear loud coughing and jingling of keys as Sawyer returns to the entrance.

I pound on Wes' chest. "Let me go, you oaf."

He chuckles and releases me. I make a beeline for his room and gratefully shut the door behind me.

Chapter 32

Wes

S awyer takes his time, and makes a tremendous amount of noise, before slowly coming inside. "You good?" he asks with a wolfish grin.

"I'm fucking awesome, man." I open a beer from the fridge and slide it across the counter to him. "Can we talk?"

"Of course."

We both sip our beers as I try to formulate the best way to approach this.

"So, you and Chelsea, huh?" Sawyer smiles from ear to ear. "Merry fucking Christmas to you."

His joy is infectious, and a smile spreads across my face as well. "Me and Chelsea."

"I have to say, I didn't think you had it in you. Did this just happen?"

"It's been happening since last summer."

Sawyer chokes on his beer. "What?"

My face hurts from smiling. It feels so damn good to finally tell someone.

"We started talking back in May, and officially...something in September. It's a bit of a moving target."

"Wait a minute." He narrows his eyes. "Did you two hook up at the World Games?"

I nod.

He sets his beer bottle down with a clatter. "We all thought you were acting really weird while we were there. Jamie seemed to know something, but would not respond to our interrogations."

I raise my eyebrow. "Jamie doesn't know. At least, I don't think he does." I think for a moment and frown. "Dammit. He probably figured it out."

Sawyer takes out his phone. "Let me ask him."

I pluck the device out of his hand. "This is what we need to talk about."

He furrows his brow before smirking. "You guys like sneaking around? Kinky."

I lean forward on the kitchen island, lowering my voice. "Sneaking around is getting old, but Chelsea isn't ready to tell everyone yet."

"Why not? Everyone loves her. It would be so fun to hang out with you guys as a couple. You could double date with Zeke and Genny." He pauses, and I see emotion unexpectedly flicker across his face. "I'm seriously so damn happy for you, Wes."

"Are you getting sappy?"

He scoffs, picking up his beer again.

"But seriously, it's really important that no one else finds out for now," I continue. "Chelsea's been hurt in the past and needs more time."

He nods. "I promise I won't say anything. Unless I screw up by accident."

"Chelsea would flay you alive."

"And I'd deserve it." He cranes his neck to look behind me. "Is she still here?"

"Yeah, she's in my room."

"Chelsea!" he calls loudly, and I wince at his volume. "Is she staying for dinner, or would you rather I just get out of your hair?" he asks me.

"It's cool. I'm hoping she sticks around, as long as you don't scare her off."

"Me? I'm an angel. *Chelsea!*"

My door creaks open, and Chelsea pokes her head out hesitantly. She squeaks in surprise when Sawyer crashes into her with a hug.

"I'm so happy for you and Wes," he says. "And I promise I won't say anything to anyone else."

She pats his back while looking at me. "What's with him?" she mouths.

I smother a laugh.

"Let me make you guys dinner as an apology for walking in on you," Sawyer says as he releases Chelsea. "My brother's fiancée sent me home with some great leftovers."

He gets as far as the kitchen island before he spins around. "Wait a fucking minute. *You're The Bear?*"

I scratch the back of my neck.

Chelsea cringes.

Sawyer zooms into the living room and quickly scans the bookshelf. He pulls out a heavily dog-eared copy of a Spicy Book Club favorite, the stalker romcom.

"Oh, shit," she says.

He skims the back blurb and looks up. "Wesley Harrison, you absolute dog. I thought this was some kind of true crime novel."

"You left that out here with him?" Chelsea hisses at me.

"He seemed oblivious," I explain.

"I now know way more about your bedroom prowess than I ever planned on, but way to fucking go, bro."

Chapter 33

Tsha'tekohsélha'
Midwinter / February

Wes

The opening guitar riff of "American Idiot" by Green Day bellows through the house as I settle in to pack for our trip. The Outlaws played in Toronto last night, and I have a quick turnaround to get ready for our flight to Wisconsin in the morning.

My phone rings as I'm putting together a toiletries bag in the bathroom, and I tap to put it on speakerphone.

"Hey, Mom."

"*Shekólih*. Did I catch you at a good time?"

I smile at her familiar voice, which I don't get to hear often these days. "I'm good. What's up?"

"Just checking in to make sure everything's still set with your trip."

"We're a go. I'll let you know if anything changes."

"Good." I hear her smile.

"Hey, while I've got you on the phone," I say, "I wanted to talk to you about something."

"What's that?"

I swallow and jump into the fire. "I haven't mentioned it, but I went to Oneida for a visit back in June."

My mom pauses for several seconds. "Oh. That's nice."

"I saw my friend Chelsea while I was out there. You know, the one I'm traveling with."

"Mmm hmm."

"Well, she introduced me to her roommate, Jessica. Her mom is your sister." I hesitate. "And we had dinner together."

It's deadly silent on the other end of the phone.

"Did you know you have a niece?" I ask quietly.

"I knew Becky had kids, yes," she says, her voice soft. "Your grandmother came out here once when you and Katie were small, and gave your dad some updates on the family."

I swallow. "Jess asked if she could tell your mom about meeting me, and I asked her to hold off until I talked to you."

"I appreciate that. Why have you waited so long to ask me? You met her months ago."

I toss my toothpaste into a bag. "She shared some things with me about why you may have left New York and, to be honest, I'm not sure if I want to meet any more of the family."

My mom clucks her tongue. "I should have opened up to you years ago about all this, and I regret that now. I don't want you to hold back on connecting with them because of how you think I might feel."

"It's not just that." I wander out of the bathroom and sit on the edge of my bed. "I'm angry with your family for not listening to you, and for keeping you in danger. I don't know if I can look past that."

She sighs. "I understand, believe me. And that's up to you to wrestle with and come to a conclusion about for yourself. But that situation led to meeting your father, and having you and Katie, and I wouldn't change anything about that now."

"I'm not sure if I can forgive them." My unfocused eyes settle on my open suitcase.

"Let's talk about it more next week," she says. "I need a chance to gather my thoughts, and we can have an open conversation about everything. You're owed that."

I smile slightly. "Thanks, Mom. I'm sorry to dredge all this up."

"Don't be. It's past time someone did."

We hang up, and I try to re-focus on packing. I'm pulling sweaters out of the closet when I hear a knock at the front door. Sawyer left for Canada this morning, and I'm not expecting any visitors, so this is unexpected.

I find Zeke on my front stoop, looking like he's ready to gnaw through his lip with anxiety.

"What's going on, Z?" I ask, tilting my head.

"Do you mind if I come in?" His breath comes out in icy puffs.

"Of course. Make yourself at home. Do you want something to drink?"

We wander into the kitchen, and Zeke sits on a barstool. "No, thanks." He looks around, eyes darting randomly across the room. "Actually, maybe some water?"

"You got it." I fill a glass for him and watch as he drums his fingers on the counter. "You good?"

He hops out of his seat to accept the water, taking a big gulp before starting to pace. "I'm not sure."

The floorboards creak under his feet as he walks back and forth.

"You're making me nervous, bro."

He pauses. "Sorry. I'm trying to figure out how to say it."

"Say what?"

Zeke reaches into his coat pocket and deposits something on the kitchen island. He immediately walks to the other side of the room, as though it's about to explode.

I stare at the small velvet box. "I appreciate the gesture, but I'm not into you that way, man."

He grunts and stomps back over. "Not *you*." He carefully cracks open the black container. "Genny."

Unexpected emotion washes over me. "I know, dumbass." I pick the box up and gently turn it to inspect the gleaming ring. "You're going to propose on your trip?"

He nods. "That's the plan. But I'm terrified it's too soon and she'll say no."

"You two were made for each other since Day One. She won't say no."

"Yeah, but I have a habit of screwing things up when it comes to her." He sits back down with a lengthy sigh. "How can she know she can trust me?"

I slide the ring box over to him. "It's a leap of faith, right? Anytime you give your heart to someone, you know there's a chance they'll break it. But would you rather miss out on a great love and never take that risk in the first place?"

Zeke turns the ring over in his fingers, his eyes solemn. "I know what my answer is, but I'm not sure how she feels."

"Genny couldn't get over you even after you ghosted her for years. I think she's stuck with you for life."

He smiles weakly. "What a ringing endorsement of our relationship."

I laugh. "I've never met two people more perfect for each other than you and Genny. If you don't get married and live happily ever after, there's no hope for the rest of us."

He gingerly places the ring back in the box. "Do you really think she'll say yes?"

"I really, really think she will."

He glances over at me and frowns. "Are you...getting emotional?"

I blink against the edge of a tear threatening the corner of my eye. "Maybe."

"Is this a Hallmark movie?"

I chuckle and brush the wetness away. "I'm envious of what you and Genny have. You've been through hell and back, twice, and came out stronger than ever. It's inspiring."

Zeke's face softens. "There's someone out there for you, too, man. You just haven't found her yet."

I bite the inside of my cheek so hard I taste blood. "I know."

We sit in silence for a minute, sipping our waters.

"Where are you heading for the bye week?" he asks.

"Wisconsin. Going to spend some time with my family."

"That's awesome. I know how much you miss them."

"Yeah, it'll be good. What about you? Where is this magical movie moment taking place?"

"Genny's always wanted to go to Montreal, so that's where we'll be." He closes the box with a soft *clunk*. "The Kahnawà:ke Mohawk reserve is nearby, and a college friend of mine is from there. We'll spend a couple of days with him, too."

"Sounds perfect." I pull him in for a hug. "I'm really happy for you, Z. This is a big step, and it shows how far you've come in the last year and a half."

He claps me on the back. "I suppose you're right, as usual."

"Let me know how it works out."

"I will. Thanks for always being the friend I need, Wes."

"Anytime."

Chapter 34

Chelsea

"**N**ow that the door to the plane is locked and you can't run away, I have to tell you something."

My hands pause as I shove my paperback into the seatback pocket. "That's ominous."

Wes fidgets with his headphones. "I may not have been one hundred percent truthful about our trip itinerary."

I angle my body to face him. "Are we secretly going to a Caribbean island? Because I wouldn't be mad about it."

"Sadly, no. We're actually going to a tundra in the middle of winter like a couple of lunatics." He raises his eyes to mine. "I told my parents we'd stop by for a couple of days, since we'll be so close to Green Bay."

I inhale deeply. "I'm...meeting your parents?"

He bites his lip. "I know I should have cleared this with you first. My mom was hoping I would come home for the entire bye week, so I had to talk her off the ledge about being nearby but not visiting."

"And they don't think it's weird you're traveling with—You know what? I'm not going to worry about that right now." I slowly and deliberately continue unpacking the contents of my purse, trying to calm my racing nerves.

A notification slides in as I'm setting my phone to Airplane Mode.

Brock: You around this week?

The device clatters to the floor as I drop it like a hot potato. *What the fuck?*

Wes leans down and grabs it for me.

"Thanks." I stare at the message for a few seconds, waiting for a panic attack to set in, but all I feel is annoyance.

"I owe you," Wes says, squeezing my knee. "I'm sorry about the family thing."

"We'll figure it out. What's more than a sock trick?"

"I'm probably on the hook for at least a baker's dozen."

"That's a good start."

I swipe to delete Brock's message, tossing my phone back into my bag.

"This place is beautiful," I say, taking in the humble cabin on the frozen shores of Lake Michigan. It's small but homey, with a cringe-worthy *"Mi casa es su casa"* sign on the buttercup yellow front door. I reach for my suitcase, but Wes grabs it first, hauling both bags out of the rental car.

He checks his phone. "The owner should be here any minute to give us the keys." He threads his fingers through mine and pulls me to him for a kiss. "I'm really going to enjoy being out in public with you here."

Gravel crunches underneath tires as a car pulls into the driveway. I pull back from Wes, but he holds me firmly to him.

"Not a chance I'm letting you go right now." He chuckles.

A woman climbs out of the vehicle and waves. "Good afternoon. Wes?"

He nods and extends his hand. "Yep, and this is Chelsea. Nice to meet you, Marianne."

"Wes and Chelsea. Gosh, aren't you two cute?" Her friendly eyes sparkle. "Newlyweds?"

I stiffen, and Wes drapes an arm around my shoulders. "Maybe."

Oh, he is so dead.

I step on his toes and feel him wince.

The owner squeals. "I knew it!"

He looks at me and I can't help but smile back. "I'm the luckiest man in the world."

"Oh my gosh, you two." She digs in her purse. "Well, I'm just going to have to stop by later with a little gift basket for you."

Wes takes a set of keys from her. "Thanks, Marianne. That's really kind of you."

"I've got all the information you'll need in a binder in the kitchen. I hope you have a *wonderful* stay in Door County."

"Who the hell was *that?*" I ask as we walk inside.

"Marianne? She's the owner I've been corresponding with over—"

"Not her. *You*."

He drops the suitcases inside the front door. "Oh, you mean my Midwestern personality?"

"Yeah, him. The newlywed."

Wes chuckles. "People here love to give you free stuff if they think you're celebrating something." He presses me against the wall, his hands framing my face. "It helps that I can't keep my hands off you."

"I hope your wife doesn't find out."

He smiles against my lips. "Would you fight for me?"

"I'd consider it. Depends on what comes in this Midwestern gift basket."

Chapter 35

Wes

"This is so fun," Chelsea says, appraising the flight of thin-stemmed glasses that were just delivered to us at the bar.

Door County is known for its wines, and visiting a winery was top of mind when I planned this trip.

"You'll have to let me know what you think of the ice wine." I tap the last glass. "It's really sweet, like dessert."

"I've never tried it, but I've always wanted to." She brings it to her nose for a sniff. "There are some wineries in southern Ontario that produce it, too."

I hook a hand under her barstool and tug her closer to me. "You look incredible, by the way."

She sips her wine as a flush crawls up her cheeks. "Thanks."

"I don't think you believe me." I drag my eyes up from her knee-high boots to the long black sweater dress she's wearing. "Which means I have work to do once we get back to the cabin."

"I can't get anything done with you around." She smiles around her glass.

"Like what? We're on vacation."

She sets it down with a sigh. "It *is* nice to have nowhere to be and nothing urgent to do. Although I do need to finish those earrings for your mom."

I trace up her calf with my fingers. "I'm really glad you finally have a chance to relax. And that I get to be here to see it."

Chelsea threads her fingers through mine and brings my hand to her lips. "I like relaxing with you."

"Speaking of which, I'm finding sneaking around is *not* relaxing."

I hold my breath waiting for her response. She runs her thumb over my knuckles as she takes another sip.

"You're right. It's not."

"Do you want to change anything about that?"

Seconds of silence tick by, and I feel every one of them.

"You've waited a long time for me," she says quietly.

"I have. And I'll wait longer." Panic dances along the edges of my nerves.

More silence. More heart palpitations.

"What do you need to feel comfortable going public?" I ask.

She looks up and catches my eye. "You're perfect. There's literally nothing you could be doing differently."

"I sense a 'but' coming."

"There's no 'but.' More like an 'and.' You're perfect, *and* I know how easily I could get caught up in you and lose sight of myself and my dreams. But I don't want to lose you." Her last sentence ends in a whisper.

"You're going to need a crowbar to get rid of me. I'm not going anywhere." I squeeze her hand. "You're worth taking a chance on."

Her eyes flutter closed. "You're a gift I haven't earned." They pop back open when I pull her stool even closer and tilt her chin up.

"You've worked so hard to achieve your accomplishments. Your college scholarship, your museum job, your bronze medal, your legions of devoted friends and family. You make me want to be a better person so I can grow alongside you. You've earned my admiration simply by being yourself."

Chelsea's eyes are glassy as they look into mine. "Dammit, Wes."

I kiss her softly, as though she's made of porcelain. "Let me love you the way you deserve, just for this week. And then we can talk, OK?"

She nods. "OK."

"I think this is a bit too Deep Woods Native, even for me." Chelsea giggles as she loses her balance.

I steady her. "You need a wider stance. How have you never been snowshoeing?"

"Listen, I'll stay and tend the fire if you want to go hunting with the warriors. My city legs are getting tired."

"All right, all right. This is good enough." I stomp down with my long, flat snowshoes to compact the surrounding powder. "I just wanted to get far enough from civilization so we could see the stars better."

"How the hell do you sit down in these things?" Chelsea helps me spread some thick blankets on the ground.

"You just kind of—" I turn my body to the side and slowly lower myself. "Like that."

She awkwardly shuffles her feet and begins to descend.

"Turn your body, not your—"

She collapses onto the snow in an undignified heap, her torso shaking with laughter.

"Don't quit your day job to become a teacher," she gasps.

I pull her up to a seated position, raining kisses on her face. "You OK, Miss Oneida? That was quite a graceful showing."

She pelts me with a fistful of snow, and we fall back laughing onto the blankets together.

It snowed earlier, and the world is cocooned in silence. We've spent the last several days exploring the nearby town, visiting lighthouses, and cooking at home. I've learned Chelsea likes sleeping in, listening to Kendrick Lamar, and watching CBS Sunday Morning while I rub her feet on the couch. I wish I could freeze time and stay in this bubble with her forever.

"The stars are beautiful tonight." She lays her head on my chest.

"They are." I watch her and not the sky.

She exhales in frozen puffs and points. "*Ohkwaliko* is out for us. He must sense you're kin."

The backend of the Great Bear constellation, the Big Dipper, twinkles brightly above us. My eyes follow the stars into the remainder of the animal shape.

"You know the story, I assume?" Chelsea asks.

"I do, but I'd love to hear you tell it."

"I'll try. I'm not much of a storyteller." She clears her throat and begins:

"A long time ago, there were three brothers living in a village. They were hunters, although none of them were very good at tracking animals. They were persistent, though, and never gave up trying.

"One day during the Big Snow moon, tracks of a Great Bear were discovered surrounding the village. It was much larger than a regular bear, and the people were very afraid. Children weren't allowed to play in the woods anymore, and the men guarded the longhouses at night. The other animals fled the area, and soon the people grew hungry from lack of food.

"There came a night when the three brothers all dreamed they tracked the Great Bear. In the dream, they found the bear and fought with him. When they woke up, the brothers discovered the Great Bear's tracks near where they slept and decided to follow them.

"They hunted the bear to the ends of the world. When they could go no further, they leapt up and continued to chase him across the skies. We can see the three hunters giving chase in the handle of the Big Dipper. In the harvest months, the hunters get close enough to wound the bear, and his blood drips down to turn the leaves red as the trees prepare for winter."

Chelsea tugs on my beard to bring my lips close to hers. "And now he's tattooed on your arm." She kisses me softly. "I really like all your tattoos."

"Tattooed guys do it for you?"

"This one does."

"Lucky me."

I'm just about to kick off my snowshoes and start a proper make-out session with her when both our phones buzz.

I groan. "That better not be Sawyer with some bullshit." I'm fumbling for the phone in my coat pocket when Chelsea shrieks.

"What's wrong?" I ask, sitting up instantly.

"Look at your texts!"

I can't get my gloves off fast enough for her liking, so she huffs and shows me her screen.

> **Genny:** *picture of her and Zeke kissing, with a sparkling diamond ring on her finger*

I grin widely. "He pulled it off! I told him she'd say yes. *Ow.*"

"You knew and didn't tell me?" Chelsea says, aghast, after smacking my upper arm.

"Well, I figured it was a secret."

"I can keep secrets!"

I fix her with a look.

She bites her lip. "That Bear thing happened, like three times!"

"Mmm hmm." I kiss that pillowy lower lip. "I'm never using you as a getaway driver."

Chapter 36

Chelsea

"It was probably not a great idea to play a game involving math right now." Wes squints at the cards in his hand as I return to the table with another round of drinks for us.

"It was your idea to teach me this weird game." I set a glass of local wine in front of him and take a sip from mine.

"Hey now. Cribbage is a beloved Wisconsin pastime." He brings his cards closer to his face before finally selecting two to discard.

"Do you want to put your glasses on, old man?" I ask. I have no idea what the best cards are to keep in my hand, so I randomly place two on the table.

"My contacts are getting dry, maybe I should." He picks up half the deck of cards and looks at me expectantly.

"What?"

"I cut the deck for you."

"What does that mean?"

"It means you flip over that card on top."

"Why?"

"Because it's your deal."

I turn over the first card in the pile. "I don't get this game."

He chuckles. "This isn't even the confusing part." He slides the four discards in my direction. "Here. It's your crib."

"I remain confused."

He laughs. "How about you think things through and I'll take my contacts out. I'll be right back."

I wave him off and study the various sets of cards before setting everything down with a huff. *I'll figure it out once he's back.*

I sip my drink and look around the first floor of the cabin. This is our last night here, and I'm downright sad about it. It's been absolute heaven getting to spend uninterrupted time with Wes for almost a week, and to do it in such a beautiful location. I'm going to miss wandering outside onto the icy deck with our morning coffees. Wes was always a few paces behind me, and would wrap his arms around my waist and kiss the back of my shoulder before taking his first sip.

We'd spent the past five days living in a dreamland where we could pretend the problems of the real world didn't exist. We could be together all the time without the demands of work, we didn't need to hide from our friends, and I could allow myself to be crazy about him without panicking that it meant I was losing control. Dread floods my system at the thought of this time being over.

"All right, let's do this." Wes returns, and a shot of desire hits me right in the chest.

"Wes," I warn.

"What's up?" He settles back in with his cards.

I ogle him in his glasses, and he smiles. "This is a huge distraction."

"I'll take my shirt off if you win this hand." He grins.

I groan. "Strip Cribbage? I don't stand a chance."

"Now you're talking." His eyes sparkle. "Loser tosses his or her shirt. Let's go."

Three hands later, I'm down to my underwear but managed to get Wes' t-shirt off. We've both gotten sloppy from wine.

"I'm not going to make it much longer." Wes watches me shimmy out of my pajama pants. He shuffles the cards, and they splutter chaotically.

"Can't handle the heat, Rookie?" I look at him over the top of my glass.

"I never could with you," he says softly.

"Are you getting mushy on me?"

"Maybe." He gets up from the table, his eyes intent.

"Uh oh." I smile in anticipation, assuming he's about to throw me over his shoulder or sweep the cribbage board off the table so he can set me on it.

Instead, he scoops me into his arms and gently tucks me against his chest. "I'm taking you to bed."

I kiss his neck as he carries me to the bedroom.

He carefully lays me down on the bed and proceeds to make love to me so reverently it startles me. He always shows passion and care for my body, but this time is different. Every touch and whisper is soft but intense.

We collapse onto the bed afterwards, the sound of our heavy breathing filling the room.

"I'll be right back." I kiss his chest and hop out of bed. I want to clean up and grab some water for us, but also have a minute to process.

That was different. There was frenzy behind his tender touch, and, to be honest, it unnerved me.

I crawl back into bed a few minutes later. "Here, drink this. You'll thank me in the morning."

He gratefully accepts the glass and chugs it. "I'll thank you now. I'm really thirsty."

I snuggle back into his chest, and he rests his chin on top of my head. I'm just about to doze off when my world comes to a screeching halt.

"I love you, Chels," Wes mumbles sleepily.

My eyes pop open. *Did he just—?*

I slowly turn my head to look up at him. His eyes are closed, and his chest rhythmically rises and falls.

"Wes," I whisper. "Are you awake?"

He remains still. His lips part slightly, and I dust a kiss across them.

He rolls onto his side and takes me with him, pulling my back to his chest as he settles in.

"Wes?" I try one more time with no response.

I'm now trapped in his arms for the foreseeable future, my mind swimming with the ramifications of what he just said.

He loved me? I'd never felt this strongly about anyone I'd dated, let alone been as cherished as I am with Wes. I'd originally fallen into this thinking it could be a bit of fun during my single era, but it quickly became much more than that. He laughs at my jokes, supports my career, and worships the ground I walk on. He's a breath of fresh fucking air, and he makes me deliriously happy.

My heart thumps painfully in my chest as he breathes steadily behind me. I don't know what to do with this information, or how to handle the conversation the morning would bring. I close my eyes with a sigh, praying that sleep will come.

Chapter 37

Wes

Waking up with Chelsea is like Christmas every morning.

She's sleeping peacefully in my arms, and I wonder how long we've been curled up together like this. I nuzzle her neck, breathing in the fruity scent of her shampoo.

She stirs as my beard rubs against her skin. I feather kisses along her shoulder.

"Morning." I gently pull her even closer to me.

"Hey." She blinks the sleep from her eyes. "How are you feeling?"

"I woke up with you in my bed, so I'm feeling fantastic."

She chuckles. "We had a lot to drink last night."

"Oh, right. I feel good, though. No ill effects."

"It's because of your youth."

I laugh and trail nibbles down her ear. "And how do you feel, old woman?"

"Bit of a headache, but OK."

I pull back and throw my legs over the side of the bed. "Let me get you some aspirin."

"Wes..."

Something in her voice gives me pause. "Yeah?"

"Do you remember everything from last night?"

Worry slices across my stomach. "I think so. Why?"

She adjusts the comforter. "Just curious."

I come around to her side of the bed and sit near her. "Did you finally beat me at cribbage?"

"Definitely not." She smirks. "We had some pretty great sex, though."

"I know. I wouldn't forget that."

She scans my eyes. "You conked out right afterwards."

I brush some hair away from her face. "Sorry about that. Wine and a beautiful woman have that effect on me."

She smiles and kisses my fingers. "I wasn't too far behind you."

"Good." I lean down to kiss her forehead. "Let me get you that aspirin so you can start feeling better."

I fix her up with some toast, coffee, and painkillers and get to work packing up the remainder of our belongings. We leave this morning for my parents' house in Green Bay, and my stomach clenches with both excitement and anxiety.

I can't wait to introduce her to my family and community. We'll only be there for a couple of days, but I want to make the most of our time.

"I love Genny's ring," Chelsea says as we pack the car. "She sent me some more pictures. It looks vintage-inspired. Very her."

"It's beautiful. Zeke did a great job." I slam the trunk closed.

I punch my parents' address into my phone and get some music going for the trip.

She sets up a mini beading station on her lap while I flip through radio stations. "Do you mind if I work?"

"Go for it. We've got about an hour and a half of driving. I don't know how you do that in motion, though."

"Just don't make any sudden stops, or we'll be picking up beads for days."

The drive passes easily, although Chelsea is quieter than usual. She seems engrossed in her beadwork, so I allow a companionable silence to pass between us.

"Do you want to swing through the rez? I need to get gas anyway, and then we can double back to my house."

She perks up. "Yeah! I'd love to see it."

I drive us past the Community Health Center where my mom works, the library, and the fitness facility. I point out familiar homes, the high school, and the longhouse.

Her eyes are wide as she takes it all in. "This place is huge!"

I chuckle. "It is. It's grown a ton in my lifetime." I put my blinker on. "Let me fill up here. Did you want to run inside and get anything?"

"Sure. I'll grab a couple of drinks for us." She carefully sets her beading tray on the floor.

I'm putting back the gas pump when Chelsea returns, looking perplexed.

She hands me a Gatorade. "Do people...pronounce Oneida words differently out here?"

I prop my arm on the car as I laugh. "I should've warned you. We pronounce all the letters you keep silent in New York. No idea why."

"The very nice cashier and I just thoroughly confused ourselves saying 'thank you' to each other."

"*Yawʌ*." I smile.

"*Ya:wʌ*," she corrects me with a grin. "But you've always said it the same way I do?"

We climb back into the car. "I pronounce Oneida the way my mom does, and she's from New York. When I'm here, I usually pronounce it their way so I don't look like a weirdo."

"Your poor mother isn't going to know what hit her when I show up."

"I truly cannot wait."

Chapter 38

Chelsea

"Here we are." Wes parks the car, smiling from ear to ear at the sight of his childhood home. It's a compact ranch with neatly trimmed landscaping, and very charming.

"This is nice," I say as we pull our bags out of the trunk.

A screen door creaks before slamming closed as a young woman with ash brown hair comes running out. She crashes into Wes and there's a flurry of limbs, ending with her in a headlock in the crook of his arm. She steps on his foot and he yelps, allowing her to escape.

"Hey, jerk." She smiles at him, her hazel eyes sparkling.

"Hey, Katie." He tucks her under his arm and beams at her.

She looks over at me with a warm smile and extends her hand. "Hi, I'm Katie."

"I'm Chelsea." I return her smile and handshake. "Is the coast clear, or are you guys about to go for round two?"

"Not sure yet." She turns to look at Wes. "Time will tell. Do you have an annoying brother, too?"

I chuckle. "I'm an only child, luckily. But I've seen plenty of this from my cousins and friends."

The door creaks again and a beautiful woman emerges, her braid long and streaked with silver like tinsel. It's a face I've seen a thousand times in old photographs, and it's surreal to see it in real life. Kay's dark eyes are kind, and she smiles warmly at me before wrapping Wes and Katie in a group hug.

"I'm so happy to see you," she whispers to him. "Thank you for coming."

"I'm happy to be home," he says. "Mom, this is my friend, Chelsea."

Kay untangles from her children and takes my outstretched hand in both of hers. "*Shekólih,* Chelsea. I'm so glad to finally meet you. Wes has told me so much about you."

I glance up at him with a murderous gaze, and he cringes. I look back at his mother and smile widely. "I can't tell you how meaningful it is to meet you, Kay. I've been close with your family my whole life."

A shadow passes over her eyes. "You're like a little piece of home. I'm delighted to welcome you to Wisconsin."

She reminds me so much of Jessica's mom, Becky.

"Let's go inside and get you something to eat. You must be tired from your trip." Kay gestures to the house.

I reach for my suitcase, but Wes grabs it out of my hands. "I got it." He winks.

"You talked to your mom about me?" I whisper as we walk inside.

"Well, I had to tell her this random friend was flying across the country with me to meet her."

"It sounds like you said a lot more than that."

"I said you're a close friend from the Oneida Nation in New York, that's all."

"You don't think your family finds it weird that you've brought a female *friend* home to meet them?"

He smothers a smile. "I'm sure they do. Just roll with it. They'll love you."

Kay and I were immediately thick as thieves. She, of course, knew both of my parents and all of my friends' families. She shared stories of their high school exploits and her time as a registered nurse working for the tribe.

Katie is lovely and pops in and out of our conversation in between catching up with her brother. We watch an NLL game together with Wes' dad, Bobby, in the living room, and these people immediately feel like home to me.

"I'll be right back," I say, hopping up. "Wes, where did you put my bag?"

"In the front bedroom," he answers. "Do you need help with anything?"

"No, I'm good." I meander down the short hallway until I find the small room with our suitcases stacked on top. I dig through my purse until I find what I'm looking for.

I sit back down near Kay. "A while ago, Wes asked if I'd make you a pair of earrings. It took me a while to get things together, but that means I'm able to give these to you in person." I hand her a dark green fabric pouch.

She smiles at me kindly and pulls open the bag. "That's so generous of you. He mentioned you were a beader." She slowly pulls out one earring and stops short. "Oh, Chelsea."

I'd pushed myself out of my comfort zone for this project. My mom had taught me traditional Haudenosaunee raised beadwork when I was younger, but I'd only worked with it a few times when making regalia. The strings of beads overlap and lift off whatever you stitch them on, giving pieces a three-dimensional element. I'd never used the technique on earrings, and it took me a while to get everything just right.

Kay puts a hand to her mouth. "These are—" She inhales deeply. "I've never seen earrings like this." She runs her fingers over the black velvet backing with green, white, and orange florals. "This reminds me of the details my mom beaded on my doll's clothes as a little girl." She sniffs.

"She's so talented, isn't she?" Wes chimes in with a proud smile.

Katie comes over and gasps. "You made these? They're spectacular."

"Can I see, sweetheart?" Bobby asks from his recliner.

Kay slides the hooks through her ears with trembling hands before walking to where he sits.

"Wow!" He sits up for a closer look. "They look like museum pieces." He tucks a stray lock of hair behind his wife's ear and smiles.

My stomach clenches with emotion.

Wes reaches over and gives my forearm a quick squeeze when no one's looking.

"How can I ever thank you enough?" Kay says, enveloping me in a hug. "I know how much time and skill goes into beadwork, especially this style."

"I wanted you to have something special, so that you knew how much you're loved and missed back home," I say softly.

Her arms tighten. "Thank you, Chelsea. What a gift you are."

Chapter 39

Chelsea

I hear a quiet *clunk* next to my ear and crack an eye open.

Wes sets a coffee cup on the nightstand and crouches next to the bed. "Good morning." He brushes the hair from my face with a smile.

"Morning." I blink the sleep from my eyes. "Did I sleep too late?"

"No, you're good." His adoring gaze gives me butterflies. "My dad and I were just starting breakfast."

"I'll come help." I push up on my side. "How'd you sleep?"

He chuckles. "Katie kicked me out around 4am. She said I flop around too much, so I spent a few hours on the couch."

"You do flip back and forth a lot." I hum happily as the first sip of coffee hits me. "But you hold on to me all night when you do it, so I can't get rid of you."

His jaw pops open in mock outrage. "Do I really?"

I giggle. "You do. But I like you, so it's OK."

Wes kisses me softly. "I missed you last night. I've been spoiled by our nights together on this trip."

"Your mom was trying to give us an out with sleeping arrangements," I remind him. "She said you could sleep wherever you wanted."

"I know, but I've already sprung this family visit on you. I don't want to turn it into a formal 'meet the parents' thing."

"I have, in fact, met your parents."

"You know what I mean." He gets to his feet. "You and I haven't even defined this yet."

But you love me? The question is on the tip of my tongue, but I don't know how I'd react to his response.

"Katie definitely sees right through us. She wouldn't stop interrogating me last night." He smiles.

"I would expect nothing less."

We're only in Green Bay for a couple of days, and our flight home is tomorrow. We spent the day visiting with Harrison family friends on the rez, including Helen and Edgar, who were Kay's first friends in Wisconsin.

Back at the house, we attempt to play cribbage together once more.

"You're looking for cards that add up to fifteen or thirty-one," Bobby says, counseling me as Wes deals.

I glare at my cards. "But last time I had thirty-one in my hand and I didn't get any points for that."

"You can only play thirty-one on the board, not count them in your hand after."

My eyes glaze over, and Kay chuckles.

"It took me a long time to get the hang of this game, too," she says. "People who grow up playing it are just built differently."

"You should take a cribbage board home with you," Katie suggests. "That way you two can practice." She winks at me and I smother a smile.

I luck into a few good hands and manage to make my inevitable defeat slightly less embarrassing.

"You're picking it up." Bobby smiles as we gather the cards and game tokens.

I guffaw. "You're very kind, but I'm not."

"Wes'll teach you. He's very patient."

I watch as Katie and her brother bundle up in their coats and head for the back door. "That he is."

"Would you like some tea, Chelsea?" Kay asks as she rummages in a cabinet.

"I'd love some, thank you. What can I help with?" I wander into the kitchen behind her.

"Why don't you grab some cookies from that container over there?" She gestures.

I pop the lid off and am hit with a mouthwatering aroma. "Mmm, chocolate chip."

The kettle whistles, and she picks it up. "I've been making them the same way for years. Got the recipe from a local woman I work with at the health center." She pours the water over tea bags in two mugs. "She gave me her banana bread recipe, too, but I wasn't ready to assimilate quite that much." She winks at me and I roar with laughter.

"How's it been, moving away from the rez?" I ask, arranging the cookies on a plate. "I'm not sure how well I'm adjusting to it."

We walk to the small, round table nestled in the corner of the cozy kitchen. From here I can see Wes, Katie, and their dad shooting around in the backyard while dodging snow piles. Wes scores a behind-the-back goal on Katie, and she shoves him in the shoulder while he laughs. I smile and tear my eyes away to look back at the table.

"Well, I didn't have much choice, so I suppose I just had to figure it out and get over it." Kay chews thoughtfully on the corner of a cookie. "But, obviously living so close to the Oneida community out here has been a huge blessing. It made it easier to raise my kids in some of the traditional ways, even though they're surrounded by white culture outside the home."

"You did well." I smile at her and gesture to the backyard. "I fill in the gaps for Wes every so often, but overall he's a great representative of Oneida Nation."

She sips her tea and studies me. "You two must be close."

I swallow nervously. "I care for him very much." It's the truth, but I'm feeling the urge to sweat.

"I can tell he cares for you, too, by the way he talks about you. And he looks at you with such admiration."

At that, I blush to the roots of my hair and quickly take a gulp of my beverage.

Kay chuckles. "I don't mean any harm. It's always been my dream that my kids find someone they match well with from the Haudenosaunee community."

I smile weakly.

"You're very lucky," she continues, "to find someone who feels that strongly about you. I had to run halfway across the country to find mine."

"Do you want to talk about why you left?" I ask gently.

She leans back in her chair and looks wistfully out the window. The room fills with silence that I'm in no hurry to fill.

"I assume you know a lot already if you know my family."

"I know a bit, but I know I'm missing the important parts of the story," I say, wrapping my hands around my warm mug.

Her eyes are unfocused. "The whole community protected Jeremy because of his powerful family. But no one protected me."

I reach across the table and grab her hand. "We failed you. So often we fail our women. We don't believe them." I squeeze gently. "I'm so sorry no one believed you."

She swallows. "He was careful not to leave bruises in visible places. His abuse was more often in words than actions, so I couldn't prove anything."

I listen quietly.

"My parents encouraged me to stick it out. That he would settle down with marriage, and that it would be such a benefit to me to marry into that family." She looks down. "I was so angry with them. I begged my mom to help me find a way out of the engagement. Looking back on it now, I think she just didn't know what to do, but I couldn't wait for her to figure it out."

"So, what did you do?" I ask.

"One morning I got up before the sun. I left a letter for my parents and just started driving. I wasn't entirely sure where I was going yet, but I knew I had to get far enough away from him that he couldn't find me."

My tea is getting cold, but I can't bring myself to look away from her for an instant.

"I'd met an Oneida woman from Wisconsin at a pow wow years before when I was on the dancing circuit. Helen, who you met today," she says. "We'd talked from time to time. I called her from a pay phone in Pennsylvania and asked if I could stay with her for a little while. She didn't think twice before saying yes."

I smile. "What a good friend."

"Yes, I'm very fortunate to have met her, and to still be able to call her a friend today. She loves Wes and Katie like they're her own. She was here the night Wes was drafted into the NLL."

I wrap a second hand around hers. "Your story is inspiring to me. I got out of a relationship over a year ago. I didn't have to endure nearly as much as you did, but he was so hateful in how he spoke to me." I take a breath. "He loved to put me down and cut me with little comments about my appearance, my career, whatever he could think of that he knew would hurt me."

She swears under her breath before looking at me intently. "Beautiful girl, that is not a man. He's not fit to tie your moccasins."

I smile warmly. "This is where I'd make a joke about him being white, but I think I've got the wrong audience."

She laughs heartily. "The audience understands there are exceptions to the rule. But I want you to know something."

I nod.

"I'm really proud of you," she says. "You were brave enough to walk away from a bad man. You loved yourself enough to do that."

I bite my lip, feeling emotional. "I've never felt brave in my life."

"But you were. And now you have a better life with a lot of potential left to come. That's incredible."

"Thank you," I whisper. "It doesn't feel that way sometimes."

"That's normal. He wants you to feel confused and lost without him. But you're not. You're finding your way."

A shout draws our attention to the window, where we see Wes and Katie fighting for a loose ball.

"Those two," Kay says fondly. "Always competing."

We watch them for a minute before I ask a question that's been on my mind for years. "Do you think you'd ever come back?"

She looks over at me with misty eyes. "I forgave my parents years ago. I couldn't keep that resentment in my heart any longer. But I don't know how to break out of this exile and admit I miss them. I miss home."

Tears prick at the corners of my eyes at her pain. "Oh, Kay." I push away from the table and hug her tightly.

"Thank you," she says. "Seeing you has brought a lot of emotions to the surface for me. I love my community here, but I've missed so much since I left."

"Would you like me to talk to your mom for you?" I ask. "I bet she'd be thrilled to see you again and meet the kids."

"I'm not sure yet," she says. "I'd understand if Wes wanted to meet her. He's an adult, and he lives so close. But I need a little more time for myself."

"That makes sense. Take all the time you need." I smile at her.

The back door creaks open, and the rest of the Harrison family enters the house with a tremendous amount of noise.

"You don't play fair!" Katie complains.

"You want me to take it easy on you?" Wes teases.

"I believe you're specifically *not* supposed to fight while playing the Medicine Game," Bobby quips.

"Yeah, don't let Creator hear you," I say with a smile, watching Wes walk by with an unfamiliar flicker of hope in my stomach.

Chapter 40

Wes

I feel life pulling us apart as soon as we land in Buffalo.

I reach for her hand as we walk through baggage claim, but she gives me a quick squeeze before letting go. She's quiet on the drive back to my place, and I'm trying not to spiral about what's going on in her head.

I've had a week with her all to myself, and it hurts like hell to give her up again.

"Did you want to come inside for a bit?" I ask as I load her bags into her car.

She shakes her head. "I need to get back and start on laundry."

I have a washer and dryer, but don't point that out. "No problem. Lacrosse on Thursday?"

She shifts from foot to foot. "I'm not sure. I'll probably be working late since I was out last week."

I swallow painfully. "Makes sense. Well, if you wind up being available, just let me know. Sawyer and I will be there at the usual time."

"OK."

I lean down to kiss her goodbye. "Is everything all right?"

Her chest rises and falls quickly. "I'm actually not feeling all that great."

My brows furrow. "Come lay down. I'll get you some water."

She sucks in a breath. "I should go."

A five-alarm fire alarm is sounding in my head, but I know that insisting she stay and talk to me will only pour gasoline on the situation. "Let me know how you're doing later, OK?"

She nods and squeezes my hand tightly.

"Hey, man! How was your loved-up vaca—?" Sawyer's face falls when he sees me enter the kitchen. "What happened?" He looks behind me. "Where's Chelsea?"

I fill a glass with water and sit across from him in the living room. "She headed home. Lots to do before work tomorrow."

He nods slowly. "I can imagine. How was your trip?"

I blow out an exhale. "Amazing. Perfect."

"But?"

"All good things must come to an end."

"Practice is not as much fun without Chelsea." Sawyer shoots the ball low, and it skips into the net.

"Tell me about it. I'm sick of dealing with your trick shots all the time." I whip the ball towards the goal.

"I'm here too, you know," Zeke protests. "And I'm lonely down in Cattaraugus without my training buddy from last season."

I cringe. "Sorry, man. I should drive down more often."

"Maybe it would be easier for Chelsea to meet us there?" Sawyer suggests.

Zeke raises an eyebrow. "You like her or something?"

Sawyer's eyes dart over to mine. "No. I just enjoy the ass-kicking she gives us once a week."

"Humph." Zeke watches him.

My phone rings that night as I'm brushing my teeth, Chelsea's photo popping up on the screen. I spit out my toothpaste and swipe to answer.

"Hey."

"Hey." Her voice is hesitant.

I miss you. I'm losing my mind wondering what's going on with you. "How's it going?"

"Good."

Silence.

My heart pounds, and I feel distinctly queasy.

"Can I say something without you freaking out?"

"When have I ever freaked out about anything?" I ask.

She harrumphs. "Fair point."

"What's going on, Chels?"

She sighs. "*I'm* freaking out."

"I had a feeling. Can I see your face?"

I stifle my exhale of relief as she sends me a video chat request.

"There's my girl." My face softens into a smile. "Best thing I've seen all day."

She exhales with a shudder. "Wes."

"What's the matter, baby?"

"I—" She covers her mouth with her hand.

It takes every ounce of self-control not to get in my car and go to her. "Tell me."

She gnaws her lip. "Our trip was the happiest I've been in a long, long time. And I'm scared."

I swallow. "I'm scared, too, if that helps." *Because you have my heart and everything you need to smash it.* "What are you afraid of?"

She takes a breath. "I'm afraid of being too much for you. Afraid of you tiring of my baggage and moving on. You've become such an important part of my life, and the thought of losing you—" Her voice fails and she clears her throat.

"Sweetheart, do I seem like a man who's tiring of you?"

"Maybe not now, but you might."

"You're just going to have to trust me, then," I say softly. "My dad spent years convincing my mom to believe that his love for her was real and not going anywhere. I've trained at the feet of the master."

She smiles weakly. "I suppose you have."

"Have I ever given you a reason to doubt me?"

She shakes her head.

"Then why do you?"

Her eyes flutter closed. "It's not you I'm doubting, not anymore. I think I need to learn to believe in myself. To trust *myself*."

"And how can we make that happen?"

She's silent for a few moments. "I have some deadlines to meet on important goals, and I want to prove to myself I can do that."

"Do you need some space? I know I'm a lot."

Her smile brightens slightly. "You're not. But yes, some space would help."

"I'm leaving tomorrow for a road game. I'll be back on Sunday if you need anything, but take as much time as you need."

"I think it'll be longer than that."

"That's OK. You know where to find me."

She sniffs. "How do you trust *me* so much?"

"Because you're worth the risk of getting my heart broken."

Chapter 41

Chelsea

Museum traffic is slow today, so Natalie pulls me into her office for a strategy meeting. The busy summer season will be here before we know it, and we need to finalize our exhibit plans.

"Now that you've been here for a few months, I'd love to hear your thoughts on how the gallery is laid out, any potential for new exhibits or artifacts, whatever comes to mind." She taps her pencil on a notebook. "This is a good time of year to think about moving smaller exhibits around to keep things fresh."

I grab a brochure with the current gallery arrangement and mull it over. "Right now the gallery presents a chronological walk through Haudenosaunee history. It's centered around the past, with some more modern exhibits." I begin sketching in my own notes. "We could consider shifting towards the story of the people's ongoing resilience and joy in the face of their changing world."

She watches as I pencil in different groupings of items.

"At Shako:wi, for example, we present basket making as a tale of survival when land and resources were scarce, not just as a traditional craft. That added detail gives the artifacts a lot of context and paints a story of strength and creativity. I think that's missing from some of the exhibits here." I look up at my boss, hoping I haven't offended her.

Natalie leans forward. "You're absolutely right. I love what we have here, but it can feel a bit...stuffy. Textbook."

"It needs some Indigenous joy." I smile. "Doing an exhibit exchange with another Haudenosaunee cultural center could infuse some color into things, and give the other nation access to artifacts they've never been able to showcase."

The corner of her mouth quivers. "Have you considered doing this for a living?"

"I thought I was?"

She laughs. "You are. But you could be a museum director one day. You've got the eye for this, plus the lived experience that most directors don't have."

I flush. "That's really nice of you to say."

She writes in her notebook and tears out the page. "I know you have your Indigenous Studies degree, but you should consider getting a Master's in something with museums." She passes me the paper. "The University at Buffalo has a Critical Museum Studies program that's really excellent, and would give you an advantage down the road."

I blink at the information she's written. I never imagined myself going back for an advanced degree, but the idea has my brain humming.

"Just something to think about." Natalie smiles and takes another look at my proposed gallery rearrangement. "The Museum has some funds for employee professional development, so we could likely help you with a Master's if you go that route."

I feel like tap dancing across her office. "I'll look into it and let you know. This is really appealing."

"Speaking of funds," she says with a grin, "how would you feel about a promotion?"

My eyes widen. "What do you mean?"

"The museum's funding has stabilized in the new year, so I can advocate for bumping you up to the title and pay I wanted to hire you at originally." She makes some notes. "I wanted to make sure you're still interested in growing your career here, and if so, I'll make the case to Human Resources."

My heart races with unexpected delight. "Yes. I would like that very much."

"I'm so glad to hear it." Her eyes dance. "I'll keep you posted on how the approval process goes, but I expect I'll be able to offer you a position as Assistant Gallery Curator."

I told Wes I needed time to take care of some things, and I'm holding myself to that. But all I can think about is sharing my job news with the person who makes me happiest.

Me: Guess who's in the running for a promotion?

The Bear: As my girlfriend? You've had the job for months, but I probably should've told you that

The Bear: Wait, you mean at work?! What happened?!

Me: You can't say things like that and just move on

The Bear: Did you get promoted??

Me: Not yet, but Nat's recommending me for a position as Assistant Gallery Curator

The Bear: I'm running out of ways to express how freaking proud of you I am, and how lucky I feel to have you in my life

Me: So, I'm your girlfriend?

The Bear: I feel like that's obvious, but I should pretend it's not so you can claim it was your idea all along

I rub my tired eyes later that night, the glow of the laptop screen the only light in my bedroom. I'm working through a list of to-dos this week, including researching the Master's program at UB and upcoming tryout dates for future Haudenosaunee national teams. I want to finish at least one more item before I head to bed.

Our Wisconsin trip has cemented for me that Wes is for real. He's all in with me, but I've continued to play it safe. I've been so worried about letting our relationship distract me from my dreams, as I've done with other men.

But what if I simply didn't let it? What if I let his endless support of my goals propel me instead?

I hover over the Submit button on registering for the upcoming WMSL season. Playing summer lacrosse lights me up, and living in Cattaraugus gives me a short commute over the Peace Bridge to my team in Ontario. I played well last year, and I know I've gotten sharper from my time training with Wes and Sawyer, as well as the experience at the World Games.

A familiar voice in my head tells me not to bother. That the team doesn't need me, and I barely made the national team last fall. *Come to think, that voice sounds a lot like—*

I jump in my chair when my phone buzzes. I squint at the time and groan when I see it's nearly midnight.

> **Brock:** I'm in Albany this weekend. Any interest in catching up?

This fucking guy.

I don't know why he's texting me lately, and I do not care. I am, however, really annoyed that it's happening.

Tapping the Block Caller button feels extra good at this time of night.

Chapter 42

Tew^hníslya'ks

Split Days / March

Chelsea

The Outlaws are playing in Rochester tonight, and Genny is coming over to watch the game with us. I went to the gym and showered earlier, so I settle into my favorite spot in the corner of the couch.

Mackenzie wanders out of her room. "Should we get the snacks and drinks started?" she asks.

"Hell yes," I answer enthusiastically, scrolling through my social media feed. "Ooh, Outlaws arrival photos!"

"Wait for me!" she calls from the kitchen, emerging a minute later with two glasses of cold wine. "Let's see 'em," she commands, handing me a glass.

I pull up the Outlaws' latest post so we can ogle the players dressed up and arriving at the arena.

"Sawyer fucking Lane," Mackenzie sighs as we drool over the sight of him in a light gray suit, his navy shirt unbuttoned at the top and his brown hair perfectly mussed.

"The man doesn't miss," I agree, taking one last look before swiping to the next photo.

"Zeke looks nice," she says, "but we really need Genny to take him shopping for a new suit."

"Agreed. It's nice, but he wears it every week." I swipe again and nearly choke on my next sip of wine.

"Holy shit," Mackenzie whistles. "Wes has upped his game."

He's played it safe with his arrival outfits since he made the starting roster, tending to favor all black items with no styling. Once he started adding a beanie to spice things up, I knew I had to step in and save him from himself. Before our trip, I went through his closet and pulled out some different combinations for him to consider, and it seems he took my advice.

He's wearing a black shirt and blazer, but he paired them with burgundy slacks and a belt. He added a couple of simple gold chains and low-top white sneakers. He has one hand in his pocket, and the other carries his stick. His beard is tidy, and his hair is casually pushed back. He looks so good I'm considering changing my plans to include jumping him as soon as he's back home.

"Hot damn," I breathe, drinking him in.

"Does he have a girlfriend we don't know about?" Mackenzie ponders, taking a drink. "Or maybe he's getting style pointers from the other guys."

"That must be it," I murmur, reluctantly swiping away from his picture. Sadly, that's the end of the photo carousel, and we both grumble in displeasure.

"Hi, gals!" Genny's voice rings out as she enters the house. She's wearing Zeke's jersey t-shirt with a pair of jeans and is looking adorable, as usual. "I brought stuff to make burgers."

When Mackenzie heads towards the kitchen, I covertly pull up the Outlaws post again and save Wes' picture to my phone. That one is definitely going to become a new favorite.

I hear the sisters tittering over the arrival photos, so I take the opportunity to send Wes a quick message.

> **Me:** You look really hot tonight, by the way

My heart races when the message almost immediately shows as read. I must've caught him before he went out for warmups. We've texted a bit over the past few weeks, but haven't met up. I've stayed focused on getting my life together, but damn, I miss him.

I'm gnawing on my bottom lip when Genny comes up from behind and startles me.

"Jesus, Gen," I squeak, nearly dropping my phone. "Why are you sneaking up on people?"

She laughs, reaching around me to place the half-empty wine bottle on the coffee table. "Why are you so on edge?" She sits next to me and pours herself a glass.

My phone buzzes, and I quickly tap to open Wes' message.

The Bear: Thanks. I had a smoking hot stylist help me out recently.

Me: Lucky girl. Does she get to help you out of those clothes later, too?

"What's The Bear up to tonight?" Mackenzie brings over a bag of chips for the group, popping a couple in her mouth.

"Oh, you know, Bear stuff," I respond nonchalantly, looking back down at my phone when the next notification comes in.

The Bear: She sure can. The door is always open for her

I bite my knuckle.

"He must not be playing tonight if he's sending you sexy texts." Genny raises an eyebrow at me, gesturing to my phone. "Or maybe he's playing out west?"

"He's an international man of mystery," I deadpan with a shrug, fingers tapping out a quick response to Wes.

Me: A tempting offer

Me: Have a good game, Rookie. I'll be watching.

Mackenzie huffs. "You have *got* to tell us who he is, Chels!" She looks over at Genny for backup.

Genny cradles her wine glass, looking thoughtful. "What's the real reason you don't want anyone to know who he is? Is he a jerk? Do the guys hate him?"

"No, he's very kind," I reply softly.

"Then what's the problem?" Genny continues. "I know you're killing it as a badass single lady, but you two have been talking and hooking up since last summer. You wouldn't give him the time of day if you didn't like him."

I shut down my phone screen and toss it onto the coffee table with a sigh. "I *do* like him. An awful lot."

"Now we're getting somewhere." Genny leans forward. "You like him, but you don't want to mess up the progress you've made since you've been single."

I wince. Genny is way too good at reading people. "No," I reply completely unconvincingly.

"Wait a minute." Mackenzie sits up. "Did you *both* want to keep this, whatever it is, a secret?"

I brace for impact. "No. It's always been me."

The two of them erupt with overlapping questions and admonitions.

"He wants a real relationship with you, and you don't?"

"So you mean we should've been rooting for The Bear all this time?!"

I groan and reach for the remote, putting on the pregame coverage.

"Let us meet him," Genny pleads. "We can help you figure out if this is a guy you should be getting serious with."

"Who said anything about getting serious?" I feel uncomfortably warm.

She fixes me with a withering look. "If this were just casual sex, you would not be on the phone with him every day. You would not be reading books together. You would not be grinning like a preteen with a crush every time he texts you!"

Goddammit. I feel an unexpected prick of tears behind my eyes and quickly get to my feet, looking for something to pretend to be doing.

I hear Genny gasp. "You *really* like him."

"I don't want to talk about it," I sniff, staring into the fridge.

"Chels," she says slowly, "do you love him?"

Why the hell am I getting emotional? I close the refrigerator in frustration, brushing a tear from my eye before coming back to the couch. "I'd rather not have this conversation, if you don't mind."

"OK," Genny says softly. "But I'm going to check back in with you about this another time."

I grumble.

"Because you deserve to be happy. And I think The Bear might just make you really, really happy."

I reach for the remote and turn up the volume as game coverage begins, trying to appear noncommittal.

I've been keeping my feelings for Wes caged for so long, and now they're spilling onto the surface. My emotions are pressing against my throat, desperate to be on the outside.

"You OK?" Mackenzie asks at halftime, leaning over the back of the couch. "You don't look great."

"I'm not feeling well," I say with a grimace. "I feel like I'm going to puke."

The sisters jump into action, ushering me into the bathroom with a hair tie and water just in case. I sit back against the wall, my breathing shaky. Genny peeks in the door.

"Hey." She kneels next to me and holds her hand against my forehead. "You're clammy. I'm worried."

"I'm OK." I smile weakly. "Go watch the game. I'm going to lie down and see if that helps."

She frowns. "I'm going to keep checking on you, got it?"

"Yes, Mom."

She helps me up and guides my unsteady feet to my room, where I immediately crawl under the covers. I'm breathing through my racing heart rate when my phone rings.

"Hello?"

"Why does it sound like you're in a cave?" Jess asks.

"I'm under the covers feeling like shit."

"Oh no." Her tone switches to concern. "What's going on? You don't need to talk to me if you're not feeling well."

I haven't heard her voice since I was home for Christmas, and her familiar cadence stirs up something in me.

"I'm all messed up, Jess. I don't know what's wrong with me. I wish you were here."

"Do you want me to come out? I could trade shifts with someone." She pauses. "Did something happen with Wes?"

Queasiness hits me again, and I groan.

"No, he's—" I stop to focus on breathing. "He's great. He's so perfect it makes me sick. Possibly literally."

"Have you told your friends about him yet?"

"No," I squeak.

She sighs. "I'm coming out there."

"Jess," I moan.

"Do you want me to tell them?"

"*No.*"

"It doesn't take a genius to see you two are head over heels for each other. He told me about your Wisconsin trip." I hear the smile in her voice. "Those earrings you made for Kay are out of this world."

"He told me he loved me." The words rush out, and as soon as they leave my mouth I feel how much they've been weighing on me.

"Oh, Chels," Jess whispers. "Of course he does. What did you say?"

"Nothing. We'd been drinking, and he was falling asleep. He doesn't even remember saying it."

"But he still meant it. I bet he's been thinking it every day."

I swallow.

"You have to tell him," she says. "You can't keep that inside. No wonder you feel like shit."

Dammit. She's right.

"Do you love him?" she asks.

"You're the second person to ask me that tonight," I mutter.

"Well, do you?"

Warmth floods my body as I close my eyes and picture Wes. Thinking of him fills me with contentment, excitement, and peace. The waves of unease settle in my stomach, and I blow out a shaky breath.

"I might."

"Then tell him. He's waiting for you to say it first, because he doesn't want to scare you away. Release yourself from this self-imposed prison."

"Do you think I'm ready?" I ask quietly.

"I know you are. Now, go get your man."

Chapter 43

Wes

The Outlaws are in a fight for our playoff lives.

After winning the championship last year, we're unexpectedly on the cusp of missing the postseason. Injuries to our goaltender and faceoff specialist have snake-bitten us, and we dropped a long stretch of games mid-season. Tomorrow night we play the Albany River Hawks, and it's a game we must win if we want to stay in the hunt for one of the final playoff spots.

"I'm impressed you're out past your bedtime, Jammer," Zeke teases.

"Trust me, it's not my first choice," Jamie deadpans, reaching for a bowling ball. "But I figured you three could use some levity the night before a big game."

He approaches our lane, pulls his arm back, and releases. The ball rolls down the center for a few hopeful seconds before careening loudly into the gutters.

"You have no idea how much it pleases me that you're terrible at something." Sawyer grins. "It's refreshing."

"I'm bad at a lot of things," Jamie says. "Trust me."

"Especially bowling." I smile as he sits down next to me with a withering look.

"How are you doing, man?" he asks, reaching for water while Zeke chooses his ball. "I feel like I haven't had a chance to talk to you much this season."

"It's been a whirlwind. Hopefully, I'm keeping Sawyer out of your hair, though."

He chuckles. "He's up in Six Nations all the time, regardless, so I can't seem to shake him."

Zeke picks off a few pins and sizes up the remainder.

Jamie nudges me. "How are you feeling about playing Albany tomorrow?"

"It'll be a tough game, but I think we've got—"

"Not that."

"Oh. That."

I figured Jamie had forgotten our pissed-off pact to dish out a bit of justice on Chelsea's ex the next time we played. We didn't have a chance in Utica, but we play his team twice in the next month.

"What're we talking about?" Sawyer plops down on the other side of me as Zeke throws his second ball.

Jamie catches my eye.

"You know Brock Pelletier?" I ask.

"Yeah, I've played on Team Canada with him. A few times in juniors, too."

"We had a run-in with him in Utica," Jamie says.

Sawyer narrows his eyes. "What happened?"

"You're up, Lanes." Zeke taps him on the shoulder as he passes.

"He tried to mess with Chelsea," I say. "He waited for her after a game and acted like a creep. They used to date."

Sawyer's jaw twitches. "Honestly, I can't stand that guy. He's a good player, but he's full of himself and treats staff members like shit. He's always nasty to the trainers and custodians, and I think that says a lot about a person."

"It would be a shame if he tripped and fell into my fist tomorrow night, is all I'm saying." Jamie's eyes twinkle.

"Am I going to have to clean up after another of your scrums?" Zeke asks with a smile.

"Almost certainly."

My pocket buzzes, and I check my messages as Sawyer takes his turn.

Chelsea: Any chance you could finagle a ticket for my dad tomorrow? He'd love to see the game

Me: Absolutely. I'll call the ticket office when it opens

Chelsea: Thanks. I really appreciate it

"What did he do to Chelsea?" Sawyer asks later, his voice low as Jamie and Zeke debate over scoring.

"He punches down, as you've noticed. He tried to get under her skin about being selected for the national team after she took a few years off lacrosse. Among other things."

"I'll remember that." He chugs some water. "Is she coming tomorrow night?"

I shake my head. "She's not, but her dad is."

"Good. We'll have to show him a good time. You doing OK?"

"I'm doing OK. But I miss her."

"I miss her, *too*."

Chapter 44

Chelsea

"I want you to come with us, Chels," Genny says with a frown as she does her makeup in the bathroom mirror. "Do you think anyone might be selling tickets at the arena and we could get you in?"

"I can call my ticket scalper," Mackenzie volunteers, fastening earrings and fluffing her long dark hair.

I bite my lip, ready to burst with my secret. "Well, actually…"

The sisters turn to look at me.

Genny's eyes light up. "What did you do?"

My teeth sink in so deeply I worry I've drawn blood. "I got a ticket."

"You did?!" Mackenzie asks with delight.

I nod. "Wes got one for me."

Genny holds my gaze. "Is this—" A grin plays at the corners of her mouth. "Is this a *date?*"

A giggle sneaks past my lips, and Genny drops her mascara wand.

"Are you and Wes—"

"—finally fucking?" Mackenzie cuts her off.

I burst out laughing, and Genny smacks her sister on the arm.

"Answer the question!" she demands, retrieving her mascara so she can point it at me. "Is this a date?"

I shrug and reach for my toothbrush. "I don't know that you could call it a *date*."

"But you're going to the game to see him?"

I'm doing a horrible job of smothering the ear to ear grin trying to break out across my face. "I am."

"Thank Creator. I never thought I'd see the day." Genny grabs me and jumps up and down. "Does he know?"

I smirk. "I told him the ticket was for my dad."

"You sneaky bitch."

I nearly choke on my toothpaste at Mackenzie's comment.

"This is going to be *so fun*!" Genny squeals. "We need to get you looking hot."

"Indigenous WAG aesthetic," Mackenzie says. "Genny's got this down pat."

"Oh, my gosh." Genny zips out of the bathroom and towards my closet. "Let me see what you've got to work with."

Half an hour and numerous piles of clothes later, I feel like a new woman. A very *sexy* new woman.

"Holy heck." Mackenzie whistles. "Wes is going to lose his mind when he sees you."

The girls helped me pair a black leather miniskirt with an orange ribbed knit tank and black blazer. My hair is pulled into a high ponytail to show off my shoulder-skimming, geometric copper earrings. Genny takes over my makeup, painting the softest of smokey eyes alongside a peachy gloss on my lips.

I feel beautiful, confident, and unapologetically me. It's perfect.

We share a squeal together before rushing to finish getting ready.

"I hope those don't hurt after a couple of hours." Genny eyes my heeled ankle boots as we pile into the car. "Otherwise, Wes is going to be carrying you home."

"It's the perfect plan." Mackenzie winks and backs out of the driveway.

My friends try to pry information out of me on the drive to Buffalo, but I keep my answers to a minimum.

"Does Wes know you like him?" Genny asks.

I smile. *You could say that*. "He does. Kind of."

"We need details, girl!"

"Let me talk to him first. Then I can fill you in."

She huffs with impatience.

"I hate to kill the mood, but the Outlaws are playing the River Hawks tonight." Mackenzie's eyes meet mine in the rearview mirror. "Are you worried about seeing Brock?"

"I'm not, to be honest. I blocked his number the other night. Did I tell you he's been texting me?"

Genny whips around. "*No*. You have a lot of catching up to do, young lady."

I shoot Wes a message as we're pulling into the parking garage.

> **Me:** Good luck tonight, Rookie. I'll be watching

> **The Bear:** Thanks. I hope your dad has a great time

> **The Bear:** I'm trying to be a tough guy and not say I miss you, but I miss you

> **Me:** I miss you, too. I'll see you soon, OK?

> **The Bear:** I can't wait

"So, uh," Genny says, "what happened with The Bear?"

I tuck my phone into my blazer pocket. "I'm ready to move on from that. It was always meant to be a short-lived thing."

"It's been almost a year," Mackenzie points out as we walk towards the arena. "Not exactly short-lived."

"And you really cared about him," Genny adds softly.

"I did. I do." I swallow nervously. "But it's time to move on to something better."

Genny pulls me to her for a warm squeeze. "Wes is absolutely the best choice."

I bite the inside of my cheek. Lying to my friends makes me feel like crap. I'm ready to be open with them, but I need to talk to him first.

The Hideout is buzzing with energy. Fans eagerly pour through the doors, decked out in every item of team merchandise they own. Little kids rush ahead of their parents wearing orange foam fingers and cowboy hats. The team store is overflowing with visitors as we pass it on the escalators.

We trek to our seats armed with bottles of water and cardboard dishes of nachos from the concession stands.

"Let's go down to the glass for warmups," Mackenzie suggests, waggling her eyebrows. "We need to motivate the troops with you two hotties."

"I'm nervous," I whisper as we make our way down the risers.

Genny squeezes my hand. "That was how I felt last year when I was trying to meet up with Zeke after the Championship." Our heels clang on the steps as we descend. "Wes is going to be so happy to see you."

We pass Dusty, the Outlaws' desert opossum mascot, on our way towards the floor. He stops dead in his tracks when he sees us.

"Dusty." Genny says flatly.

The mascot leaps into a nearby aisle and out of our way.

I look back and forth. "Do you two have history?"

"Something like that," Genny mutters.

Dusty runs across and hides behind me.

"How on earth do you have beef with an opossum?" I laugh and boop the mascot on the tip of his pink nose.

He wraps me in a hug, and Genny scoffs.

"Oh, sure. You like *her*."

"I hate to break up this touching scene," Mackenzie interjects, "but warmups are starting."

"Bye, Dusty." I blow him a kiss, and we continue on.

The Outlaws run out from behind the bench, full of energy. Some of the players immediately scoop up balls and toss them to kids behind the glass, smiling and waving. The goalie jogs into the net and locks in, blocking shots from teammates.

Zeke, Wes, and Jamie pass to each other before taking turns shooting on net. Jamie notices us and says something to the other two, nodding towards the glass. Zeke sees Genny and lights up, jogging towards our position.

Wes turns and his eyes lock onto mine. My stomach drops somewhere around my ankles, and I smile nervously. Surprise, joy, and confusion flash across his face as he walks over.

Mackenzie grabs me and dramatically sweeps her arm in front of my body. "Look at her!" she yells over the glass to Wes.

I elbow her in the stomach.

His eyes drag from my face down past the sliver of exposed skin on my abdomen and over my legs. He trips over his feet while checking me out and looks at the ceiling in embarrassment.

I smile broadly, my heart racing at the sight of him.

"I'd be willing to bet Wes hasn't looked at another woman since he met you," Mackenzie says.

I blush when his eyes meet mine again. I hold my palm up to the glass.

He looks longingly at it but doesn't move. "What are you doing here?" he calls over the noise of the crowd.

"I'm—"

Genny and Mackenzie cut me off. "She's here to see you!" they yell.

Zeke whips his head around to look between me and Wes with surprise. He says something I can't hear, but Wes doesn't answer. He's too busy staring at me like he's seeing me for the first time.

Jamie jogs over and pokes them with his stick, angling his head towards the goal. It was time to continue with warmups.

Wes nods before raising his hand and placing it against mine on the other side of the glass. We stay like that for a few seconds before Zeke taps him on the helmet.

Wes raises his hand to his ear. "Call me," he mouths.

I smile and nod, and he jogs away.

Chapter 45

Wes

B rock slithers over to me during warmups while I'm stretching my quads.

"I remember you," he says without looking at me.

I ignore him, looking out into the crowd to where the girls are giggling and looking at one of their phones. *Probably perusing the arrival photos*, I think with a smile.

"You're with Chelsea, right?"

I turn to look at him, hatred infusing my veins. "I don't believe that's any concern of yours."

He chuckles. "Maybe not. I can't get her to return my calls anymore."

That's my girl.

Sawyer comes over to stretch with me, and Brock thankfully moves on.

"I'm taking every chance to trip him tonight," he says, glaring at Brock's departing figure.

"Same."

"Is that Chelsea I see over there?" He playfully elbows me. "I thought she wasn't coming."

I grin. "It is. I'm not sure what happened, but she's in the seat I set aside for her dad."

"Maybe she wanted to surprise you?"

"She's good at that."

Once the game starts, Brock makes a beeline for me at every opportunity on the floor.

"I can't blame you for getting with Chels," Brock says as I cover him in the defensive zone. "She's real cute, especially if you ignore her a little bit."

I grit my teeth and hold myself in check.

"You seem a little too nice for her taste," he says as we battle for a loose ball in the corner. "I'm surprised you're still hanging around."

I kick his shin and pretend it's an accident.

The River Hawks are playing tough. They're just as desperate for a playoff spot as we are, and our two teams have never liked each other. My blood pressure continues to rise the longer the game goes on, especially since we're behind on the scoreboard. Brock's asshole powers seem to grow with every Hawks goal.

"Don't let him get to you," Jamie says quietly as we line up for a faceoff. "That's his objective."

"I know. I'm trying."

"Go hit something at the gym after this, instead." He winks.

By the fourth quarter, we're losing by three goals and can't get out of our own way. We keep missing passes and taking bad penalties, and we're running out of time.

Zeke's pass to Sawyer gets picked off *again*, so we're down in our own end *again*. I'm so sick of defending Brock, but we're right back on top of each other. Again.

He's wearing on me, and it's taking more and more effort to keep myself from taking cheap shots against him.

Brock cross-checks me near the net as we monitor the passes cycling around us. I accidentally-on-purpose hit his stomach with the butt end of my stick.

He grumbles as we jostle for position. "I have to admit, Harrison, you're not who I would've guessed she'd go for after me."

I intercept a pass aimed at Brock and launch the ball past the restraining line. Unfortunately, there's a River Hawk player nearby to chase it down before it crosses the midline for an over and back.

"I really could not care less what you think about me, man."

He ignores me. "You'll get tired of her soon, I assume. Not enough going on upstairs with that one."

"You talk a lot about a girl you claim you don't like."

Brock finally catches a pass and spins around, sending the ball between our goalie's legs and scoring right in front of me.

I'm accidentally knocked down by an Outlaws defender in the process, tumbling into the crease feeling pissed off and ready to be done with this shit. I plant my hand on the ground to get to my feet when I feel a searing pain.

"Whoops. Sorry about that." Brock's saccharine tone washes over me as I watch his sneaker painfully dig into the back of my hand. I glance up to find him smirking at me, and I. Have. Had. It.

My left hand is pinned under his foot, so I swing with my right and make contact with his groin.

He doubles over, his stick tumbling to the floor. I gratefully pull my hand free, shaking out the pain.

"Oops," I say pointedly as I walk by him.

His eyes turn dark as he swears, still bent in half with discomfort.

"Sorry in advance, Jammer," I apologize as we approach the bench.

"For what?" he asks.

"That jagoff isn't going to take—"

I feel a sharp slash across the back of my head before everything goes black.

Chapter 46

Chelsea

I had never experienced a living nightmare before seeing Wes crumble to the ground and not get back up.

I gasp when Brock, clearly seeing red from the skirmish after his goal, stomps over and uses his stick to cross-check a defenseless Wes in the back of the head. I fly to my feet in horror, watching as he collapses to the turf like a sack of potatoes.

"Oh, my God!" Genny exclaims, jumping up next to me.

It all happens within moments that feel like hours. Jamie winds up and clocks Brock, sending his helmet flying off. Gloves go airborne as the two of them begin trading punches. Brock is considerably taller, but Jamie is faster, broader, and absolutely furious. Another River Hawk player attempts to go after Jamie, but Zeke grabs him by the jersey and hauls him out of the way like a petulant child.

"Why is he not getting up?" I rasp, watching as Sawyer gets to his knees next to Wes. He frantically motions to the training staff to come onto the turf, even as fisticuff chaos swirls around them.

She grabs my hand and squeezes tightly. "He's OK. Let's give it a few more breaths, and he's going to be OK."

Wes isn't moving at all. He's deathly still, and I want to puke.

"He's OK, Chels. He's probably just stunned."

"He's not moving," I whisper.

Out of the corner of my eye, I see Brock's feet go up as Jamie slams him into the turf. The crowd roars at his victory, but I'm too busy trying not to have a heart attack.

A trainer I recognize is on the floor. She gently touches Wes' arm and shoulder. He fell on his right side, his helmet popping halfway off his head.

The refs have broken up Jamie and Brock and sent them to the locker room, but Jamie is refusing to go until they let him check on Wes. He takes a knee next to him, and Coach Travis jumps down from the bench to join him.

"Gen." My voice trembles.

She continues clutching my arm as The Hideout falls silent.

"He's breathing," Mackenzie says, answering a question I was too afraid to ask. "I can see his chest rising and falling."

After what feels like an hour, I notice his head turn slightly to the side.

I let out a shaky breath I didn't realize I was holding. "Did he just move his head?"

"He did. I saw it, too," Genny says.

Wes is facing away from me, so I can't see if his eyes are open, but I notice Jamie smile and start talking to him.

The crowd tentatively starts clapping as Wes rolls slowly onto his back, becoming louder and louder as the trainer helps him sit up.

"Thank God." I blink back tears as Jamie and Sawyer each grab one of his hands and carefully pull him to his feet. He hooks his arms around their shoulders and slowly begins to walk towards the locker room.

"Do you want to go see him?" Genny asks, watching curiously as I wipe my eyes.

"Can I do that?"

"Let's see if I can sweet talk my way into the locker room."

"I'll check online for any details that get released," Mackenzie offers.

"Thanks, Kenz. We'll be back," Genny says.

Genny leads me on a winding path through the arena, and I hope she knows where she's going because I'm too distracted to be keeping track of our twists and turns.

"I'm honestly not sure we can get there from here, but let's try." She squeezes my hand and tugs me towards the room where friends and family can meet players after the game. It connects to the backstage of the Hideout, which houses the locker room and training facilities.

The room is locked since the game is still being played, but we track down a passing security guard.

"I'm sorry, Miss. I can't let you back there," he apologizes. "You'll have to wait until the game's over and your player exits."

"Are you sure you can't, just, let us in? It's an emergency." Genny's voice is thick with sweetness and desperation.

He shakes his head. "I really can't. I'd lose my job."

We find a bench nearby, and I pull my knees up to my chest, hugging myself tightly.

"He's in good hands. The Outlaws have a fantastic training staff." Genny wraps her coat around my legs. "He walked off the floor, which is a really great sign."

I take a few deep breaths to keep some queasiness at bay.

We sit silently for a few minutes, watching custodians sweep up popcorn and vendors wipe down counters. The concourse is quiet, but we hear the goal horn and some muted crowd noise.

"I love him, Gen."

She rests her head on my shoulder. "He's The Bear, isn't he?"

I lift my torso to look at her in surprise. "How did you know?"

Genny smiles. "I've known for a while. I figured it out when our phones both dinged at the same time during training camp. Then I started to realize all the signs were there, but I didn't want to ask and throw you into a tailspin. So, I pretended I was clueless."

I rest my forehead on my knees, a deep laugh building in my core. "You knew all this time, and watched me bend over backwards to keep it a secret?"

She nods. "I tried to get Sawyer to confirm my suspicions, but he wouldn't crack. I assume he found out at some point, but he's a vault."

My shoulders shake with laughter. "I thought for sure he would let the cat out of the bag almost immediately. What a pleasant surprise." I pick my head up. "Wait, does Zeke know?"

"No, I didn't tell him. Mackenzie either. I wanted to respect your wishes to tell us when you were ready."

I pull her into a tight hug. "Thank you. Although I probably needed someone to smack some sense into me a long time ago."

"You would not believe how many times I had to physically hold myself back from telling you I knew."

I chuckle. "I can imagine."

We rest our heads against the wall behind us.

"So, what now? Do you want to watch the end of the game if there's any time left?" Genny checks the clock on her phone. "I wish I had contact info for the training staff."

"Oh!" I dig in my pocket. "I noticed the trainer on the floor was the same one from the World Games. She gave me her number after I got injured."

"Do you still have it?" she asks excitedly.

I scroll through my contacts. Paige Bomberry. *Bingo.*

I nearly drop my phone in my eagerness to tap her number.

"Hello?"

"Paige? This is Chelsea John, from the Haudenosaunee team in Utica."

"Oh, hi Chelsea. What can I help you with?"

"I'm so sorry to bother you in the middle of work, but I'm trying to get an update on Wes Harrison. I'm at the Outlaws game, and he's...my boyfriend." My voice quivers.

I can hear her smile. "I'm so glad you called, because Wes asked someone to reach out to you, but I got distracted."

My heart leaps.

"I'm at the hospital with him now," she continues. "They just took him back for a CT scan to rule out any serious brain injuries."

I just barely hold back a whimper, and Genny squeezes me again.

"Does he—" I run out of air and lose my words.

"He has a concussion. I want to make sure there's nothing worse, given the severity of the hit. He was out cold for close to a minute. But as long as his scans are clear, he can rest at home and be back on the floor in a couple of weeks."

"Thank goodness," I whisper. "Thank you for letting me know."

"Of course," Paige says. "I'll let him know I talked to you once he's done here."

"What's the scoop?" Genny asks once I end the call.

"Concussion, and they're checking for more. But hopefully that's all."

"Good." She holds out her hand and helps me to my feet. "Do you want to wait for Kenzie here, or go back inside?"

"Let's go check the score and go from there."

"You got it."

Chapter 47

Chelsea

We return to our seats and are stunned to find the Outlaws have tied the game in the dying seconds, forcing overtime.

"What the hell happened?" Genny asks, gaping at the scoreboard.

"You've missed a lot," Mackenzie replies, her long hair messy as though she's been anxiously grabbing at it.

"I see that." I plop down into my seat.

Mackenzie shakes her head. "Nothing's been announced here about Wes, and the lacrosse reporters I follow online don't have anything yet. Did you make it to the locker room?"

"No, but I talked to a trainer. He has a concussion and is getting scans at the hospital. Not sure when we'll know more." I bite my lip.

"I'm so glad you're here tonight," Genny says with a smile. "It's awful seeing them hurt, but he's going to be so happy to see you once he's back."

My leg bounces. "I need time to pass more quickly."

"Well, luckily for us, if not our nervous systems, we've got an overtime period to watch," Mackenzie says.

Our eyes stay glued to the floor as the Outlaws settle into their offensive zone, cycling passes around the Hawks' goaltender.

"So, catch us up," Genny says. "When we left, the Outlaws were down by four and looking like crap."

Mackenzie begins ticking items off her fingers. "Brock got ejected from the game. I wouldn't be surprised if the league suspends him, too. Jamie was given a misconduct for fighting, so he went to the locker room. The Outlaws were pissed as hell about Wes getting hurt and scored a bunch of goals in the final few minutes. Zeke and Sawyer are on the warpath."

"Holy heck." I watch as Zeke throws his sizable frame into a River Hawk and knocks him off the ball.

"That's hot," Genny and Mackenzie murmur together.

I laugh, reaching for my phone and keeping one eye on the gameplay.

> **Me:** Not sure if you have your phone on you, but I wanted you to know I'm thinking about you. Let me know how you're doing when you have a chance

> **Me:** I lied. I'm worried sick about you. Please be OK

The two teams battle back and forth, both getting dangerous shots on goal and spectacular saves from the goalies. With half of the overtime period remaining, Albany loses possession on a foul, and the Outlaws have a few seconds to re-group.

"Here we go," Genny says as Sawyer slowly jogs down the center of the floor, waiting for the rest of the offense to join him from the bench.

Zeke trots by in the opposite direction, and Sawyer flicks the ball up as they pass. Their sticks are positioned on top of each other, but the ball comes back down in Sawyer's pocket.

I roughly grab Genny's forearm. "Hidden ball trick!" I hiss.

"Is it?" She cranes her neck to watch Zeke speed up and cradle with his stick, as though he has the ball. He draws several defenders, moving everyone closer to the net where he's most dangerous.

Meanwhile, Sawyer walks to the other corner, watching Zeke.

"He's got the ball," I say.

"I'm not sure—"

Zeke makes a move near the crease, and the River Hawks close in around him, attempting to block his progress.

Sawyer takes two short steps forward, winds up, and slings the ball into the wide open side of the net without anyone noticing.

The best part of pulling off a hidden ball trick is when the goal horn blares and nobody has any fucking clue what just happened. Especially the goaltender.

I jump up with an ocean of seated and confused fans around me.

"Oh my God." Genny laughs and stands beside me, applauding hard. "Sawyer's been trying to pull one of those off for years."

The Outlaws pile on top of Sawyer to celebrate their win. He points at Zeke through the melee, crediting him with selling the trick play so well. The team is one step closer to the playoffs with only a few games left to go.

We gather in the friends and family room afterwards, and the atmosphere is jubilant. My eyes stay laser-focused on the locker room door, looking for Wes in every player that enters, but he never comes.

Jamie approaches and pulls me in for a hug as Zeke and Genny embrace.

"Good to see you again, Chelsea. How're you holding up?"

"Could be better, but could be a lot worse." I smile weakly.

"Our boy's tough. He's going to come out of this just fine," he says with a reassuring squeeze.

"Have you seen him?"

He shakes his head. "Not yet. But Paige has him, and he couldn't be in better hands."

I gesture towards his blossoming black eye. "Are you trying a new makeup trend?"

"You like that? I thought it looked nice." He grins. "I'll wear this one proudly, because I earned it for you *and* Wes."

My eyes widen, and he chuckles.

"I didn't like the way that asshole talked to you in Utica. And I hold grudges."

I'm swallowed up by a pair of muscular arms before I can reply.

"Chels! I've missed you!" Sawyer crushes me to his chest.

I manage a breathless squeak, and he loosens his grip.

"Sorry. Just excited to see you." He flashes a megawatt smile. "You're good?"

"I'll be better once I see him."

My stomach clenches watching players and families begin to file out of the room, with no sign of Wes.

"If anyone wants to come over, we can hang out and wait for Wes to get released," Sawyer offers. "Our place is just a few minutes from here."

Everyone murmurs their agreement, and we begin to drift towards the exit.

Progress is slow. Mackenzie visits the restroom. Jamie stops to chat with the custodians cleaning up. Sawyer gets asked to pose for a dozen pictures with cute girls.

I'm still rattled and desperate to get out of this building.

"I'm going outside to get some air. I'll meet you all in the parking lot, OK?" I say to Zeke while he signs an autograph.

"OK, Chels. We'll be out in a couple of minutes," he says.

I move quickly down the hallway to the player lot. The cold March air hits my face when I push the door open and breathe deeply. My nerves are shot, and the icy breeze feels calming.

"We keep meeting this way."

The last time I heard that voice my blood ran cold. This time it runs fiery hot.

"*You*," I spit at Brock. I see the River Hawks team bus across the lot, so he must be on his way there.

He grins wryly, but his eyes betray his nervousness. "Miss me?"

"You fucking psychopath!" I push him with both hands against his chest. It catches him off guard, and he trips backward.

"What the fuck, Chels?"

"Excuse me? *I'm* the unreasonable party here?" I step towards him, and he takes another step back.

"Yeah, you're acting crazy."

I legitimately want to throttle him, but I won't give him the satisfaction. "You have brought nothing but hurt to my life since I met you. That would be bad enough, but now you're putting my loved ones in the hospital."

Brock has the decency to flinch. "My coach already chewed me out about the hit, so I don't need to hear it from you, too."

"You fucking *drilled him in the head with your stick*, you absolute sicko," I yell. "For what? So you could keep tormenting me for existing?"

He scoffs. "Don't flatter yourself. I don't care about you."

"I know you don't. So why won't you let me go?"

He crosses his arms across his chest. "It pisses me off that you won't talk to me anymore." His jaw ticks. "I can't believe you blocked me."

"We're not together anymore! Why would I still talk to you? You've got plenty of groupies, so go bother them."

He huffs and adjusts the strap of his duffel bag. "Maybe I will."

"Great. Bye. Lose my number." I spin on my heel to walk back into the arena, where my friends are emerging from the exit door.

My arm is wrenched back as he grabs for it. "Chels, wait."

I drop my elbow into his solar plexus and he releases me, gasping for air.

"Leave. Me. Alone." I say.

Zeke is at my side in an instant.

"Is there a problem?" He glowers at Brock.

Brock shakes his head, trying to catch his breath. "No problem. I'm going."

"Stay gone this time, Pelletier," Sawyer says, appearing on the other side of me.

Brock scowls but scurries off when Zeke takes a half step forward.

How did I ever believe anything this loser told me about myself?

The door creaks again, and I turn back in that direction.

Jamie and the girls walk out, and he holds the door open behind him.

Wes slowly emerges looking disheveled, and my heart leaps in my throat.

"Look who we found straggling out of the locker room," Jamie says with a smile.

I run the remaining distance between us and bury my face in Wes' neck. "Is this OK? I don't want to hurt you."

"This is perfect." He squeezes me. "God, I missed you so much," he says quietly.

I pull back slightly and take his face between my hands. "I'm coming home with you tonight," I say. "I'm not taking no for an answer."

He searches my eyes. "You told them?" he asks in a whisper.

"Not all of them." I grin and pull him closer. "Now please kiss me and never scare me like that again, you jerk."

He barks out a laugh and dips his mouth to mine.

Our friends whistle and clap in appreciation as he kisses me deeply.

"Are you allowed to make out with a concussion?" I ask against his lips.

He chuckles. "Absolutely. It's part of my treatment plan."

"Wait a minute!"

My head snaps over at Zeke's outburst.

"Is—" His eyes are the size of dinner plates. "Is Wes...The Bear?"

Jamie clears his throat. "Are you—are you just figuring that out now?"

We all collectively turn to stare at him, and he shrugs.

"I thought it was obvious."

Chapter 48

Wes

I lean on Chelsea as we wait for Sawyer to unlock the front door. My entire right side aches from dropping my dead weight to the turf, and my head is throbbing.

It occurs to me that I'm easily able to rest my head on her shoulder, and I glance at our feet.

"Are you taller than me in these heels?" I ask, my mouth curving upwards.

Her eyes dance playfully. "Does that threaten your masculinity?"

"Nothing I can't handle." I kiss her softly.

"Personally, I love tall women," Sawyer chimes in, pushing the door open. "Tell Creator to send me an Amazon goddess, if you wouldn't mind."

"You look hot as hell, by the way," I murmur in her ear as we walk into the house. "So completely unfair to show up looking like that before I had to play."

Chelsea giggles. "Sorry. Blame Genny and Mackenzie."

"I blame your smoking hot body and nothing else."

Our friends had sent us home with promises to catch up another night once I was feeling better, and I'm grateful for the opportunity to be alone with her sooner. I haven't seen her in weeks, and I'm craving her touch.

"I'm going to bed, and I'll be out cold until the morning," Sawyer announces on his way through the kitchen. "I'll have a movie on in my room and won't hear anything."

I grin. "I think it's going to be an early night for us, so don't go to too much trouble."

"I'm just saying. Pretend I don't exist." He grabs a Gatorade and backs away into his bedroom. "See you two in the morning. Let me know if there's an emergency."

Chelsea and I look at each other from across the kitchen island.

She clears her throat. "Do you have discharge instructions for what to do over the next few days? I want to make sure you have everything you need tonight."

"I have everything I need right here." I smile at her.

"Wesley."

"So serious tonight." I pull my phone from my pocket and slide it to her. "Paige said she'd send me information. Would you mind looking for it? I'm supposed to avoid screens."

"Yeah, of course." She sits on a barstool and scrolls through my messages. "Are you hungry? I could make you something."

"I'm not hungry." I bring one of her hands to my lips for a kiss.

She scrolls with her other hand. "Let's get you some Tylenol and lots of water."

"Sounds good."

"And you need to rest. A lot."

"Could that involve staying in bed with you? Because I'd be down for that."

A smile tugs at her lips. "It could. Genny's going to bring me some clothes tomorrow so I can stay a few days. I'll just need to go into work starting Monday, and put Sawyer on babysitting duty."

"I'd much rather have you as my nurse." I tenderly kiss down her neck, and she sighs contentedly.

"You need to rest," she says.

"This is resting." I pull her closer to me. "Come to bed."

"Hydrate. Medicate. Then bed," she says sternly.

I gulp down water and Tylenol as she reviews my care instructions. "So, what's new with you?"

Her eyes flick up to mine. "This is awkward, isn't it?"

I chuckle. "Not really. I knew you'd find me again once you were ready."

She sets my phone down and wraps herself around me. "I'm ready." She dusts a soft kiss across my lips. "Are *you* ready to be stuck with me?"

"Like glue, baby." Her mouth is soft and eager against mine.

"That promotion came through." Her eyes light up. "And I applied for a Master's program."

"You did?" I press her into the island. "You're already out of my league, and now this?"

That delightfully saucy giggle is better than I remember. "And I signed up for Nationals tryouts this summer. The

Haudenosaunee have some pre-Olympic qualifiers coming up in the fall."

"I must be Creator's favorite." I nip at her lower lip. "What did I do to deserve you?"

"You're everything I needed," she whispers.

"Likewise."

Chelsea tugs me carefully towards the bedroom, pushing my navy suit jacket down my arms as we walk.

"Let me undress you." She positions me against the wall and feathers kisses along my jaw. "Please."

I swallow. "I'm all yours."

She pulls my white shirt from my waistband. "We can't do anything tonight, though." Her mouth moves to my neck as she ever so slowly begins unbuttoning me. "Paige said no strenuous activities for at least several days."

Her lips follow the path her fingers reveal as she undoes another button. "What if the activities aren't strenuous?"

She chuckles. "I'm not taking any chances."

"Dammit, Chels."

She hums in appreciation when she reaches my abdomen, running her lips across my muscles and flicking open my belt buckle.

I close my eyes. "We may be entering strenuous territory."

Her palms flatten against my chest. "I'll be good, don't worry." She peels my shirt down my shoulders. "Which is honestly a sacrifice, considering how good you look."

I thread my hand through her hair and pull her closer. "I look like hell tonight, and you know it."

She scoffs. "You do not." The button-down falls to the floor, and she gasps softly. "Oh, Wes."

Her eyes fill with tears as she takes in the bruising already darkening down the side of my arm, chest, and leg.

"I'm OK, baby. It looks bad, but I'm in good shape. Nothing serious."

Chelsea's fingers gently skim over the colorful line of bruises. She rests her head on my shoulder, and I feel wetness on my skin.

"I'm so sorry he hurt you because of me," she whispers.

I wrap her in my arms. "First of all, you are not responsible, in any way, for his actions. Second of all," I continue with a smile, "he hurt me because I punched him in the junk."

Her jaw pops open. "You didn't."

I grin. "I did. And I'd gladly do it all over again."

Her head falls forward in laughter, her body quivering against me. "I love you so much."

I still, certain I misheard her. "You—"

She pulls my lips to hers. "*Kunolúkhwa.*"

I cradle her face in my hands to deepen our kiss. "I love you, too. So, so much."

"I know."

Chelsea smiles against me, and I drag my mouth away from hers. "Excuse me?"

She bites her lip. "I have a confession."

"I'm all ears."

Her smile is as bright as the sun. "Our last night in the cabin, you told me you loved me while you were falling asleep."

I swear. "I'm sorry. That must've freaked you out. No wonder you needed space."

Her hands drift back to my waist and flip open the button of my pants. "It did, but I needed that. I realized I didn't need the boundaries I was stubbornly sticking to with you."

My suit pants puddle on the ground as she makes quick work of my zipper.

"I'm going to need you to tell me you love me a few hundred more times tonight, if that's all right," I say, stepping back towards the bed with her.

"Who's keeping count?"

I strip her blazer off and sink my hands into the ribbed softness of her tank top. "I will, because you're going to be keeping track of something else."

"Hey!" she protests as I unzip her leather skirt. "What did I tell you about strenuous activity?"

"Making you climax is downright relaxing, sweetheart." I carefully pull out her long earrings and set them on the nightstand. "It sounds like just the kind of physical therapy I need."

She later falls asleep in my arms with promises to play cribbage and listen to an audiobook with me tomorrow. I'll take my recovery one day at a time, but knowing Chelsea is really and truly mine makes life feel like a breeze.

"*Kunolúkhwa*, Chels," I mumble as we drift off.

"*Kunolúkhwa*, Rookie."

Epilogue
K̂ kwi.té / Spring

Chelsea

"Why do I have to sit in the back?" Katie whines.

"Because you're the youngest," Wes responds with a grin.

"I can sit back there, no problem," I offer, stepping towards the car.

Wes snakes an arm around my waist and pulls me firmly to his side. "No way. You're with me."

It's been two months since we've officially been "out" to everyone, and I still get a little zip of glee from his open affection.

"One of you is going to get left behind if you don't decide soon," Bobby says from the driver's seat, where he's punching an address into the GPS.

Katie huffs and folds down the middle row of the rental SUV. "Fine. But I should get time served for sitting back there the whole three-hour drive from Buffalo."

Wes' family came to visit after the Outlaws' season ended. The team made it deep into the playoffs, but ultimately lost in the semifinal round. Wes and I both start our summer lacrosse leagues in another week, so the Harrisons' trip comes at the perfect time.

Jess met us at the hotel in Oneida this morning. She was the perfect icebreaker, because she and her Aunt Kay immediately clicked and put everyone at ease. We probably should have put those two in the back of the car to continue chatting, but Wes' dad needed Jess' navigation help in the passenger seat.

"You ready for this?" I ask Wes as he slides into the seat next to me.

He threads his fingers between mine. "We're as ready as we're ever going to be."

I watch Kay as the familiar sights of the reservation roll by our windows. She's muted, aside from the occasional burst of questions for Jess about various family members.

Katie's head pops up between us, and I jump. "So, what's the strategy here?" she whispers. Her new beaded robin earrings swing from her ears.

Jess is pointing out some newer buildings, so Bobby and Kay's attention is diverted.

"What do you mean?" Wes asks.

"How do we want to approach this? Should you and I get out of the car first?"

"That's a good idea," I say. "The two of you could get out with Jess, and I'll stay behind with your parents."

"She might want to be alone with them first," Wes says. "We should ask her."

"That's the dumbest thing you've said since your concussion." Katie scoffs.

He fixes her with a withering glare. "My head is fine. I just want to be sure Mom's feelings are the priority here. She's been through a lot."

"I know, but it's probably better if she doesn't overthink this."

"It probably doesn't hurt to ask," I say, and Katie harrumphs.

We pull into a gravel driveway in a sleepy cluster of homes. It's a house I've been to countless times in my life, but today is different.

"How do you want to do this, Mom?" Wes asks, ignoring the daggers shooting from his sister's eyes.

Kay draws a deep breath. "You kids can go first, if you'd like, and I'll follow."

"You sure you're OK with this?" I ask.

She gives me a shaky smile. "I am. I'm ready to put this chapter of my life behind me."

"Ready to go?" Jess asks her cousins, and they nod.

I give Wes a kiss before he exits to let Katie out. "I love you. Good luck."

"I'll see you on the other side." He winks and moves the seat for his sister.

"I can stay back with you if you'd like," I say to Kay.

Her eyes meet Bobby's in the rearview mirror. She nods imperceptively at him, and he gets out of the car.

"I think I'll be all right. I just need a few minutes." She squeezes my hand.

Bobby opens her door, and she scoots to make room for him.

"I'll give you some privacy. Just know we're here for you."

He opens his arms, and she folds into his chest with visible relief.

I know the feeling of melting into a Harrison man.

"Thank you, Chelsea," he says, wrapping his wife in his embrace. "You've been such an enormous help with this process."

"Of course. Take all the time you need."

My sandals crunch on the gravel as I approach the rest of our group. Wes holds out his hand to me as Jess knocks on the front door.

Diane and Gerald Patterson's home is small and full of love, its white siding and black shutters beginning to show their age. Jess and I would often play here with her brothers while our parents helped with projects or made food for upcoming community events.

Kay's presence hung around like a ghost, as her photos remained on the walls and her bedroom was preserved as she'd left it for years. The family finally converted it to an office when we were in middle school, and even then I realized what a hard decision it must have been to move on. I used to study the photos of Kay, mystified as to why a beautiful, successful young woman would have left her people and never come back. Jess and I would come up with stories about where she was and what her life looked like. I never could have imagined that years later I'd find myself in love with her son, helping to facilitate a long-anticipated family reunion.

The screen door creaks open and Diane emerges, her eyes shining.

"Wes and Katie are here to meet you," Jess says, giving her grandmother a side hug.

Katie approaches first, without hesitation. "Hi, Grandma."

"Look at you," Diane says with awe. "You look just like your mother."

They embrace, and I squeeze Wes' hand. "You've got this."

He kisses my knuckles and heads onto the porch as Gerald comes through the front door.

Katie says something to make everyone laugh, and pretty soon there's a group hug happening. Diane ruffles Wes' hair, and his easy smile melts my heart.

A car door shuts behind me, and I turn to watch Kay slowly approach, clutching Bobby's hand.

Jess catches my eye from the porch, and we exchange nervous smiles.

Game time.

Wes appears at my elbow as the family descends from the porch.

"Everyone doing OK?" I whisper.

"Yeah. For now."

Kay and Diane watch each other, and I'm pretty sure we all collectively hold our breath.

"*Aknulhá*," Kay whispers, taking a step towards her mother.

Diane rushes forward, wrapping her in her arms. "*Wa'kenha:t□*. I'm so sorry."

Kay's sob nearly breaks me, and I reach for Wes' hand.

He pulls me into his chest with one arm and drapes the other around a sniffling Katie.

"I'm sorry too, Mom," Kay says. "I punished you for too long and didn't know how to take a step back."

"You have nothing to apologize for," Diane insists. "Let us hold that wound and work together to repair it."

Gerald joins his wife and daughter, his movements hesitant.

"Don't cry, sweetheart," he says, his voice thick with emotion. "We're so happy to see you again."

"*Lake'níha*." Kay opens her arms to him, and now we're all crying.

Gerald kisses Kay's head and looks up at Wes' father. "Thank you for loving her and taking care of her all these years. You saved her."

Bobby crosses the distance between them and places a hand on Kay's back. "She's the best thing that's ever happened to me. And she saved herself; I was just there to encourage her."

Kay smiles up at him, and my heart skips at the look of love that passes between them.

"See?" Wes whispers to me. "I told you I learned from the best."

I kiss his cheek, and he holds me close.

"You two are going to make me vomit," Katie says quietly before dodging her brother's kick.

Diane wipes at her wet eyes. "Would you all like to come inside for some corn soup?"

"Yes!" Katie pumps her fist. "I've waited my whole life for my own grandmother's corn soup."

Diane smiles at her. "Be sure to tell your friends that your *aksótha* makes it best."

"She really does," I agree. "Don't tell my mom I said that."

Wes and I bid good night to his family after a successful afternoon at his grandparents' house.

"Thanks for letting us spend the night with you, Jess," I say. "The hotel room was a little cozy last night."

"Yes, my back thanks you after sleeping on the pullout couch." Wes smiles.

Jess laughs. "No problem. I'm glad for the company." She unlocks the door and we enter.

"It's good to be back." I look around the familiar apartment.

"I've only ever seen this place on video calls." Wes looks around.

"It's not much, but it's home." Jess fills a glass of water. "I hate to cut and run, but I've got to head into work at the casino in a few minutes. If you need anything, just text me."

"Will do." I pull her to me for a hug. "Thanks for making all this happen today."

She holds out an arm for Wes to join in. "I didn't do much. I'm grateful Kay was willing to come out and reconnect."

"Thank you, Jess." Wes squeezes her. "We couldn't have done this without you."

"You're the best thing that's happened to me since your darling girlfriend came into my life." She smiles.

"Ditto." He grins.

"So, this is where you called me from that first night?" Wes says as I close the bedroom door behind us.

Jess briefly had another roommate after I moved out, but the room is largely unchanged from my time there.

I chuckle. "It is. And all the times after that, as well."

He wraps his arms around me from behind. "Can I make some of those dreams of yours come true tonight?" His beard tickles my skin as he kisses down my neck.

"I'm counting on it." I drop my head back onto his chest.

"Speaking of the best thing to ever happen to me..."

"Yes?"

"You're the linchpin in everything that's happened with my family. If I hadn't met you, I probably would've driven out here once or twice but never would have known how to connect with my grandparents or cousins." He drops a kiss on my lips.

"Your mom was such a mystery to me growing up," I say. "It's amazing to think I played a small part in her finally coming back."

"You played more than a small part, Chels." Another kiss. "Thank you for loving me, and for loving my family like they're your own."

"Well, as someone once told me, you're easy to love."

He turns me to face him. "Sounds like a smart guy. You should keep him around."

"I plan on it."

Acknowledgements

Niawen'kó:wa to the Haudenosaunee community across Turtle Island for the welcome I have always received as a *Kanien'kehá:ka* woman who grew up off-reserve. There's always more to learn, and it is a joy to do so.

Thank you to my friends and editors: Reannen, Carole, Connie, and Kirby. My books grow so much under your thoughtful feedback and encouragement.

I am deeply grateful for my husband, Brad, who steers our family's ship while I spend every free moment writing. He is my North Star and lacrosse vibes checker.

Growing up as an urban Native of mixed ancestry, the opportunity was there for my parents to disregard our Mohawk traditions. Instead, they fought for them. *Konnorónhkwa*.

I consulted a number of authentic voices in my research for this book:

Selections from Thanksgiving Address: Greetings to the Natural World. English version: John Stokes and Kanawahienton (David Benedict, Turtle Clan/Mohawk). This translation of the Mohawk version was provided courtesy of Six Nations Indian Museum and the Tracking Project.

Oneida Nation of New York
(https://www.oneidaindiannation.com/)

Oneida Nation of Wisconsin (https://oneida-nsn.gov/)

Milwaukee Public Museum
(https://www.mpm.edu/content/wirp/ICW-156)

Oneida Language Resources
(https://www.oneidaindiannation.com/languagelearning/)

The Great Bear and the Big Dipper
(https://oneidalanguage.ca/oneida-culture/oneidalanguage-stories/the-great-bear-and-the-big-dipper/)

About the author

S.E. Martin is an enrolled member of the Mohawk Nation at Six Nations of the Grand River reserve in Ohsweken, Ontario. She grew up in Niagara Falls, NY and currently resides in New England with her husband and children. She's been writing personally and professionally since her teenage years. She has always been captivated by the power of a good story. She's writing The Medicine Game series in order to share the beauty of Haudenosaunee culture and the game of lacrosse with a wider audience. When she's not reading or writing, you can find her losing years off her lifespan by cheering for Buffalo sports teams.

Connect With Me

The Medicine Game Series

- **Over and Back:** A childhood friends-to-lovers, second chance romance on the Seneca Nation

- **Hidden Ball Trick:** A friends with benefits, secret dating romance featuring the Oneida Nation

- **Trick Shot**: A frenemies-to-lovers, second chance romance involving the Tuscarora Nation